BICYCLE DAYS

A Novel

JOHN
BURNHAM
SCHWARTZ

SUMMIT BOOKS
NEW YORK · LONDON · TORONTO · SYDNEY · TOKYO

Summit Books
Simon & Schuster Building
Rockefeller Center
1230 Avenue of the Americas
New York, New York 10020

This book is a work of fiction. Names, characters, places and incidents are either the product of the author's imagination or are used fictitiously. Any resemblance to actual events or locales or persons, living or dead, is entirely coincidental.

SUMMIT BOOKS and colophon are trademarks
of Simon & Schuster Inc.

Designed by Ellen Korbonski/Levavi & Levavi
Manufactured in the United States of America

10   9   8   7   6   5   4   3   2

Library of Congress Cataloging in Publication Data

Schwartz, John Burnham.

Bicycle days : a novel / John Burnham Schwartz.
p.   cm.
ISBN 0-671-66600-2
I. Title.
PS3569.C5658B5   1989   89-4177
813'.54—dc 19   CIP

For Margaret McElderry Lunt

CONTENTS

Home is where one starts from.

—T. S. Eliot
Four Quartets
East Coker; III

I

TREMORS

The noise of the silver balls was deafening. It enveloped the senses, locking Alec in no less than the Japanese men who sat transfixed, rows and rows of them, their faces inches from the pachinko machines. Every few seconds a ball would hit home, sending another stream rushing out through an opening at the bottom. Without once interrupting the motion of their thumbs as they worked the levers, the men would collect their new supply, occasionally wiping a bead of sweat from their cheeks with a twist of the shoulder. But always the noise. The vibrations would rise to a crescendo as a new jackpot was struck, only to sink again. The rhythm rose from these constant pulsations, a whirlpool of anonymous men and silver balls.

Alec pulled his face away from the window front, erased the trace of his breath with his shirt-sleeve. The air was muggy, and he felt for a moment as if there weren't enough oxygen in it. He stood on the wide, busy stretch of Waseda Avenue, his bags scattered around him, just a few blocks from the Japanese homestay family with whom he would be spending the summer. His watch read seven o'clock. He couldn't remember if he had reset it when he arrived. The confusing bus ride from the airport, much more than the flight from New York, had robbed him of all sense of time.

He had woken with the sense that something was wrong. His first thought was that he had missed his stop. Terrified, he looked around him. It was the same bus he had been on before he had fallen asleep, filled with the same people, the driver wearing the exact same pale blue hat. The bus looked like every other bus Alec had ever been on. The red vinyl seats reminded him of the Greyhound he used to ride to his aunt's house in Vermont. He took a deep breath and rubbed his head where it had been knocking against the window. A young woman sitting across the aisle looked away when he noticed her; he was sure she had been staring at him while he slept. His head felt as though someone had been pounding on it with a rubber hammer. He traced the ache to his left ear, which was being attacked by a constant stream of freezing cold air. It surprised him that the air-conditioning could be so accurate. When he sat back, his head against the synthetic white cover, the air went directly into his ear. But he couldn't figure out where it was coming from—there was no vent visible, no way to turn it off.

Beyond the window, the sparse greenery of the suburbs between Narita Airport and Tokyo was merging with the outskirts of the city itself. The block forms of tall apartment complexes, gray and gold in the twilight, rolled out to greet him. Laundry flanked the balconies like children gathered for a parade. There was no longer any green, only solid, urban matter: slabs of concrete and sheets of iron; timber walls and tile roofs; the glistening bodies of Hondas and Toyotas bumper to bumper, stretching off the highway and down into the streets below. Neon signs had come on all over the city, cloaking the buildings and streets in electricity, promising an explosion of light when the sky turned dark.

The bus eased off the exit ramp, and Alec felt Tokyo close in around him. The highway had been elevated, and he had looked out over the entire city, the distant observer. But the bus was in a maze of narrow streets now, and the city had moved close to him. Everything was concentrated; the neon brighter, garish, the buildings tall and dark above their electric signs, the people pushing, moving.

He sat back in his seat for a moment, too tired to do anything else. It had been like this since his graduation from college, three weeks before. That afternoon his family and friends had formed a circle around him, crying and congratulating him. His father had hugged him. It was a brief, fierce, awkward hug, followed by an embarrassed silence as Alec bent down to pick up his mortarboard from the ground. His mother had hugged him, too, but then held on longer than that, stepping away with her hands tightly gripping his arms, her eyes on his, as if she had finally caught sight of him after a long absence, only to realize that he was about to disappear again. She told him to come home soon, or whenever he wanted to. And to write or call collect anytime, because she would be there to talk to him. Anytime. And it seemed to Alec as if the day had ended with that word, because he couldn't remember what came after.

The bus was stopped at a light, and Alec looked down a side street. An old bicycle with a metal basket leaned against a dark one-story house. A teenage boy in a white apron and paper hat walked swiftly out of the house, carrying a tray of stacked empty dishes above his right shoulder. The light turned green, the bus jerked forward. Trying to see, Alec craned his neck against the glass. The bike was moving fast, gaining on the bus. Alec gasped as the boy came abreast of the bus, a flash of white, weaving and dipping and somehow managing not to lose the tray, which he held aloft on one hand, the one solid part of a sculpture that was all fluid motion. And then, at the next corner, he was gone.

The driver's voice came over the loudspeaker, announcing his stop, Takadanobaba Station. Alec quickly checked his sheet of directions, then jumped to his feet to gather his bags. The aisle seemed endless as he hurried toward the front of the bus, his luggage catching on the seats, dragging over them, hitting the silent, staring passengers on their heads.

But the bus ride was already a memory. Alec bent down to pick up his bags and felt sweat begin to trickle down his side. A roar from across the street caught his attention. An ape was suspended from the second story of a building, its chest covered with Japanese characters spelling King Kong. At regular intervals, the ape would beat its chest with both hands and growl. Alec looked at it for a moment, then moved on.

Up ahead was a gas station. He checked the directions and veered left down one street, then right at the next corner. He was now only about two minutes beyond the neon chaos of Waseda Avenue. People lived here—in pillbox houses of wood and tile and tin, down streets barely wide enough for a car to pass through.

Alec walked to the end of the street, then turned left again, checking the numbers on the doors as he struggled with his luggage. He stopped in front of a four-story house with a garage taking up most of the first floor. "Hasegawa Company" was written on the glass door in adhesive Japanese characters. He put down his bags, looked once more at the sheet of directions, then back at the door. Poised, a stone lion sat just to the left. Alec repeated a couple of Japanese phrases to himself, ran a hand through his hair, and rang the doorbell.

A teenage girl came running to the edge of a steep flight of stairs and squinted down at him. She continued to peer at him, making him even more uneasy. As he began to turn away, the girl seemed to see him for the first time. After screaming something in Japanese, she sprinted down the stairs and let him in. She wore a striped knee-length dress that looked brand-new. And black knee socks.

"You're Alec-san," she said in Japanese, turning the "l" in his name into an "r."

"Yes," he said. "Please excuse my lateness."

The girl made many rapid sounds after that, but Alec didn't

recognize any of them. He gathered his bags and followed her inside.

On the landing, shoes were neatly lined up against the wall. He tried to untie his high-tops while still standing. The girl laughed at him but clamped her hand over her mouth as soon as he looked at her. A white miniature poodle came running down the short hallway and jumped on him. A short barrel of a woman in a puffed and pleated evening dress came after it, yelling, "Chiko! Chiko!" The dog started chewing Alec's right foot. Alec was still trying to get his sneakers off.

The pain started just below his knees and went shooting up into his thighs. Alec looked around the low table at his new family. They were all dressed as if they might be going out for an evening at the theater. Exhausted, far away from himself, he sensed that he was smiling and saying small things in Japanese every once in a while. He remembered the many times he had been to Japanese restaurants at home, how he had always liked the idea of sitting at a low table, liked how simple it was.

He took a piece of sushi in his chopsticks, dipped it in soy sauce, and guided it into his mouth. Mrs. Hasegawa had ordered it especially for his arrival. He felt the eyes of the entire family on him as he chewed. Did Alec really like sushi? Yes? Laughter.

He thought he was beginning to understand the rhythm of the conversation, if not the words. Mr. Hasegawa's speech was unintelligible. Short and slim with a crewcut, he made constant grunting noises that seemed to come from somewhere deep inside him. This was at first confusing, but Alec soon realized that each grunt was a sign of assent. Again and again, he would stop in the middle of a sentence to search for a word, only to see Mr. Hasegawa leaning forward, his hands resting on his thighs. Like a seismologist reading the tremors before a major earthquake, Alec knew then that a grunt was coming, and this knowledge gave him enough confidence to struggle through the sentence. Then the grunt would actually erupt, accompanied by an audible sigh of relief from everyone at the table, especially Alec.

Yoshi, the eldest of the three children, was talking, mixing in a few words of English with the Japanese. Alec thought this a good sign. The summer before, when he was sixteen, Yoshi had spent a couple of weeks in the States on a group tour. He had seen Michael Jackson in concert. Yukiko, his fifteen-year-old sister, said that she preferred Bruce Springsteen. Hiroshi, twelve, was more interested in professional wrestling. Had Alec heard of Hulk Hogan?

Alec looked at Mrs. Hasegawa sitting across the table from him, not exactly cross-legged. She had brought a plate of sliced apples from the kitchen and was eating one, chewing with a great, sweeping rotation of her jaws. When she finished, she took a toothpick from a small jar on the table and scraped her teeth. Throughout, she never stopped talking.

Alec must eat a lot of beef, she said. And it was surprising that he wasn't taller—most Americans are so big. She didn't mean that he was short, but he certainly wasn't tall. Did he have a girlfriend? What was that? No girlfriend? But he must be so smart and handsome to have graduated from a school like Yale, such a famous university. How could he not have a girlfriend?

Alec shook his head. No one seemed to notice. He ate a slice of apple.

I like American girls, Yoshi said. Especially California girls.

Alec grunted, took a sip of beer.

2

BLANK TAPE

H e rolled over and looked at his watch: four-thirty in the
morning. He closed his eyes and tried to go back to sleep
but knew there was no point. The room glowed from the one
window, which looked directly into a neighboring house. For a
moment, he didn't think at all about where he was. It was just
a room, nothing else. Alec lay in it and thought of his first
summer away at camp, how empty and alone he had felt on his
first night there, lying awake on the top level of a bunk bed in
a bare, wooden cabin, listening to the breathing of seven other
boys his own age. He had not wanted to go away then. He had
cried and screamed at his parents. It hadn't been his decision—
not the way it had been later, when he went away to school, or
even now, coming here. But the feeling was not so different.
This room was not so different.

Alec felt suddenly afraid then, the room seemed so small. He
thought he should get some air. Rummaging through his suit-
case, he pulled out a blue-and-white-patterned yukata that his

mother had bought for him at Bloomingdale's. He put it on and slid open the wood-and-paper screen of his room, and then the glass door to the balcony. The air was cool and comfortable, and he stepped into it as though into a hot bath: gingerly at first, then completely, with satisfaction. He breathed deeply. The sky was cloudless, and Tokyo lay sprawled out before him, silent and waiting, offering him his own private viewing.

About an hour later, Alec stood in a closet-size room, his yukata hanging on a hook behind him. He was looking down at a Japanese-style toilet and felt much more naked than he normally would with no clothes on. The toilet was just a porcelain hole in the ground with a single pipe curving out of it and into the wall. There was nothing to indicate the proper mounting procedure. He supposed it was something like a bidet and did not want to be facing the wrong way when the time came to flush. He squatted over it but lost his balance and had to grab on to the pipe for support.

When he had finished, he walked down the stairs, stopping on the third floor. It was still only five-thirty in the morning, and the house was quiet. The bedrooms were open, and he looked in at the black heads of the family resting against the white of their futons and comforters. He stood there for a while, hardly breathing, until the sleeping bodies blurred before his eyes. He blinked and focused on them again. But they seemed no more real or comprehensible to him than they had before, and a sudden wave of loneliness came over him. He turned and walked away from the feeling, down the stairs, and into the bathroom.

The bathroom was damp, covered in tile. Removing his yukata, Alec squatted on a low, plastic seat in front of a faucet, which jutted out from the wall as though it had been placed there by mistake. He filled a plastic bowl with water and dumped it over his head. Next, shampoo and soap. He scrubbed himself with a cloth that felt like sandpaper against his skin. He finished by dumping another bowl of water over his head. Rinsed and clean, he stood up and rolled back the cover of the small, deep bathtub. A cloud of rising steam hit him in the face. Alec looked at the bathwater, wondering if it was really supposed to be that hot.

He entered the tub left leg first, the heat making him feel as if the skin might peel right off his body. It went like that, one limb at a time, until five minutes later only his head was still above water. He sat back in the tub, knees up, and considered the possibility that he had come to the wrong country.

He sat at the low table, dressed in his new pin-striped suit. Yukiko came in from the kitchen and set down a tray of dishes in front of him. She said good morning without looking at anyone and immediately disappeared. Hiroshi, the youngest, sat to Alec's right, barely awake, slumped over his food. Alec picked up his bowl in his left hand, ate some rice with dried fish flakes on it. He looked at Hiroshi.

"What time do you usually go to school?" he asked in Japanese.

Hiroshi looked up at him through bleary eyes. "Around eight o'clock."

"So, how do you like it?" This time Alec smiled.

"It is okay," Hiroshi said. He didn't smile back.

Alec gave a mild grunt and ate a few more dried fish flakes. He thought of all the hours he had spent studying Japanese in college. None of it seemed to be of much use in actual conversation.

He tried to concentrate on his food. As he choked down a bowl of raw egg and soy sauce, he noticed that Hiroshi was nibbling at a plate of buttered toast and fried eggs.

"Excuse me," he said, gesturing toward Hiroshi's food. "Do you eat this kind of food every day?"

Hiroshi stopped nibbling. "Yes. It is delicious." He started nibbling again.

"I see. What about this kind of food?" Alec motioned to his own Japanese-style breakfast.

"I do not like it very much."

Mrs. Hasegawa came bustling in from the kitchen and set down a dish of fried shrimp in front of Alec.

"Please eat," she said.

"Thank you. It looks delicious," he said, already full.

She sat down across from him. "Where is your office building?"

"It is in Toranomon. Twenty-two Mori Building."

"Eh? Toranomon? It is a very good area—the best for business. Your company must be very important. Yes? Eh! Good. You will take the subway to Toranomon like a Japanese. My friend, Yoshimura-san, will go with you today. In twenty minutes." She held up two fingers. "Do you understand, Alec-san? Twenty minutes."

Her words had been partly muffled as she chewed a large shrimp taken from his plate, and Alec wasn't sure he had understood. "I am working at an American company," he said.

She shook her head until she had finished chewing. "The subway," she said. "You will ride it to work. Yes?" She began to act out the role of a subway passenger, her arm raised upward and bent at the elbow, her thick body rocking violently back and forth.

"Oh, yes, yes. I see. I am sorry." The Japanese words collided against each other in his mouth. "I understand. Yes, thank you."

Yukiko spoke up from the corner where she was finger-combing her bangs in front of a mirror. "Your Japanese is very good. Did you really go to Yale? You are very smart."

Alec saw Mrs. Hasegawa moving toward him with another platter of shrimp.

"Don't you like the shrimp?" Mrs. Hasegawa said. "Eat."

*   *   *

Alec had never seen so many people. They poured into the subway station, moving rapidly, silently, with purpose. Hundreds and hundreds of Japanese, most of them men in nondescript suits, bought their tickets or simply showed their subway passes and walked through the electronic gates. Painted lines on the platform told them where to stand. Electronic signs indicated a train's departure from the previous station, while uniformed men with white gloves shouted out the final approach. Everyone stood close together, mopping their foreheads with multicolored handkerchiefs. And they read: newspapers, magazines, novels; violent, erotic comics bound in thick paperback volumes.

And then the next train was there, doors hissing open to unleash another wave of people. Those getting off surged forward, fighting to make it through the doors, almost running directly into the wall of people waiting to board the train. But the white-gloved men were always there to keep order. Directions purred over the loudspeaker in ultrapolite Japanese.

Feeling himself pushed forward by the weight of the crowd behind him, Alec struggled to maintain his position next to Mari Yoshimura, the guide Mrs. Hasegawa had arranged for him. But it was no use. His new briefcase—a graduation present from his father—had suddenly become a hazard, trapped as it was between the bodies of three men who were being shoved to his left. Alec held on to the handle and felt his arm being painfully twisted. Fear held him for an instant before he tore the briefcase free and pressed forward. Luckily his head was slightly above the crowd, so he was able to keep his eyes on Mari—if he lost track of her, he might never get to work, or even back home. He watched her being jostled and shoved by men almost twice her size. Her pale, round face was expressionless, as though nothing were happening at all. But her eyes were anxious, looking at him, and Alec wondered if she regretted being his guide. He struggled harder, until he was standing next to her.

Then they were in the car, jammed together in the stifling air. Unlike the bus, there was no air-conditioning, only fans spaced just far enough apart to be ineffective. The wave of people stopped for a moment, and Alec tried to create a little space for himself, only to be knocked deeper into the car as the white-gloved attendants made their final push. The doors slid closed, the train jolted into motion.

"You are from New York, Alec-san?" Mari said in excellent English. "I have been there many times with my husband. It is a wonderful city, I think."

Breaking through the silence of the car, Mari's voice sounded embarrassingly loud to Alec, and he suppressed a sudden urge to put his finger to his lips. He noticed that people were glaring at her but merely stealing quick glances at him, their mouths compressed into tight lines of disapproval.

The train pulled into another station, the loudspeaker came to life again. People flowed out and back, prodded by the white-gloved men.

And then Alec heard his own voice in the silent car, telling Mari that he liked New York, too, that it was his favorite city. It was an uncomfortable voice, loud and foreign, and it seemed to him somehow tainted with the disapproval of everyone around him. There was no response from Mari, and Alec could only stand dumbly beside her, listening to the muted rattle of the train, because there were no other sounds to listen to. Hundreds of people crammed together, pushing and shoving, reading and sweating, and not a single word. No apologies. No good mornings. As if the mouths of everyone were closed too tightly to ever open again.

A newspaper flapped in the breeze from an open window. Alec thought he could still hear the echo of his own voice; the train seemed unbearably small. He noticed a young man by the doors with a thin cord leading from his ears into a shoulder bag.

What kind of music was he listening to? Maybe it was just a blank tape.

The train came quickly to a stop, the doors opened.

"We change here to the Ginza line," Mari said.

Shhhh, Alec thought as the white-gloved men herded them off the train.

3

CHRISTMAS CAKE

Awakened by a hidden electronic eye, the building's sleek
metal doors parted soundlessly. Alec walked through
without breaking stride. The second row of doors fell away,
closing behind him as soon as he was inside. There was no
turning back now; he had the feeling that the electronic eye only
worked in one direction. A security guard in full uniform, with
a hat just barely covering his close-cropped hair, bowed to the
waist and said good morning. He repeated the gesture automatically for every person who came in. His voice never changed
tone, he never bowed lower or higher than he had the time
before.

The elevator opened for him on the fourteenth floor, and Alec
stepped out quickly. His legs began walking almost without
him, pulling him around the corner toward two tinted glass
doors with "Compucom, Inc." printed above them in bold
letters. Through the doors he could see the receptionist at her
desk, talking on the telephone, her head bobbing up and down

as she spoke. Alec watched her for a moment, thinking that her ponytail made her look like a schoolgirl. Then he pushed through the doors.

The receptionist was looking at him. "Yes, herro. Can I help, prease?"

Distantly, Alec noticed that she was no longer on the phone. "Oh. Yes."

She gave him a hesitant smile. Almost encouraging, he thought. "And, so, who see?"

"I'm Alec Stern," he said.

"Just moment, prease." She started flipping through a little book, found a page, and traced a list of names with her finger. The finger went to the bottom of the page, then back up again.

Alec shook his head. "*I'm* Alec Stern. I'm supposed to start work here today. First time."

She let out a brief giggle, and her hand flew to her mouth to cover it. "First time, too," she said, indicating herself by touching the tip of her nose with her index finger.

"Really? Your English is very good." Switching to Japanese, he added, "What is your name?"

Her face turned red, the hand went up again, curved and feminine. "Keiko."

He put his own hand forward, holding it just above the desk. "I am Alec. Nice to meet you." As he said it, he realized that the literal translation from the Japanese was something like "Please look after me."

Keiko went through a brief struggle over what to do with her hand. Alec watched as it hesitated between the two points. Suddenly she grabbed his hand, shook it once, then quickly covered her mouth again.

Keiko took a moment to compose herself. "Please wait while I call Boon-san's secretary," she said in formal Japanese.

She punched a couple of buttons on the telephone. Alec looked around the waiting room. High-gloss photographs of various computer parts hung on the walls. The sofa and chairs were bright orange. Company brochures and spec sheets lay on the glass coffee table. Absently, he picked up a brochure and leafed through it.

"Excuse me," Keiko said. "Boon-san will see you now. His office is on the right."

He gave a slight bow, really more of a nod. "Thank you very much. I'd like to talk to you again sometime."

She blushed again. "Oh no, it is nothing. Your Japanese is so good."

Alec had run out of things to say, so he shook his head, smiled, and hurried through the door. He straightened his tie, walked to the right and around a partition.

The central space was crowded with little clusters of desks. There were about twenty people, most of them on the phone, trying to be heard over the noise. Occasionally a telephone message would be yelled from one cluster to another, resulting in a flurry of messages back the other way. Off to one side, two men, one Japanese and one Western, were arguing in Japanese in front of a computer terminal. Alec could barely catch a word. Beyond them was a clear Plexiglas wall, through which he could see several people working in semiprivate offices.

He felt a hand on his shoulder. He turned around.

"Morning, Alec. I'm Joe Boon."

"Hello, Mr. Boon. I'm sorry."

Boon smiled. "For what? Don't be sorry."

He was tall and thin, with a long, sloping face. Looking at him, Alec thought that it was the odd shape of Boon's face that made him handsome, stretching and softening features that might otherwise appear too sharp.

"I was nosing around a little," Alec said.

Boon nodded. "I know. I was watching you from my office." He indicated a large, private room behind him. "I guess it's a slightly different atmosphere from one you'd find in the States."

They walked into Boon's office. Alec sat on the edge of the sofa. Boon sat across from him on a deep leather chair. A computer system was set up to the side of a large, glass-topped desk. The screen showed a bar graph in fluorescent rainbow colors. The walls of the office were lined with photographs of Boon with various Japanese dignitaries. In each one, Boon towered above the others.

"You arrived, when—yesterday?" Boon said. "You must be exhausted."

"Yes, I suppose so. And maybe a little queasy."

Boon laughed. "Good. I can remember feeling that way myself in the beginning. I've heard it's a sign that everything will turn out all right."

"I've never heard that before."

"Trust me, Alec. So aside from your physical ailments, is everything all right? How's the family?"

"Fine, I guess. I mean, it's hard to tell right now. None of them speak any English."

"That's the way it should be."

Alec nodded but couldn't think of anything to say. Boon looked anxious to finish the meeting, his eyes darting around the room. He cleared his throat.

"Okay. So what's the deal again? You stay and work here for the summer. If you like it, you stay longer. And if you don't, you don't. Does that still sound good to you?"

"Yes."

"Good. This is a great opportunity for a guy your age. I could almost guarantee you'll want to stay on."

"Guarantees make me nervous," Alec said, trying to smile.

Boon looked at him intently for a moment. Then he reached over and opened the doors to a bamboo cabinet. Alec couldn't see, but he heard the suction release of the refrigerator door. Boon brought out a large bottle of Sapporo beer and two small glasses. He poured, handed one to Alec, and raised his own.

"Be patient, Alec," he said. "Everyone has a tough time their first few days here. I did. And that was a long time ago."

Alec took a sip of beer and wondered if Americans in Japan always started drinking this early in the day. He looked across at Boon, liking him.

Boon stood up after a while and took Alec on a brief tour of the office. There were five secretaries, all of them Japanese, all named Satoh.

When the tour was finished, Boon left him to get acquainted with two of the Japanese professionals, a man and a woman, who shared one of the small offices located along the far wall of the main office. Takahara appeared to be in his late thirties, stocky, with a broad, flat nose and thick eyebrows that connected above the gold rims of his eyeglasses. He continually tapped his chest with his first two fingers to emphasize the importance of what he was saying. His English was raw and heavily accented, and its tone made Alec think of Mr. Hasegawa's overly masculine, grunting Japanese. Distracted by all the chest tapping, Alec was not really listening to what Takahara was saying but thinking instead of Kawashima, the young woman sitting at the other desk. He wondered why she had not turned around to face him. He had only caught a glimpse of her face when Boon had first introduced them, enough to tell him that she was attractive and probably in her late twenties. She had turned quickly back to her work then, and Takahara had done all the talking. Alec wished he would be quiet. Finally, Takahara said he had a meeting and left.

Alec stayed in the office with Kawashima, staring at her black hair, waiting for her to say something. Still reading, Kawashima began twirling a pencil between her thumb and forefinger. Alec got up from where he was sitting and moved to the chair behind Takahara's desk. He could see most of her face clearly now. It was a good face, he thought, but a little sad. Her nose was small and delicate, like so many of the Japanese women he had seen. But the bones of her face were different. Her chin was straight, almost mannish, and her cheekbones high and sharply defined. In the midst of such strong lines, her mouth seemed soft and unsure, as though she might cry. Her shoulder-length hair hung in bangs across the middle of her forehead and swept down behind her ears. Alec wanted to lean over and touch her hair, it was so black.

"You are staring at me." She said it matter-of-factly in English, without turning around.

Alec expected to feel embarrassed, but didn't. "I guess I am. Sorry."

"It is okay." Kawashima turned around to face him.

She was older than Alec had originally thought, and prettier. Faint lines turned down at the edges of her eyes, reflecting her mouth's suggestion of sadness. Her neck was like a dancer's, long and smooth.

"It's a bad habit, staring," Alec said.

Kawashima almost smiled. "Sometimes it is not so bad."

He let that one sit for a moment, mulling it over. "How long have you worked here?"

"This fall it will be three years."

"Really? Three years is a pretty long time."

"You will find that time goes fast here."

"That's what people keep telling me." He looked out the window at the building across the street, hoping it might offer something witty to say. Fragments of sunlight shot back at him from the reflective glass. "Your English is great. You must have studied abroad."

Kawashima looked pleased. "Yes. Four years at the University of Michigan and then two more working in San Francisco. I enjoyed it very much."

"I've never been to Michigan," Alec said. He began to marvel at his capacity for inanity.

"I remember that it was very cold in winter. Colder than Japan's snow country. But not as beautiful, I think. Do you know of the snow country?"

"Only from reading Kawabata."

She leaned forward in her chair. "You have read *Snow Country?*"

"Yes. For a class at school."

"I am surprised," she said.

Alec nodded but said nothing. They looked at each other for

what seemed to him like a long time, sometimes openly, some-times surreptitiously. Then Kawashima gracefully swiveled her chair so that she looked out the window.

"Michigan was some years ago. I am thirty-three now." She paused. "Does that surprise you?"

"Maybe a little. But being surprised isn't so bad. You're surprised that I've read Kawabata."

"Yes," she said, and he couldn't tell if it was bitterness that he heard in her voice. "But sometimes my age surprises me, too."

"How long have you been sharing an office with Takahara-san?"

"Only three weeks. Now, time does not move so quickly." She smiled, but it was painful. "It was supposed to be a good thing for me, a promotion. But Takahara-san does not like the idea of sharing an office with a woman. Maybe he would not mind if I were young and beautiful, but as I am he is only angry."

"He obviously has no taste."

Kawashima looked down at the floor.

"Couldn't you ask Mr. Boon for a change?" Alec said quickly. "Maybe you could switch with someone down the hall."

She shook her head to signify there was no hope. "Such a thing would cause Takahara-san to lose great face, so one of us would have to leave the company. It is a very bad thing to make someone lose face. Things are never again the same."

"It seems to me that a change is exactly what you need," Alec said. "I mean, if he's so rude to you, why make sacrifices just to accommodate him?"

"People do not think that Takahara-san is rude."

"He doesn't even let you speak. He expects you to sit there and be quiet while he goes around tapping his chest all day."

"You have to understand, Alec-san, that I am a woman. In Japan sometimes that is the most important thing about me." Kawashima paused, noticed that she was still twirling the pencil. She put it down on the desk. "Most women are never allowed to work at an interesting job. And they are told that if they do not get married by age twenty-five, no one will want them. Some men have a name for women like me: it is called 'Christmas cake.' If the cake is not sold by Christmas, these men say, no one will ever buy it. And so I am lucky, I think, because I like my work. Of course, sometimes it is difficult."

Kawashima was quiet after that, staring at the floor. Her cheeks were flushed. Absently, she pushed her hair back behind her ears. Finally, she looked up at him.

"I live with my aunt." She said it like a confession.

Alec nodded his head slowly, looking at her dark eyes. "That's okay."

She smiled faintly. "Yes. Perhaps it is."

The coffee machine was in the communications room. Alec stood beside it, fixing himself a cup. Electronic noises buzzed around him. The fax machine slowly spit out a document. One of the secretaries leaned over the copying machine, adding more paper. A man in a lab coat peered into the circuitry of a PC terminal, then back into his tool bag. The nondairy creamer had stuck to the bottom of the jar. Alec tried to loosen it with a spoon.

Takahara flew by, heading down the hallway toward another part of the office. Ten seconds later, he was standing next to Alec, grinning.

"It was you, Alec-san, so I stop. Maybe we have lunch together? I know very good soba restaurant. Very delicious and very close. So, we go?"

Alec managed to scrape out a half-spoonful of powder. He stirred it into the coffee and took a sip, thinking about his options. No one else had invited him to lunch. And Takahara was blocking the doorway.

He said, "I would like that very much, Takahara-san. Thank you for asking."

As they walked out, Alec threw the coffee in the trash can.

*　　*　　*

Bowl and mouth were connected by long strands of pasty white soba. Chopsticks were held poised in midair at the median, offering limited structural support to the wavering band of noodles. Droplets of brownish broth hung suspended on every surface, waiting. And then the noise began, the noodles disappeared, the drops splattered.

The soba shop was small and crowded. The walls, tables, and counter were made of plain wood of identical grain and color, as if they had been carved from the massive trunk of a single tree. Red paper lanterns with dark touches of Japanese calligraphy hung lightly from the ceiling beams. The counter was filled by a row of solitary men in dark suits, who bent their heads down into the large ceramic bowls of noodles and slurped loudly until there was nothing left. They departed in a hurry, their jackets still half-off, wiping invisible droplets of broth from their chins with the crumpled corners of paper napkins. Other dark-suited men stepped forward to fill the empty spaces. Orders were barked out in semicode, heaping bowls of hot or cold soba were served up from behind the counter. A customer called roughly for a raw egg.

Seated at one of the few tables, Alec studied Takahara's broad, flat face. Yet all he saw was the mouth, cavernous and hungry. And the noodles, limp and helpless, being sucked up and devoured. They had just been served, and Takahara was nearly finished. Alec had not started yet; it was hard to eat with all the noise, as though a huge mouth were sucking on a melting popsicle right next to his ear. He noticed a spot just below the collar of Takahara's textured, sky-blue button-down shirt where the broth had splattered and, behind it, the outlines of a sleeveless T-shirt.

Alec tried to make noises when he ate. With his chopsticks, he dragged the soba from the bowl to his mouth and pursed his lips like a fish; he sucked in hard. The noodles moved a little bit, but not with the same snap as Takahara's. He wondered if he was relying too much on his teeth, chewing instead of sucking. He caught his breath and tried again. Movement was a little better, but there was still no noise. His face felt hot and sticky. He decided to forget about his teeth and concentrate on his lungs; noise would only come with power. The soba stood suspended from his chopsticks, hesitant, like a snake charmer's rope.

Takahara looked up from the remains of his food when he heard the sounds coming from Alec's mouth and gave a faint grunt of approval.

On the way back to the office, Takahara grew talkative. He complained that being put in the same office with Kawashima, a woman, would make his rise to the top of Compucom more difficult. He said that Boon didn't understand how unfair this was to a thirty-seven-year-old Japanese man like himself, who was already divorced, who had expenses and a lonely life. He lived in an apartment in Ikebukuro, sometimes alone, sometimes not. When he wasn't working or in his apartment, he spent his time sailing. He had bought a boat after reading that women are secretly excited by the water. But he usually ended up going out alone, because most women were like Kawashima, old and boring.

"I am too sensitive for most women," he told Alec with sad eyes. "Do you have a sister?"

It was later, around six-thirty. Alec sat at his desk, wondering whether it was all right to leave for the day. He had spent most of the afternoon copying phone numbers onto his Rolodex and filing the papers he was supposed to read. As Boon had explained it, Alec was to be the assistant manager of Compucom's government and industry relations within Japan. This was a relatively new position, and Boon had emphasized the fact that Alec was only the second person to fill it. The original man had not been young enough, Boon felt, to keep up with the constant eating, drinking, and late nights that the job required. His marriage had broken up.

Alec took a deep breath, telling himself to take time and see how things developed. He felt someone looking at him, turned, and saw Park, who occupied the adjacent desk. Park was in fact much nearer to Alec than the position of his desk would have indicated: for some reason his glasses weren't quite right, and he tended to lean very close to whomever he was talking to.

Park was Korean but had been raised partly in Japan. He had already spent two years in the Korean military, received a law-business degree from a prestigious Japanese graduate school, and earned a black belt in judo. Alec had learned these facts from Boon, who had recently hired Park but still seemed to be trying to figure him out.

Park sprang back when Alec turned to face him, almost falling over in his chair. His eyes blinked continuously. "I am very sorry, Mr. Stern," he said in English. "I hope I did not disturb your work." Park spoke fluent Korean, Japanese, and English, though his English tended to be a bit textbook.

"No, not at all," Alec said. "I wasn't doing anything. Just sitting."

Park nodded his head slowly. "I understand, Mr. Stern."

"Please call me Alec if you want. I mean, you were in the military and have a graduate degree. I just graduated from college."

Park's head moved up and down again. "I am Korean, Mr. Stern, so I feel more comfortable if I call you 'Mr. Stern.' I hope I am not rude."

"You're not rude at all, Park-san," Alec said. "In fact, I sort of like being called 'Mr.'—it doesn't really happen that often."

Park's face was inching closer again. "I understand, Mr. Stern. If I may ask, where are you currently residing?"

"In Takadanobaba. You know, on the Tozai line, near Shinjuku. The company arranged for me to live with a Japanese family for the summer. Then maybe I'll move to my own apartment."

Park put his face within a few inches of Alec's. "You are living close to Shinjuku," he said in a half whisper. "Have you yet to visit those wonderful places they call 'Turkish bath'?"

"Actually, I haven't yet. I just got into Tokyo last night. But I've heard they're interesting. How about you? Do you visit them often?"

"All the time," Park said. "Many things relax."

Alec picked up a calculator pen from his desk, began clicking the point in and out with his thumb.

"Perhaps sometime we go together?" Park's eyes were blinking very fast now.

"Sure, Park-san. I'd like that a lot."

Park didn't smile but still managed to look pleased. He pulled his face away from Alec and stood up. "Would you like tea?"

"Yes, I think so."

"It is good for the digestion," Park said, and walked away.

Alec watched him go, feeling suddenly the weight of his exhaustion, the way he had felt it the night before when the Hasegawas were all speaking to him in Japanese, drowning him with questions.

Park returned with the green tea, muttering something about its being an aphrodisiac. Alec nodded encouragement, thinking about caffeine. He thanked Park, took the mug, and held it under his chin, letting the steam bathe his face. Around him, keyboards clicked furiously as the secretaries tried to finish their last letters before quitting time. Behind this noise, the printers buzzed from the terminal room, and people on the telephone seemed to speak louder just to be heard. The desks appeared to have drawn even more tightly together; there was no room to move.

Alec closed his eyes and thought of home.

4

LOST AND FOUND

It was simple at first, a kind of still-life: sky the color of smoke; a crowded street; a small boy and his mother, holding hands. And then the picture began to fill itself out. Like an old film, it flickered to life.

Alec thought it funny that he recognized himself by his walk—even then, at five years, there were signs of the heel-to-toe rock, the slight side-to-side swagger. And his mother, with her usual briskness, slowed just enough to allow for the shortness of his legs. They were walking along Fifth Avenue, just in front of Rockefeller Center. She held his hand through his thick wool mitten. Holding hands was their lifeline, she said—protection from the crush of the Christmas crowd come to see the skating rink and the great tree.

Alec's hand was sweaty and he was tired and he didn't like all the people. He wanted to go home. She told him to stay close, tried to pull him to the left, around a dense crowd that had formed in the middle of the block. But he was already moving to the right, in his own direction, and the crowd came between them, moving into them, forcing them apart. He heard her call his name, and the fear in her voice jabbed at him. But by then he had felt the mitten pulled off his hand, and he knew that she must have been holding it still, even though he could no longer see her through all the people.

The world changed suddenly after that. He was no longer attached to someone who was life-size, big enough for the world and all its dangers. Now he stood alone, and his smallness terrified him. He moved in frantic circles, pushing into the crowd, looking for his mother. He wondered whether or not she would keep his mitten. He began to cry. The crowd of people moved like a flooded river, branching out, creating distances around him.

Finally, Alec stopped moving and waited. He watched and listened. Shiny black shoes scraped and battled against one another, while thin, pointed ones sounded like teeth against the cold sidewalk. Skirts and pants rustled close to his ears, the bony knees coming at him, threatening.

The darkening sky pushed down on him, making him even smaller. A bell was ringing somewhere and, behind it, a faint voice over a loudspeaker and the hum and rattle of passing cars. Alec continued to cry, but he was patient, too, as though time might wait for him. He noticed that the sidewalk was dirty. And then he noticed a pair of gray pants coming toward him—a suit that looked soft, like his father's. The pants led to a pair of black shoes that looked shiny but old, as if they had been worn many times before.

Alec raised his eyes and saw the face of a man who looked about the same age as his father. The face had the warmth he wanted, and he stepped in front of the man, but couldn't speak when he tried, because he was crying too hard. The man stopped walking then and bent down. Alec felt the long arm come around his shoulders, sheltering him from the people rushing by, soothing him with the gray softness. He felt himself being lifted up onto the man's shoulders and knew that he was connected to the world again. There was too much happening at once, and he could only point when he saw his mother at the edge of the sidewalk, his mitten held tightly in one hand. She stood in front of a Salvation Army sign, beside a skinny man dressed as Santa Claus. Again and again, she called out his name, while Santa Clause rang a bell and sang Christmas carols.

It seemed to Alec that it took a long time to finally reach her. He wasn't being carried anymore. And then she was holding him, his red face hard against her chest, both of them crying. It would never happen again, she said. Never. Never, Alec said. He turned around, but the man in the soft gray suit had disappeared into the crowd. There was only Santa Claus, his bell ringing and ringing.

But there was more to it than that.

There was the way people used to tell them how much they looked like each other, Alec and his mother. It seemed back then as if they couldn't walk more than a couple of blocks without someone—usually an old woman or a shopkeeper—saying how remarkable it was, how perfect. Alec's hair had been lighter then, like his mother's, and the women would touch his head with their wrinkled hands and scrunch up their eyes and pucker their lips at him, until he thought they looked like the fish swimming in the tank in his room. He didn't mind it, though. He could see how everyone liked her, how pretty they thought she was. And it was enough to make him feel as though he were holding her hand even when he wasn't.

Alec was seven and eight and nine and ten in those years, but somehow he always felt younger than he knew he was. Often it was his brother, Mark, who made him feel that way. Mark was only a year older, but he was much bigger; already he had the beginnings of their father's broad shoulders and his strong cheekbones and jaw, his dark brown, curly hair. Looking at his brother, Alec felt none of the flush of pride that came to him when told that he looked like his mother. He felt only that there would always be someone older and bigger than he was, someone to stand between him and the wider, more important world.

They fought constantly. It was a large, sprawling apartment, and Alec made use of it in trying to escape to safety. There were times when he would hit Mark and start running before he had even finished his swing, his heart beating so fast that it hurt. His goal at those times never once changed: to find his mother fast became the most important thing in the world. Sometimes he would begin his sprint without knowing where she was in the apartment, and he would have to pass through almost every room just to find her. Then, tears in his eyes, he would race by her and hook his arm around her legs to slow himself down, finally coming to stand behind her with a firm hold on her skirt, around which he could peer at Mark's angry face.

She protected him in that way, and Alec came to expect it of her. It seemed now that nothing was ever settled in those fights, merely swept behind a curtain of pleated skirts. Alec could not remember Mark's fierceness ever once being talked out and understood, only pushed back inside for a little while. But Mark had always been like that, everything under the surface. Sometimes when they played together Alec felt the differences between them, the way he would talk and laugh and cry all the time, all nonsense and melodrama, while Mark kept to himself, not mean, but quiet and tight and far away. Alec wanted to bring him closer, make him talk. A good fight could do that. Sometimes it only took a few seconds to get things started. Being younger helped. He could flaunt the fact that the two of them had all the same television and bedtime privileges, even though he, Alec, was a whole year younger.

Most weekends the four of them drove up to a house they rented in upstate New York. But occasionally they would stay in the city. They lived uptown then, and on those days they would take walks down Fifth Avenue and into Central Park. Alec wondered what other people thought when they saw them together, whether they even guessed that they were looking at a family. He and Mark never talked about how different they looked, how much they each resembled a different one of their parents.

Alec remembered the football his father always brought along, and how they would throw it back and forth among themselves while they walked. Every once in a while his father would surprise them all by tossing the ball to his mother. She would catch it, laughing, and throw it back. The walk always ended at Sheep's Meadow. And she always sat on the same bench, reading the newspaper, while the three of them played touch football. Now and then her head would appear over the top of the paper. When one of them made a difficult catch or a long run, she would carefully set down the paper and clap her hands.

When he was on offense, Alec liked to huddle close before each play, watching while his father used his forefinger to map out the route of the pass play on his palm. Go down-and-out, his father would say, and the finger would do a perfect down-and-out on the hand-size playing field. Or it would fake a buttonhook and go deep, too quick for any defender. Then the snap of the ball, and Alec would be off and running for real, feeling Mark's hand on his back, trying to run out from under it. More often than not, he would drop the ball, or Mark would knock it away. Things would be quiet after that, except for Alec's breathing. He remembered that quiet, and the way his mother's head would disappear again behind the newspaper.

The times when he caught the touchdown ball, he thought he could remember every one of them: feeling the hard football settle into his thin arms, the snug strength of it trapped against his body. Not stopping until he had run right through the makeshift end zone, turning to see his father standing far down the field, his arms raised above his head like a referee. The sound of his mother's clapping was always crisp and strong, and it seemed to Alec in those moments as if they were the only people in the park.

5

GRAPEFRUIT JUICE

Dinner with the family, a couple of nights later. Alec had bathed already. He sat at the low table, pulling now and then at the hem of his yukata to keep his underwear from showing. Mrs. Hasegawa and Yukiko passed in and out of the kitchen, carrying dishes of sukiyaki and small bowls of rice and brightly colored pickled vegetables. Mr. Hasegawa already had his chopsticks in the main serving dish, which was placed at the center of the table. Seated across from Alec, Hiroshi ate some rice by bending his head down to the bowl, putting his lips over the rim, and loudly sucking up little clumps of the grain.

The television was on, turned as usual to a baseball game. The Hiroshima Carp were leading the Hanshin Tigers by a score of 3–2. The Tigers were at bat. A burly American with a beard stepped up to the plate.

"Eh!" Yoshi said. "He is going to hit a home run."

"He is fat," Alec said.

"He is strong," Yoshi said.

Hiroshi looked up from his food. "That's Por-ta. He is American. Do you know him, Alec-san?"

Alec said, "America is a big country, Hiroshi."

Mr. Hasegawa laughed loudly, showing the food in his mouth. "Alec-san is very funny. The funniest American I know."

Mrs. Hasegawa and Yukiko sat down at the table. Alec noticed that his underwear was showing. He pulled again at the hem of his yukata. The sounds of eating grew loud. Arms reached into the center of the table and returned to their small plates and rice bowls with thin slices of beef, glass noodles, crescents of onion, flattened tubes of scallion, half-leaves of cabbage that were withered and soft from cooking. Hiroshi licked sauce from his plate like a cat. Mr. Hasegawa belched with great satisfaction. Porter fouled off four balls before hitting a home run.

"*Sugoi!*" Yukiko said. She looked quickly at Alec, her face turned red.

"Por-ta is strong," Mr. Hasegawa said, more of a grunt than a sentence. "Big and strong because he is American. Eh, Alec-san? And hairy, too. Do you understand *hairy,* Alec-san? Too much hair—like a monkey. It is because of the diet."

"Because of the diet," Alec repeated.

Mr. Hasegawa grunted, lifted his bowl, and shoveled in two mouthfuls of rice. "Yes. It is strange that you are not as big as Por-ta, since you eat the same food. But you have a lot of hair like him, eh? Hair on your head and hair on your arms and legs. Because of the diet."

Alec looked at him. "Like a monkey?"

Everyone laughed. Hiroshi said, "Alec-san is like a monkey! Like a monkey!"

Mrs. Hasegawa used her chopsticks to pile Alec's plate with more food. "Eat," she told him. "Even if you are like a monkey."

"The sukiyaki is delicious," Alec said.

"No. It is terrible," Mrs. Hasegawa said, looking pleased.

"Alec-san needs a haircut," Mr. Hasegawa pronounced.

Alec touched his hair. He looked at Mr. Hasegawa's crewcut, at the little spots of scalp shining through. "Haircut?"

Mr. Hasegawa grunted. "Your hair is long. I will take you to my barber. He cuts the hair of company presidents like me."

Yoshi laughed, reached over, and rubbed the top of his father's head. "Alec-san does not need a haircut like this one."

"He needs to change his diet," Mrs. Hasegawa suggested. "Then he will have less hair. The Japanese have the best diet in the world. Isn't that so?"

Everyone agreed.

The baseball game ended, and players from both teams greeted each other on the field. Alec was thankful that the family's attention could for the moment be focused on something other than his hair. Using a remote control, Yoshi began changing channels. MTV came and went. Several news and talk show programs flashed on the screen. A Japanese aerobics instructor called out the number of sit-ups she was doing. She vanished as quickly as she had appeared, succeeded by a herd of zebra scattering across an African plain at the approach of a lion. The voice of the off-screen Japanese narrator was disturbingly uninflected.

Mrs. Hasegawa and Yukiko began to clear the table. Alec stood up to help but sat down again when Mrs. Hasegawa shook her head and made a clucking noise with her tongue against the back of her mouth. She brought out a tray piled with mango, grapefruit, and kiwi.

"These are from my husband's business," she said. "In Japan, fruit is very expensive. But it is better than American fruit. Here, eat this."

She put a grapefruit on Alec's plate. He looked at it for a moment, aware that it had a much greater value in Japan than it did in America. He wasn't sure he wanted to eat it. He felt everyone looking at him. Finally, Mrs. Hasegawa sighed loudly. She reached over and began peeling it for him, her stubby fingers easily breaking through the yellow skin. Alec watched her, thinking of his mother, of how she had peeled grapefruits for him in just the same way. They were Florida grapefruits—the kind that relatives sent in boxes at Christmastime—and they were sweet.

Mrs. Hasegawa broke off a section of grapefruit and handed it to him. The family looked on in silence as he chewed. He could taste the juice running into his mouth. It was sweet the way the others had been sweet, no bitterness at all, and he wanted to close his eyes for just a second, so he could be alone.

"It is good," Mr. Hasegawa said. "Eh, Alec-san? Number one. The best in the world, these grapefruits."

Alec nodded his head. His eyes moved to the television. The zebras were gone, displaced by chimpanzees picking lice from each other's heads.

"Eh! Look!" Hiroshi said, pointing. "Alec-san's on television!"

Alec laughed along with everyone else, until he could no longer taste the grapefruit's sweetness on his tongue.

6

BRISTLES

Alec stared through the tinted windows of the Hasegawas' indigo Mercedes sedan, feeling victimized by fate. He was looking at a dead-end street, half lit by four streetlights. Oddly shaped one-story houses stretched in two tight rows, like pieces cut to fit the wrong puzzle. Some of the roofs were made of corrugated tin that extended out over the eaves in sharp-edged canopies. Other houses were capped by dark green tiles that curved over one another to form graceful, protective shells. Resting above the dim glow of the streetlights, the tiles appeared sea dark and ancient, like relics of another time and place that had been set down mistakenly in a jungle of tin and asphalt.

Evening had only just set, but the neighborhood appeared to be empty of people. No children could be seen playing together on the street, no adults talking outside to cool down. Alec found it hard to believe that every family ate dinner at exactly the same time each night. In the driver's seat, Mr. Hasegawa grunted with satisfaction as he stopped the car in front of a small, dingy building that looked like a tool shed with windows. A barber-shop pole encased in Plexiglas stood in front, revolving inter-mittently, as though wounded. They got out of the car. Mr. Hasegawa grunted again as the central locking system operated with a quiet whirr. Alec looked at him across the hood, at the bristly outlines of his crewcut. He ran his fingers through his own hair, suddenly afraid of what might happen to it. He liked hair—it felt human. Bristles were for hedgehogs.

As they approached the barbershop, Alec saw that it was more dilapidated than he had thought. The exterior wall was scarred with gauges and discolorations, the white core of the wood showing through the original dark brown. And the cor-rugated tin roof had been severely dented where it extended out over the street. The front window appeared to be the only part of the building that was undamaged. Alec peered through it into a clean, well-lit room almost bare of furniture. A broad-faced man in a black-and-white-striped apron sat in the single barber's chair with his feet propped on a stool, reading a newspaper. He inhaled deeply from a cigarette. His forehead seemed unusually long, and Alec realized it was because he had no eyebrows. A woman, her face pale and lifeless from too much makeup, sat in a chair to the man's left. She looked absently at her fingernails, as if she already knew the condition of each one. At the back of the room, a gaunt teenage boy in a plain white apron stood stiffly with his arms folded across his chest.

Still standing outside, Mr. Hasegawa pointed two fingers through the window at the man without eyebrows and the woman sitting beside him. "The proprietor and his wife," he grunted. He directed his fingers toward the boy. "And the apprentice. Do you understand, Alec-san? A Japanese barber-shop."

Alec nodded, not quite sure what it was he was supposed to understand. Then he watched Mr. Hasegawa make enough of an entrance for both of them, knocking and grunting and finally striding through the hanging strips of cloth and into the bar-bershop like a feudal lord returning to his fiefdom after battle.

He might have laughed, except that Mr. Hasegawa had a firm grip on his arm, pulling him into the room behind him. Their entrance was greeted by immediate action. The proprietor vaulted from the barber's chair and folded the newspaper in a single motion. His wife and apprentice covered the room in a few quick steps. And then they were all standing in a row, bent to the waist, telling Mr. Hasegawa what an honor it was to see him again. The proprietor called him "Sha-cho," a term of great respect used for company presidents. Mr. Hasegawa seemed to stand taller, grow larger. He introduced Alec to the proprietor and his wife. He boasted about Alec's intelligence and his skill in Japanese, about the high social standing of his family in America.

The proprietor ran his fingers through Alec's hair. The apprentice looked on intently, studying the older man's technique, the way he touched the hair, his understanding of its texture. Alec looked at both of them, wondering who cut *their* hair—it was as short as Mr. Hasegawa's. Spots of scalp showing through. And bristles. A room full of hedgehogs. He touched his own hair again, trying to calm himself. The proprietor's wife led him to the barber's chair. Her fingers moved softly up and down his arm. The apprentice disappeared into a back room concealed behind an orange curtain and reappeared carrying a tray of steaming white towels. Alec closed his eyes as the proprietor coiled the hot towels about his face. He could hear Mr. Hasegawa's continued boasting and the faint cooing sounds of admiration made by the proprietor's wife.

The towels came off. Alec opened his eyes. The proprietor was already bent over him, applying warm shaving cream with a brush. Over his shoulder, Alec saw the apprentice taking towels and passing implements. The proprietor reached out his hand for the straight-edge razor. Alec had never been shaved before, and he felt his body go rigid at the sight of the blade. The proprietor leaned down over him. Small beads of sweat had formed on his forehead, on the smooth skin where his eyebrows were supposed to be, on his equally hairless upper lip. Behind him, Alec saw the apprentice pause in confusion: now that the master was at work, he didn't know where to stand. As though performing some kind of ritual mating dance, he began to move in short, jerky steps behind the proprietor, his head bobbing closer and then farther away, trying to find the most unobtrusive place from which to observe.

When the shave was finished, the proprietor wiped Alec's face with a scented towel. Alec noticed that he seemed preoccupied, his eyes darting sidelong glances toward the chair where Mr. Hasegawa now sat. Reflected in the mirror he saw the proprietor's wife standing behind Mr. Hasegawa's chair, his face in her hands, her red-nailed fingers massaging his temples. The back of his head was resting against the pillow of her breasts. His eyes were closed, and he was still grunting and boasting, though more softly now, brief comments about the success of his business. She did not once look up from what she was doing, and after a minute Alec realized that the proprietor had stopped glancing at her altogether and resumed his work.

The haircut was beginning. The proprietor shook a milky substance into his palms, which he quickly cupped over Alec's head like a helmet. Alec closed his eyes as the hands warmed his scalp. Then the hands lifted and the fingers began to work. They started with his hair and moved to his temples, the back of his neck, behind his ears. Knuckles of smooth stone kneaded his skull as though it were dough, while agile fingertips pressed heat into unseen areas of pain and tension. Minutes passed. Alec felt himself floating. The sound of clipping scissors came to him from far away. It was a dream, his head somehow suspended above his body, his hair rising still higher, infused with the warmth and energy of the proprietor's sure hands. He kept his eyes closed and listened to the cutting of his own hair and thought that he had never in his life met such wonderful, dedicated people. Such noble people.

It was not right then that he noticed how quiet the room had grown. It seemed that Mr. Hasegawa had run out of boasts for a while, and the proprietor's wife had stopped cooing. It was not then that Alec noticed their absence from the room, but later, when the apprentice was already opening the many different bottles of tonic to be used when the haircut was over. And the first of those tonics had already been massaged into his scalp by the time they returned from the back room acting as if nothing had happened. Alec's eyes were open then, and he looked over at Mr. Hasegawa, who was sitting again in the straight-backed chair, and then back at the mirror, at the hairless face of the proprietor, for some sign of understanding or recognition of what he knew had taken place. But nothing had changed. The proprietor was all fierce concentration, all points of energy, the way he had always been. He was finishing the job he had set out to do.

For a moment, Alec thought he might see himself get up and walk out of the barbershop, away from his own soiled notions of dignity and dedication. But he didn't move a muscle. He stayed where he was in the barber's chair, staring at the newly visible patches of his scalp, as one scented tonic after another was massaged into his hair.

7

HOSPITALIZATION

There was a note from Boon sitting on Alec's desk when he arrived at the office Thursday morning. This in itself was not unusual—Boon had told Alec that he was a message writer by nature, constantly scribbling here and there, leaving a trail of paper scraps throughout the office. This message was even more cryptic than usual, and Alec had to track Boon down in order to translate it.

"Oh, that," Boon said, rummaging in his closet. "I want you to head over to MITI this afternoon around two-thirty. There's this guy over there—I think his name is Nobi Sato, or something like that. Anyway, he's only twenty-seven, but they're already giving him a lot of responsibility in the high-tech trade area. So I thought it might be a good idea if you and he got together, got to know each other a little bit. Besides being a help to us, he could probably introduce you to some people. You know, socially. Hey, here it is." He pulled out an old tin of black shoe polish, then stuck his head back into the closet. "Now where's the brush, for Christ's sake?"

At two-thirty, Alec was nervously pacing back and forth in the elevator of the MITI building. MITI stood for the Ministry of International Trade and Industry, the most powerful of Japan's government ministries. The bureaucrats who worked there represented the top of Japanese society, both professionally and socially. Alec wondered what exactly it was that he represented. He thought of the job he used to have at a neighborhood movie theater when he was fifteen.

He stepped out of the elevator and walked down one long hallway after another, following the directions he had been given over the phone. The building was clean and well lit—much better, he had heard, than some of the other ministries. But it still seemed oppressive, with hundreds of doors lined up in a row on each floor. One of these doors belonged to Sato's department. Alec pushed it a couple of inches and poked his head into the room.

Scuffed metal desks and filing cabinets covered the square space, all of them buried under stacks of unfiled papers, half-empty Styrofoam cups, and ashtrays overflowing with cigarette butts. The windows were propped open with books, a single fan circulating the hot air. Behind the papers, a battery of young white-shirted Japanese men pored over their research.

A couple of heads looked up when he entered, then back down at their work. Alec cleared his throat. In Japanese he asked if, by any chance, Sato-san was in the office. From behind the tallest stack of papers, a hand shot up.

"Hi. Alec, right? I am Nobi."

They shook hands. Alec said, "Nice to meet you. Your English is terrific."

Nobi smiled. "Not true, but thanks anyway. I studied in America." He waved his hand in the direction of the door. "This really is not the best place for conversation. Perhaps we should go downstairs for some coffee."

They took the elevator to the basement, where the ministry coffee shop was located. The room was partly filled with older ministry officials, many of them peering at each other through heavy black-rimmed eyeglasses. After they were seated, Alec watched Nobi while he ordered iced coffee for both of them. He spoke to the waitress in masculine Japanese that sounded abrupt, almost guttural. She responded without seeming to be there at all, the word *hai* coming from her mouth like electronic beeps. Absently Nobi waved his right hand, the waitress hurried away.

"My director here at MITI has heard very good things about you from Mr. Boon," Nobi said.

"Thanks, that's nice to hear," Alec said. "But I haven't even been here a week yet, so I can't really say I've been much of a help to the company. I've been mostly, you know, getting settled and stuff."

"Are you here for a long time?"

"I don't know. At least for the summer, though it'll probably be longer. It's kind of a trial period, in case things don't work out. I got the job through a professor of mine at school who knows Mr. Boon."

The waitress arrived with two glasses of black coffee on ice. She was very careful not to look at either of them. Alec waited until she had left before speaking again.

"So how did your English get so good?"

"Well, I joined MITI after I graduated from Todai—Tokyo University," Nobi said. "I had been through the usual school English program, but, like many Japanese, my English was still not good. So the ministry paid for me to study economics at Stanford for two years."

"Do you ever think about going back?"

Nobi looked surprised. "To America? No—well, perhaps sometimes. You probably have heard how it is: a person leaves Japan for too long a time and cannot ever really return—he becomes too different. I think sometimes that I returned just before it became too late. I was having such a good time in

California, with an American girlfriend and everything. Two or three months longer and perhaps I would have decided not to return to Japan. But I do know that I have a position in Japan that I would never have anywhere else. And, of course, I am Japanese."

"It's not easy to arrive in a new country and feel comfortable the way you did," Alec said. "Not that easy for me, anyway. Not here, where things are so different. I mean, I knew it would be different. But it's . . ." He paused. Nothing came to him. "I don't know. It's just really different." He felt his face getting hot, took a sip of coffee.

"That is exactly how I felt when I arrived in California," Nobi said. "Time makes some differences less strong, I think."

"Which differences?"

"Which differences are important to you?"

Alec shrugged. "I don't know. Too many."

"How about a girlfriend? Do you have one?"

"A girlfriend? No. Not at the moment."

"So there is one thing that can change. Yes? If you have a Japanese girlfriend, other differences will disappear. It is the best way."

"I don't doubt it," Alec said. "But I don't know any women here. And I don't know how to meet them, either. Not in Japanese. That combination can be sort of prohibitive."

"Not prohibitive," Nobi said firmly. He took a sip of coffee and leaned closer to Alec. He looked as though he was enjoying himself. "You have to be very careful with Japanese women when you first meet them. American women are more aggressive. In America, you walk up to a pretty girl and ask her to dance. Yes? They expect you to. But it is not like that in Japan. Here you have to be patient. The women learn to expect a certain kind of behavior from men, and when they do not get it, they fly away. And then it breaks our hearts. Yes?"

Alec fiddled with his spoon and anything else he could find on the table. "Okay. So let's say I go to a club. Right? And I see this woman over by the bar—she's beautiful, and I want to meet her.

What then? I mean, if I can't ask her to dance, there are only so many things I can say to her."

"But you must not think of it in that way," Nobi said. "Remember: this is Japan. There is much less flexibility in relationships between men and women here. First date, second date, third date, on each one she expects that you act a certain way, that you do and say certain things. It might not sound so exciting now, but it is." He wiped his forehead with a handkerchief, put it back in his pocket. "All right. So you see a beautiful woman and you think you will die if you do not meet her. Yes? That is very good—everything will be right because of that feeling. You must walk up to her slowly and compliment her. Not like a big movie star, but quietly. I would say that quiet confidence is very important. So, you compliment her beauty and her clothes, everything, and you make her laugh. And then you suggest dancing. Before you leave, you tell her that if you do not see her again, you will become very ill, you will be hospitalized. When she hears that, she will give you her phone number. That is the first meeting."

Alec was laughing. "Come on. Hospitalized? That's the worst line I've ever heard."

Nobi was trying to look indignant. "Of course. But there is sympathy for anyone who would take rejection so hard. Yes?"

"This must be a purely Japanese phenomenon," Alec said. "From my experience, not even the threat of suicide works in New York."

Nobi laughed loudly. A group of MITI officials at a nearby table looked over, their expressions severe. Alec saw them and cleared his throat. Nobi looked up, quickly pulled himself together, and signaled for the check.

On the way out, Nobi invited Alec to a party at his apartment that weekend. He wrote out the address and phone number and told him that there would be many beautiful women there, and many opportunities for hospitalization.

8

ACCOUNTS

Alec wavered a little outside the door, steadied himself by placing his hand on the head of the stone lion. As usual, the glass door was unlocked, and he pushed through it hard, catching it just before it slammed into the wall. The stairs were almost too steep for him. He took his time, leaning forward, grabbing the handrail with his left hand. Midway up there was a small landing where he stopped to regain his strength and sense of balance. A wire bird cage stood against the wall, almost even with his own height. Within the cage, two lovebirds sat together on a perch, their beaks touching. He thought they looked very pretty. Tentatively, afraid of being bitten, he stuck his forefinger between the wires and touched one of the birds on the wing. The bird didn't move. He touched it harder; both birds fell off the perch, landing with a thud at the bottom of the cage. He desperately wanted to put the birds back on the perch but couldn't figure out how to get his whole hand in the cage to do it. The birds looked funny with their feet sticking up in the air and little tufts of stuffing sticking out from under their wings. Realizing that it might be easier in the morning, he started climbing the stairs again.

At the second-floor landing, he kicked off his loafers, then glided in his socks along the short hallway toward the next set of stairs. A light was on in the eating room, its edge brightening the wood floor ahead of him. Mrs. Hasegawa was still awake. He could hear her harsh, openmouthed breathing, could picture her sitting at the low table, the house account books spread out before her. Often in the early morning when Alec went downstairs for a bath, he would walk into the eating room to find her asleep on the tatami, the account books still open on the table. He knew that she only slept a few hours a night and would try not to disturb her. But she would somehow sense his presence and awake on her own, like a bear emerging from a period of hibernation. She always stood up and moved slowly, as though her legs caused her considerable pain. They looked heavy and unused, her legs, and Alec worried that her circulation was not good. But he had once seen her riding a bicycle.

She always wanted to talk in the morning. And she would want to talk now, too. She would ask him questions about everything he had said and done since he had left for work. She would try to feed him. Alec took the stairs guiltily, one at a time, trying not to make a sound. He held his breath: two more and he would be up and around the corner, home free.

"Alec!" The voice made him jump.

"*Hai*," he responded automatically, walked back down the stairs to the eating room. The scene was just as he had imagined it: Mrs. Hasegawa sat, beaming, on the tatami floor, the account books open on the table. She stood up when she saw him.

"Come. Sit down." She pointed to a spot at the table. He sat as close to it as he could manage. She peered at him, began laughing, her breasts shaking. "Alec! Have you been drinking beer again?" Then her mouth stopped smiling; she looked suddenly very wise. "*Mugi-cha*," she said, and disappeared into the kitchen.

Alec tried to remain seated but no longer felt strong enough to support his upper body. He lay back on the tatami. The white plaster ceiling and plain wooden crossbeams seemed unusually bright. Resting comfortably, he pulled at his tie to loosen it, began unfastening the buttons on his shirt.

Mrs. Hasegawa came back into the room carrying a glass of dark brown liquid. Alec was lying on his back, half-undressed, scratching his stomach. She started laughing again, almost spilling the drink as she handed it to him. Propping himself up on one elbow, he took a sip. The cold, bitter tea felt alive in his dry mouth. He drank off the rest of the glass. Mrs. Hasegawa returned from the kitchen with a liter bottle of the tea, refilled his glass. Looking very pleased, she sat down at her place again.

"Where did you go tonight?" she asked.

Alec looked at her, sideways and up, from the floor. A response in Japanese wasn't forthcoming, so he smiled at her until he could put together an answer. "I went to a party at the house of my friend from MITI."

Her eyes widened. "Is that so? A party? What sort of party? Were there girls?"

"It was a party to watch the summer fireworks," he said slowly, piecing the backward grammatical constructions together in his head. "There were a lot of girls. Japanese girls."

Mrs. Hasegawa looked shocked. "Eh? Japanese girls? Do you like them? What did you talk about?"

Alec felt inadequate in the face of her hunger for information. "I told them that they were beautiful and that I liked their clothes. One girl in a red dress, I asked her to dance, but her husband said that she couldn't. His face was the same color as her dress."

"You should not ask a married woman to dance," she said severely. "Japanese women are different from American women, you know."

"I have heard that, Hasegawa-san."

"Call me Mother."

"Mother," Alec said softly.

"That is very funny. What else did you say?"

"Mother," Alec repeated.

She shook her head patiently. "No. At the party."

If he just lay on his back and closed his eyes, Alec found that the talking itself didn't require a great deal of effort. "I told every girl I met that if I did not see her again, I would become very sick. I do not think they understood." He opened his eyes, rolling his head to the side in order to see her expression.

Mrs. Hasegawa looked severe again. She was making her favorite noise of disapproval: a loud clucking. Alec thought she sounded like a chicken. He almost laughed but stopped himself by turning over on his stomach, cradling his face in his arms.

"There is a very important thing about Japan that you do not yet know, so I will tell you," she said to his back. "Even though you are not very tall, you are handsome. You are not fat. Your family must be very important—it is a good family. So, you cannot have just any girl for a girlfriend; she must also be of good family, eh? Do you understand?"

He heard the pouring sounds as she refilled his glass. "Yes, thank you. You are right," he said, his voice muffled by his arms. "You are right."

There was a break in the conversation. Alec wondered if she had gone back to working on the account books. Mr. Hasegawa had inherited the family business of wholesaling fruits and vegetables to restaurants and supermarkets throughout the To-kyo area. It appeared that the business was thriving. An indigo Mercedes was parked in the garage of their narrow, four-story house. They had an extra bedroom. They ate mango and kiwi. Yet it seemed to Alec that, outside of these material rewards, all Mrs. Hasegawa really had to herself were the account books, which she spent at least an hour every night updating. They were her responsibility, not her husband's. She chose to work on them late at night, when everyone else in her family had gone to bed. Alec wondered whether there was a kind of freedom in that routine—in the chance to have, for just an hour or two, a job and place of her own, free of her children and household chores.

In that sense, the account books were more real to her than was her husband. Aside from meals, Alec had yet to see the two of them together. Mr. Hasegawa's office was on the third floor of the house, and he could be found there at all hours of the day, unless he was at the low table, watching the baseball game on TV, his wife and daughter wordlessly serving him dinner.

"Do you like Scotch?" Mrs. Hasegawa asked.

Alec looked up. "What? Yes."

Slowly she stood up, walked into the kitchen. When she returned, she set a bottle of Scotch and two glasses with ice down on the low table. She mixed two drinks with a little water, handed one to him.

"*Kampai*," she said.

"*Kampai*." He took a sip of the strong drink.

She sat down on the tatami again. "Sometimes I get very tired."

"You are always working, Mother."

"Working? No, I am not working. I am only taking care of the house."

"But taking care of the house takes a lot of time. Perhaps more time than your husband spends working." He said it without thinking.

Something in her eyes seemed to light up, focus on him more intently. "My husband?" She laughed, but he didn't hear any humor in it. "In the house, my husband only does work. But he leaves the house often; I almost never leave. And when he comes back, he starts to work again. He does not tell me what he does when he leaves. He does not talk to me."

Alec took a sip of Scotch and felt something open up around him, between them, as if they had crossed some sort of line together by talking. Then he turned away and lay down on his stomach, afraid that if he looked at her too long, she might stop coming into focus.

"What about your children? Do you talk to them?"

She shook her head slowly. "My husband and I, we are not from Tokyo. Eh? We are from Tohoku, in the north—from a very small village. But our children, they are from Tokyo. And so, sometimes it is difficult to talk. Sometimes I think they are children of Tokyo, not of me."

They were quiet after that, Alec knowing that she expected him to speak but not quite sure what to say. Finally she picked up her pen, went back to working on the account books.

But he knew something about her now, and he felt in her silence the truth of what she had told him. Watching her, he saw the tedium of her daily life; saw, too, the intensity of her excitement at his return and the chance for conversation. Dizzy, he rolled over and sat up. Mrs. Hasegawa stared up at him with curious, almost hesitant eyes. He smiled at her, took another sip of Scotch.

"I want to tell you a little about my friend Nobi," he said.

9

HEADACHE

The restaurant was distinctly European. Crystal chandeliers shed soft light throughout the dining room. Earthen-colored Tuscan floor tiles blended with chairs of mahogany and leather, giving the room a sense of opulence and comfort. Crisp and white, the tables stood at attention, uncrowded, inviting. Japanese waiters floated from place to place, attentive and discreet, cutting sharp figures in their starched black-and-white uniforms.

It was a business dinner, Alec's first, and Boon was being no help at all. He sat as though in a trance, his fingertips touching in front of his half-closed eyes. A dessert menu lay open before him, but there was no motion in his face, not even a hint that anything was taking place within his head.

Alec was getting a headache. He imagined himself as an inverted pachinko machine, his shoulders and neck producing little silver balls of muscular tension, which, one by one, were bouncing their way up into his head. Noise reverberating in his brain. Levers clicking. Balls clattering. A cacophony of sound and pain. He looked around the table in the hope that someone else might be sharing his experience. It seemed unlikely. The two men from the Japanese electronics firm mirrored Boon's neutral countenance. Imamura, the senior executive, sat like a schoolboy in church, his hands in his lap, his eyes cast downward. Occasionally he would glance furtively at his partner, Ayada, who was acting as both translator and *atendo*, caretaker and protector of the higher-ranking man.

Silence had overtaken the table as if by consensus. Heads had bent down to study the dessert menus and had not been raised again. Alec could not understand what had happened. The meal had gone smoothly up until then, formalities mixing easily with talk about baseball, women, and drinking. With each glass of wine, the faces of both Japanese men had evolved into deeper shades of red, while Alec soon believed himself to be a native speaker. His tongue felt loose, athletic. He was talking to Imamura about the benefits of bachelorhood. He was laughing with Ayada as they discussed the dangers of drinking too much sake before telling the bar hostess that her pert breasts were the only true national treasures of Japan. And he was aware that Boon was taking it in, not necessarily understanding all the Japanese, but knowing what was behind it, watching him.

It had been an easy dinner, Alec thought. A good dinner. And he had contributed to it, had kept the conversation flowing just the way he thought it should. Only to have Boon ruin it now with his determined silence. Alec waited, but still no one said a word. Finally he cleared his throat loudly and looked at Imamura.

"Do you follow American baseball, Imamura-san?"

Startled, Imamura mumbled, No, and glanced questioningly at Boon. Alec was about to ask him another question when he saw Boon staring at him. He closed his mouth, looked hard at the menu, and decided not to speak for the rest of the evening.

In the pachinko world of his head, a jackpot had been struck. Little silver balls of pain were bouncing everywhere.

"I think this is my favorite view of Tokyo," Boon said. "There's always a mist, or cloud cover, or something. And with those great skyscrapers poking through. It hardly looks real."

It was just the two of them now, and it was late. They sat sprawled in deep lounge chairs on the top floor of the Akasaka Prince Hotel. Alec took a sip of beer and followed Boon's gaze through the huge picture window. Above its blanket of mist, the city seemed to shoot off in every direction; to snake and sprawl, to rise skyward, lifting him with it. He felt his exhaustion turn to awe at the play of shadow and light. To the left, Boon pointed out the dark outlines of the grounds of the Imperial Palace, a vast expanse of land in a city where so little was available that a golf club membership could cost a million dollars.

Boon pushed his glasses up and rubbed his eyes with his thumb and forefinger. Tonight was the first time Alec had seen him when he wasn't bursting with energy. He felt closer to him because of it, as though he had been let in on a secret.

"You look kind of tired." He said it timidly, not sure that it was the right thing to do. He waited.

Boon stopped rubbing his eyes, his glasses fell back into place. The corners of his mouth turned up a little. "Yeah, I guess I am. Sometimes it just catches up with me."

"Please don't stay up for my sake, Mr. Boon. I can just finish my drink and head home. It's really no problem."

"Not at all, Alec," Boon said. "You'll find you get used to being tired over here, the hours are so much longer. Also, I guess I'm getting a little older—forty's not so young anymore. Though it doesn't always feel like forty. There's so much to do." He paused. "And please, call me Joe. Japan's so formal I almost never hear my first name anymore. I kind of miss it. Okay?"

Alec nodded his head. "Good," Boon said, then slapped his thigh. "Anyway, I didn't bring you up here to subject you to my ramblings. I want to know what you thought of the dinner, what kinds of things you picked up from it."

"Maybe you could tell from my behavior at the table that I wasn't really sure what was going on," Alec said.

"Yes, actually, I could." Boon smiled suddenly. "But that's okay. Just tell me what you thought."

"Well, I thought the dinner was going fine until everyone stopped talking. Then, suddenly, it all felt very awkward. That's when I made the mistake of asking Imamura about baseball. Then you gave me that look and I shut up for good. How's that?"

"Fair enough," Boon said. "I decided about halfway through that it wasn't the time to talk business. It was clear that they were expecting some serious discussion of the proposal—Imamura is the highest man they've sent over so far—and I sensed that it might be in our best interest to keep them a little off balance. So, the dinner was really just another chance to feel them out, to get a better understanding of who we're doing business with." He took a sip of his drink. "I wanted you there for a couple of reasons, the most obvious of which was to give you the chance to see firsthand how people do business over here—or, in this case, how they choose not to do business. But you were also a very active participant in the dinner. Your being there made them uncomfortable at first, because they weren't expecting you. In general, bringing surprise guests is not something to be recommended. But I thought they would like you, and they did. That's what allowed me to run the dinner that way. I didn't realize your Japanese was good enough to really talk to people."

"Neither did I," Alec said. "After a few drinks, though, I just seemed to pick up speed. I probably won't be able to speak a word tomorrow."

"Knowing the language can be a great asset. Maybe I should've put more time into it when I was younger."

"Maybe so," Alec said, "but I got the feeling at dinner that you understood a lot more of the Japanese conversation than you let on. What there was of it, anyway."

"Yeah, I guess you could say that. Remember: when you don't understand much, you have to be very shrewd." He gave a quiet laugh, as though it were a joke he had heard many times.

Alec had been looking away, out the window, but there was something in Boon's laugh—in the softness of it—that made him turn back to Boon for just a second, almost to make sure it was still really him. He remembered hearing his father laugh that same way once before. It was a laugh of modesty and warmth, so unlike his usual laugh, which had always sounded harsh to Alec, something thrown at people across the dinner table. This was a laugh of unconscious moments, and Alec looked more closely at Boon, feeling that he had somehow been let in on another secret, this one less clear and more important.

"Joe?"

Boon looked surprised for a moment at hearing his own name.

"I was just wondering about your family. If you have one, I mean."

"Sometimes I wonder about my family, too," Boon said. Then he smiled. "Don't look so serious, Alec."

"Sorry."

"And don't apologize. Okay? My wife and I split up a long time ago. Diane was never really happy here. She tried to make it work for a couple of years. Then, one morning, she said she thought she had to leave, to go back. Things were just starting to work for me at the company, and I felt I had to stay on. For my career. So that was pretty much it. Of course, there were other problems, too."

"Do you have any kids?"

Boon held up his index finger. "One. A daughter. She's at school in Connecticut, where her mother lives. She'll enter tenth grade this fall. I haven't seen her in a year."

"You miss her."

"Yes. Sure."

"Do you get lonely sometimes?"

"Lonely? Not really," Boon said, looking out the window. "Not anymore. There's too much to do. But life's not all one way or another, Alec—not all loneliness or happiness. I guess I don't believe people can separate the parts of their lives like that. And if you spend your life thinking you can, or even trying to, I think you always end up a little disappointed."

They were both quiet then. Alec found himself caught in the strange, bittersweet mood of the nearly empty bar. Waiters in red jackets emptied ashtrays and wiped the tables clean. Chairs were put up, lights were turned off; the room became a patchwork of shadows. The bartender glanced nervously at the two foreigners, not wanting to speak to them, hoping they would realize on their own that it was time to leave. Looking out from the darkened interior, the glowing, mist-covered sky appeared otherworldly, an apparition.

10

MOTORCYCLE DREAMS

The steam rose from the water of the wooden bathtub, fast and then slow. Suspended, swirling, it cloaked the walls and ceiling of the small room in layers of billowed white gauze. And with it came the heat, wet and sensual, all energy in the confined space.

Alec reached up and pushed the window open a crack. Steam poured out the opening, briefly painting the darkness a cloudy white before disappearing. He rested the back of his head against the rim of the small, deep tub. Eyes closed, he listened to his breathing as it became more and more relaxed. He crossed his arms underwater, hugging himself.

His mind filled with pictures. Some of them were real, some imagined. His mother appeared in every one of them. In one she was playing Chopin on the piano, a half smile on her face as her fingers danced and hopped across the keyboard. In another she was reading aloud to him as he sat next to her on the sofa, her finger following the words so he would know where she was in the story. But the most frequent picture was of the kitchen table. It was old and unvarnished, thick and bare like a chopping block, with burns, nicks, and gauges on its surface. Its length fit snugly against one wall of the large kitchen, so that there was just enough room for a wooden stool at each end and two folding chairs along one side. In the mornings, Alec liked to sit on his stool across from Mark, watching his mother make breakfast.

Mark had already begun playing team sports after school, leaving Alec to come home alone after classes were done. His mother was almost always in the kitchen, preparing dinner. In between trips to the stove she sat at the table, on Mark's stool, with a couple of magazines open in front of her. The sleeves of her blouse were rolled up, and there were light streaks of flour on her dark green apron. Her blond hair was tied back from her face. She drank lukewarm coffee with milk in it from a gray pottery mug.

Alec learned that there were no rules in the afternoons. She would look up from her magazines or from the counter where she had her hands in a large cooking bowl and ask him questions. She wanted to know if he was scared when he went to school on the first day of classes every year or what he remembered of the books she used to read to him when he had been small. Some of the questions were hard in that way, and he had to think for a minute before answering.

She encouraged him to ask her questions. She said once that there was nothing he could ask her that she wouldn't answer. Nothing. Alec felt older when she said that; he took it seriously. Once he asked her why he sometimes heard her and his father yelling at each other at night through the closed door of their bedroom, when they thought he and Mark would be asleep. Her face tightened then, he knew it did, and she told him that all parents fight once in a while, even when they love each other very much.

*   *   *

It was hard to know exactly when the look and feel of the pictures in his mind changed permanently. But whenever it was, it seemed to Alec that suddenly the pictures were too sharp and clear to belong to anyone, least of all himself. There were no fingerprints on them, nothing to show that they had ever been touched.

Things might have changed when he was eleven, on the afternoon when his mother left the apartment to begin her job. It was a good job, she said, teaching piano a few afternoons a week at a nearby music school. He heard her voice through the closed door of his room, where he had taken his glass of milk. She said that sometimes she needed to get out of the house, too. Alec didn't tell her what he was feeling, even though she asked him twice. He drank his milk and stared at the wall of his room. He didn't tell her anything.

After that, he came home to the empty apartment three times a week and began to make tours. He would drop his knapsack on the floor, walk into the high-ceilinged living room, and sit on the formal chairs. He would lie down on the long sofa, imagining people sitting around him at his own dinner party. He would light cigarettes and set them in the ashtray to burn.

Then he would go into the library, where the upright piano stood against one wall. He would lift the lid of the keyboard and lay out sheets of music as though he were going to practice. Only he would get up then and turn on the television and the stereo. He would sit down at his father's antique rolltop desk, uncap the lacquered fountain pen, and fill one sheet of notepaper after another with the signatures of his family. He would sign imaginary letters and contracts and school forms, working at it every afternoon until he could write four different signatures, all of them perfect, his own included.

He always saved his parents' bedroom for last. He went through their closets. The hanging clothes brushed against his face. He breathed in the smells of mothballs and flannel and leather, and traces of his mother's perfume. He looked into their bureau drawers, felt the gold weight of a pocketwatch that had belonged to his grandfather. And then he walked out of their bedroom, closing the door behind him. He stood a few feet away from it, his body pressed tight against the wall, and imagined that he and Mark were listening to another one of their parents' fights, adding their own mental pictures to the words they heard. He thought of his mother teaching the piano to strange children, of his father running a business that his family didn't really understand, of Mark playing football with the older boys because he was as big as they were. He remembered how much he had liked sitting at the kitchen table after school. And he felt fear come to him as he stood in the short, dark corridor that connected his parents' room to the rest of the apartment. It held him and pressed him harder against the wall until his shoulders and back began to hurt, until he slid down and sat on the carpet.

He didn't often go into his parents' room after that; the apartment began to seem dangerous. He stayed in his own end of the house. His was the smallest room—he always assumed it was because he was the smallest person—but during those afternoons he rarely left it. There was a black-and-white TV he could watch if he felt like it. But mostly he just sat by the window, looking out over the reservoir and Central Park.

He began to daydream, sometimes for hours at a time. He became good at it. He went places and did things and never told anyone about any of it. Often he was a famous child actor or a tennis star. Or both. He owned a motorcycle and rode it across the country. He stopped in places where he had never been before, but where everyone seemed to know him. And then he rode off again. He never needed anything else; he took it all with him wherever he went.

One afternoon, he went with his class on a trip to a children's museum, where a traditional Japanese house had been built. He saw plastic figures dressed in stiff robes sitting around a low table. There was no other furniture, and he thought it must be strange to live in an empty house. And the floor wasn't really a floor at all, but large woven mats placed together with no space in between. The teacher told him that the mats were called *tatami*, and that Japanese people never wore their shoes inside the house. When Alec took off his shoes, he felt the reed floor tickle his feet; it moved when he did, as though it were alive in some way. And it smelled good, like running barefoot in the country.

The house was all clean emptiness and he felt close to it, as if he knew it. The wood was what he thought wood should look like, it wasn't painted or stained. There weren't any pictures, only tall, beautiful flowers in a bowl with white pebbles. The flowers sat on a shelf in one corner of the room where the table was.

When he got home that day, Alec told his mother he didn't want to wear shoes inside the house anymore. But she didn't ask him any questions this time about what he had seen and done and felt. She just smiled absently and touched his hair.

She never asked him about Japan, so he never told her how often he thought about it. Never told her that the motorcycle dreams were all gone now, that he was no longer a famous child actor or a tennis player. He never mentioned how a family had grown out of the picture of the house he had seen. It was his family—a second family—and they lived in Japan, which was his, too, because it looked just the way he thought it should, all wood and reed and tall, beautiful flowers. He had a sister in his new family, and they played cards together. His Japanese parents stayed home most of the time, as though neither of them had a job at all. And no one ever mentioned how different he looked from everyone else. Not a single word about it.

II

FUJI-SAN

Alec had not expected to be where he was the next weekend, away from Tokyo, standing on the slatted porch of a family-run inn overlooking the resort area of Yamanaka Lake. The trip had been Boon's surprise gift to everyone in the office: a company offsite designed to strengthen their fraternal ties and loyalty to Compucom. The result had been a Saturday spent locked away in meetings to discuss future business strategy. But it was almost evening now, and the meetings had finally ended. Alec stood alone on the porch. Behind him, through the sliding glass door, the rest of the Compucom staff had gathered in the Western-style living room for coffee.

Alec took a deep breath, closed his eyes. The air was just beginning to cool. He thought he could smell the color of the pine trees as they darkened with the passing of the day's light, each successive shade of green somehow richer than the one before it. He noticed the odd pattern of the trees when he opened his eyes again. They were rooted to the hillside at all angles, a permanent and respectful audience for the lake below. A luminous cone of clouds rose straight up in the distance, almost obscuring the dark blue silhouette of Mount Fuji.

Alec heard the door behind him slide open and then closed.

"It is very beautiful tonight," Kawashima said softly, standing beside him.

He turned, saw her face pale against the dusk. "Yes, it is. Makes you wonder how people can ever stand to live in Tokyo."

"My mother's family is from the country, from northern Japan. Sometimes I feel that is where I belong, not in Tokyo."

"I've heard the north is practically a different country."

"In some ways, yes," she said. "The people there do not see the land as something to defeat or sell for billions of yen. They understand that it is their history and culture. And so they treat it with respect and try not to change it. We should all be more like that, I think."

She was looking intently at something in the distance. Alec followed her eyes and saw a hawk soaring powerfully above the trees. Its flight was leisurely, rising and falling, utterly trusting in the air currents.

"In the north these birds are everywhere," Kawashima said, still staring at the bird. "No other animal is so free, so strong and beautiful. When I was small, I wanted more than anything to become this bird, so I could always be strong and fly where I wanted." She looked quickly at him and giggled, a little girl's embarrassed laugh. "But that is silly to speak of now."

"There's nothing silly about that."

She looked at him then.

He turned to look out over the woods, which had suddenly grown dark with shadows. "I used to imagine things all the time when I was a kid. To the point where that was all I'd do some afternoons—just sit and make up things. And I think I remember every one of those daydreams. Maybe it's because at that age they feel as if they're the only things that really belong to you. I mean, you don't need anyone else to imagine something, just close your eyes and you're somewhere else, someone else. There's a lot of freedom in that. The problem is it's never real. But it's not silly."

"When you were small, Alec-san, what did you want to become?"

The question surprised him; he looked up and caught her eyes for an instant. "I don't know. I guess it's not what I wanted to become so much as where I wanted to be. I think I just wanted to be someplace that felt as if it belonged to me—the kind of place that I would think of whenever I heard the word *home*." He paused. "But I guess *that's* silly: home run, hometown, homework . . . there's no end to it. No wonder I'm crazy."

Confused, she smiled and shook her head. She crossed her bare arms to keep herself warm. "You are very strange, Alec-san. You make jokes when inside you want to be serious, I think."

"It's what I do when being serious gets scary," Alec said. "You can think you've thought something out to the point of understanding yourself. But then sometimes things come out while you're talking, and you realize that if you keep going, all you'll discover are how many things you really don't understand."

"You do not sound happy," Kawashima said.

He shook his head. "Maybe waiting is harder when you don't know what you're waiting for. But there's got to be something out there—something worth the wait. Sometimes I think the idea of it is almost more important than whatever it might turn out to be. Anyway, I'm going on too long about this. Maybe we should go inside."

She dismissed his last words with a slight frown. "You said that when you were small you desired to be in another place." Her voice was steady and quiet. "What place?"

They were almost touching. "Right now this porch looks pretty good to me."

*　　*　　*

The next day there were no meetings—Boon said he wanted everyone to relax and enjoy themselves, that he had another surprise. He led them down to the lake after breakfast. The sky was cloudless. As he emerged from the dense cover of the pine trees, Alec saw Mount Fuji. The distant peak was snow-capped, but not completely: like the full moon, there were traces of a human face, thin scars and discolorations where the snow had melted. And like the moon, the peak appeared suspended above an invisible base, disembodied.

At one end of the lake, families lay along a bare strip of beach under striped umbrellas. On the paved path, a narrow band around the lake, children expertly weaved their bicycles through the crowds of pale, middle-aged men and women in hats and sunglasses. Boon led the group to a dock where an elderly man with one cloudy eye rented pedal boats, each one in the shape of a swan. The huge birds flocked expectantly, the long necks arching gracefully skyward, the glass orbs catching the sun as the boats bobbed gently on the water.

When Boon went to pair everybody up, Alec turned, found himself standing next to Kawashima's office-mate, Takahara. He groaned inwardly, remembering the disturbing ferocity with which Takahara had eaten soba during their one lunch together. But there was no time to change position in line. Like Noah's animals, they stepped by twos into the great white birds. The old man winked his cloudy eye and sent them off with a strong shove.

Once out on the lake, Alec turned to Takahara, who was busy watching the stem of ash on his cigarette grow longer.

"We might go faster if you pedal, too."

Takahara was wearing a maroon velour warm-up suit. Thick-rimmed sunglasses covered most of his face. With the part that was still visible, he looked surprised.

"Me pedal, Alec-san? I am sailor, not bird boater." He turned back to his cigarette; the ash was improbably long.

Alec looked carefully at the cigarette, at the face, at the velour suit. "I see," he said.

"I should be in big sailboat," Takahara said.

"You're telling me."

Takahara didn't get it. "With many women." He gave Alec a conciliatory leer.

Ahead and to the right, another swan boat moved steadily along. There was a glint of sunlight reflecting off glass, and Alec knew it must be Park. Drawing closer, he saw that Kawashima was with him, her hair tied back from her face. Moving slowly in opposite directions, the two boats drew momentarily abreast of each other. Park and Kawashima smiled and waved, Alec returned the gesture. Beside him, Takahara remained inert. Looking over his shoulder, Alec caught a glimpse of Kawashima's legs working the pedals, her white cotton shorts cuffed at the thigh. He hoped he would dream about her that night, so he could be alone with her. This time he would kiss her.

Takahara threw the stub of his cigarette into the water. Within seconds, he had lit up a new one. "And so, good thing not be in bird with those two. Eh, Alec-san?"

Alec looked over at him, at the legs that weren't pedaling. "Actually, they looked to me as if they were having a good time."

"Good time?" Takahara scoffed, thick smoke pouring out of his nostrils. "Not good time. Terrible time. Why?" He laughed. "Because he is Korean. And she is a strange woman. Yes, very bad to be in that bird."

Alec tried to keep his voice neutral. "You're wrong. She's not strange, and neither is Park."

"I tell you, Alec-san, she is strange. Yes, old and strange. And he is Korean, and Korean and Japanese for long time do not like the other. Japanese are always very good. But Koreans are not so good; always, they work so hard, and do not laugh. They see Japanese and become angry that we have better living."

Alec wondered whether Takahara's idea of better living had something to do with his freedom to wear maroon velour warm-ups; or to smoke more cigarettes than any human on earth; or to attack more unsuspecting females in the berth of his boat than Bluebeard himself had ever managed.

"So why don't you work for a Japanese company?"

"It is simple," Takahara said, cigarette still burning between his middle fingers. "At Japanese company, there is no freedom, no weekends. I have no time to go sailing, or ask women to come to the water."

Alec's legs were killing him. He glared at Takahara, whose warm-up suit looked as if it had just been pressed. It took all his restraint to keep from hurling him into the water.

Takahara grunted. "You have girlfriend, Alec-san? Maybe beautiful American girl?"

Alec said, "No, she's Japanese. A model who's secretly related to the imperial family."

"What?"

"Nothing. A joke. No action for me."

"No action? You should buy boat, Alec-san," Takahara said, and started laughing loudly.

Alec punched him playfully on the arm. "That's funny, Takahara-san." He turned away from him to look at Mount Fuji in the distance.

Takahara noticed him staring at the mountain. "Fuji-san is beautiful today. Eh, Alec-san? Maybe later, we drive to snack bar at top."

Alec could not take his eyes off the luminous peak. The swan boat drifted, leaving only the hint of a wake.

12

MAKING SUSHI

It wasn't a dream. Once, twice, three times Kawashima rubbed her wet hands down the front of Alec's T-shirt. She started at midchest and pulled downward to his navel. The little finger of her right hand brushed against his nipple. He almost shivered. Three times, then her hands were dry. Laughing, she said: "Now it is your turn, Alec."

Alec moved his eyes from her hands to her face. "My turn to what?"

"To make sushi," she said.

It wasn't a dream. They were alone in Nobi's apartment, making sushi. The afternoon hadn't begun this way, just the two of them. Nobi had not mentioned her when he invited Alec to lunch. He said only that another friend might show up, but he didn't say who. It wasn't until he was already inside the one-room apartment that Alec saw her. The kitchen was separated from the rest of the room by a three-part screen painting of an emerald-green Chinese dragon. Above the screen the back of a woman's head was visible. She was looking down, concentrating on something, her shoulder-length hair falling away to expose the pale skin of her nape. Her hand reached up absently and tucked a few loose strands of hair back behind her ear. Alec stood still in the doorway, watching her, certain now who she was. He felt Nobi's hand on his shoulder, guiding him into the room.

"Alec, you must know Kiyoko Kawashima," Nobi said. "Yes? She is my old friend."

Alec said, "Old friend?"

"Yes. Like a sister. Our fathers have been in business together for many years."

She had turned at the sound of their voices. Her body remained hidden by the screen so that it appeared as if her long, graceful neck rose straight from the fiery coil of the painted dragon. But the image only lasted a moment. Then she was around the screen and whole again, dressed in a lavender skirt and a white blouse open at the throat.

She was looking at her feet. "Alec."

Alec said her name, Kiyoko, trying it out for the first time. Nothing came to him after that. They stood in silence for a few seconds until Nobi brought out folding chairs so the three of them could sit down. And then Nobi was telling the story of his and Kiyoko's friendship, the history of their growing up together. Alec listened quietly and tried to think of something interesting to say. Words slipped away from him. All he could think of was his fifth-grade teacher, Miss Sherwood, how full-breasted and maternal she had been, but sexy too, and how confused she had made him feel. He had found it almost impossible to talk to her. She would call on him in class, and often he would open his mouth only to find that nothing came out. Entire days where he didn't speak to her, couldn't speak to her, unless he absolutely had to. Nights where he dreamed about her. And never being able to tell her—not even feeling able to answer her questions in class. For a whole year. A feeling that didn't seem all that far away now, with Kiyoko sitting next to him in the little apartment. It never occurred to him that fifteen minutes later she would be drying her hands on the front of his shirt.

It was Nobi who made the difference. He checked his watch and stood up, announced that he had forgotten to buy sake for lunch. He left before anyone could offer to do it for him. They watched him go. Kiyoko looked as alarmed as Alec felt. He smiled nervously at her. She said she had to finish preparing lunch, got up, and went around the screen. Alec studied the painted dragon.

He was looking at the back of her head again. He guessed he would know it well by the end of the afternoon. It seemed somehow more possible to talk to her this way, with the dragon between them. He wondered whether she thought so, too. Then she spoke.

"I am making sushi, Alec."

"I like sushi," Alec said. His tongue felt as useless as when he had said her name for the first time.

"At this moment, I am cutting pieces of *maguro,* what you would call tuna. I am using the knife of my grandmother."

"One of those long heavy ones? Like a sword?"

"Yes. You must not cut the fish the way you cut other things. Not too hard or too soft. Not too straight."

Alec was still looking at the back of her head.

"Now the rice," Kiyoko said. "And then wasabi. A small amount, because the taste is very strong. Too much wasabi and the fish has no taste."

Alec could picture her hands. There was grace and lightness in them, in her long fingers. They were swift and they touched everything. Fish was not simply cut, but caressed. Like soft clay, rice was sculpted into small, rounded blocks, wasabi dabbed on as though it were paint, the final touches of color.

By the time he finally decided to approach her, he was too late. He had missed the performance. He walked around the screen to find her already washing her hands. They were just as he had imagined them. Thinking of a television commercial he had once seen, he said: "Great hands."

She turned to look at him. "I do not understand."

"I mean, you have beautiful hands."

Kiyoko began to giggle. "I think you must be crazy, Alec."

"I've heard making sushi does that to people—makes them crazy."

She was turning off the faucet. Still giggling. Shaking her head. Hair flying loose.

"Or maybe it's the wasabi that does it," Alec said. "Strong stuff."

She was laughing now, holding her dripping wet hands out in front of her. Alec saw her eyes move from her hands to him. That was when she did it: dried her hands on the front of his shirt. Once, twice, three times. It wasn't a dream. He didn't see her even look for a towel.

She told him it was his turn to make sushi.

"It's too late," he said, pointing to the platter full of sushi she had made. "You've already done it."

"I have not yet made *maki*."

"I like *maki*."

"Good. Then you can make it. Yes?"

Alec felt his head nod up, then down.

She handed him a small, flexible mat made of thin strips of bamboo tied together with string. He placed it flat on the counter. Over it he fitted a paper-thin square of dried seaweed, called nori. He stuck his hand into a cooking bowl half-filled with cool, sticky rice. He groped for a handful, then squeezed too hard. The grains molded together, became indivisible in his palm; the consistency of rough mud. He cursed quietly and dumped it in the trash can. Kiyoko put her hand over her mouth to keep from laughing. Alec looked at her, trying not to smile.

"You're making me nervous. How about if you stand on the other side of the screen until I finish?"

"That is the way it used to be with women in Japan," she said, suddenly serious. "Always hidden behind screens."

Alec nodded, unsure how to respond. He grabbed another handful of rice but this time hardly squeezed at all. He imagined he was holding a live bird. He piled it on the sheet of nori, then spread it out by patting lightly with his fingertips. Now there were three layers: bamboo, seaweed, rice. Wasabi was next, making little streaks of green on the white of the grains. And then the tuna and cucumber, both of which Kiyoko had already cut into long thin strips. As though preparing to seal an envelope, he wet his fingers and rubbed them along one edge of the sheet of nori. Then he began to roll up the bamboo mat. He did this slowly, using his fingers to realign the nori and to poke little bits of rice and cucumber and fish back into the tube that was forming.

Kiyoko said, "It is very large, Alec. Maybe there is too much rice."

Alec finished rolling. Now that he looked at it, the tube did appear to be thicker than usual. He tried to flatten it using his palm as a spatula. A light tearing sound came from inside.

"It'll be fine," he said. "Nothing to worry about."

Kiyoko smiled. "I am not worried."

"Good. Okay, here we go."

Alec quickly unrolled the bamboo mat. The *maki* was inside. He carefully picked it up in both hands. "How about a bite?"

She had not stopped laughing since the unveiling of his creation. "You are supposed to cut the *maki* into pieces, I think."

"Pieces. Yes." He picked up the sushi knife and sliced off a misshapen circle of *maki*. Palm up, he held it out to her. She reached to take the piece, but Alec lightly closed his fingers around it.

"Here. Let me feed it to you."

Kiyoko shook her head.

"Why not? Just one bite."

She didn't move away.

"Kiyoko," he said. "Please."

His arm was still out toward her, but bent at the elbow now, closer to his body. He opened his fingers again. The *maki* sat on his palm, looking battered and pasty. He watched her take a small step forward, watched her dancer's neck as it extended toward him, her mouth smiling as it opened to take the food from his hand. And it seemed the most natural thing in the world to touch her, to reach out with his free hand and touch her neck, to slide his fingers down until they found her breast. He held her for an instant and felt as if it were not hours he had waited, but ages, longer than his time in Japan.

His mind was too full to notice how rigid her body became the moment he touched her, how quickly she slipped away from him. Too full to even realize that the *maki* was still in his hand. It was not until she had turned away from him and moved to the other side of the kitchen that he understood what had happened. But by then it was too late. He heard a key turning in the lock, the door swinging open. Nobi entered the apartment with the rustling of plastic bags and the clinking of glass bottles. He swept into the space, waved to Alec above the screen.

"Too many people," he said. "The crowds were very big. And things here? How is lunch? I also bought beer."

Alec nodded, looking at the floor. "I'd say we're just about done here."

Nobi came around the screen carrying the groceries. "That is good. I am hungry."

Kiyoko stood at the edge of the kitchen, her back turned. She seemed very far away to Alec. Nobi was between them, humming to himself as he unpacked the bottles of sake and beer.

Alec said, "I guess I'll wash up before lunch, then."

Nobi stopped what he was doing long enough to point behind him toward the door. "I am sorry, but it is not private. Because of ministry housing, yes? To the right and down the hallway."

The bathroom was empty. Alec splashed his face with double handfuls of cold water. Drops splattered his shirt. It seemed the coolness was the only thing that could relieve him. More and more water. He let it splash into his short hair, into his ears, down his neck. The tiled bathroom echoed like an indoor pool. The emptiness gave back to him all his sounds and movements, his splashing and breathing, until not even the coolness could take him away from himself. All because she had dried her hands on his shirt. Because now he knew exactly what it felt like to touch her.

He turned off the faucet and, his hands still dripping wet, went out the door and back down the hallway to the apartment.

Nobi was waiting for him alone in the doorway. "Kiyoko apologized many times, Alec, but she said she had to leave on business."

Alec didn't move. "What business? It's Saturday."

Nobi shrugged. "She said she just now remembered something she promised Mr. Boon she would finish by today. She was very sorry. I am also sorry."

"Yeah. Me, too. I was only gone a couple of minutes."

Alec noticed for the first time that Nobi's futon in the corner of the room was moss green in color, and that the dining room table, which was set for three, was in fact a gray metal desk taken from the Ministry of International Trade and Industry. He stepped past Nobi into the room and saw that there were only two windows, both without blinds, that the lights were all bare bulbs, that the walls were made of rough concrete. He looked toward the kitchen, to where he and Kiyoko had stood together only minutes before, and thought how ridiculous the painted screen looked now in the naked light of the room and how utterly stupid it was for the bathroom to be down the hallway to the right, a couple of minutes away.

Nobi was looking at him with an odd expression on his face. "Perhaps we should go out for lunch," he said.

13

THE CLUB SCENE

The area was called Kabuki-cho. The business appeared to be sex. The guide was Park. The weather: raining, mid-July heat.

Alec stood stiffly in front of a run-down building, holding his umbrella so that it partly covered his face. Beside him, a Japanese man wearing a plaid sports jacket called out to passersby to come and sample his show. Alternating between Japanese and halting English, he graciously offered a free look downstairs. Park was a taker. He disappeared down a steep set of stairs.

Alec peered out from under his umbrella. The sex shops and pornographic movie houses around him were lost in the buzz and glow of multicolored neon. It spread over the rain-wet streets and cars, over the moving pedestrians and their black umbrellas, over the corner vending machines, until the entire neighborhood was bathed in eerie fragments of wild, electric color. Shrill voices announced opportunities for sex and voyeurism. Quick, eager hands closed around crisp bills and whisked dark-suited men down into unseen basements. The men were of all ages, many still dressed in their business clothes, as solemn and upright as rush-hour commuters going home to their wives. Alec thought they looked like obscene moving advertisements, these men, caught in the flashing neon of sex shops, their destinations etched in their faces like smiles. Then it occurred to him that he must look even worse: a dirty young man straight from Times Square. He was almost relieved to see Park emerge from underground.

"This place is very good," Park gasped. "Very good." He waved Alec down the stairs.

The theater was dark and hot, the air like steam. Several dozen folding chairs were set up in rows around a circular stage, most of them occupied by the types of men Alec had seen on the streets above. He and Park kept to the back, standing with their backs against the wall. Alec realized that there were actually two stages, one round and central, the other a glass-bottomed rectangle that moved on tracks above the audience. The stage lights were dim, mysterious. Strange, almost tribal, music played over the loudspeakers.

Suddenly, five men sitting close to one another in the audience jumped to their feet and formed a circle. Shouting in unison, throwing their right hands into the center, they played Rock, Paper, Scissors. Alec couldn't believe he was seeing a game from his childhood used to determine who would participate in a live sex show. Two men dropped out, then a third. The two remaining men leapt up on stage. One of them was barely five feet tall, with the scrawny legs of a young adolescent. He eagerly climbed a ladder to the floating bed above. The other man was overweight, his stomach hanging thickly over his belt. He stood next to the woman on the central stage. Leaving on their shirts, ties, and socks, both men stripped off the rest of their clothing. The music grew louder, beating through the small room. From vinyl bags, each woman brought out clear plastic gloves and a Wet-Nap—the kind Alec had seen advertised on television to wipe babies' bottoms. Like surgeons preparing for a routine operation, they put on the gloves, one finger at a time, and then roughly wiped the men's genitals.

Park put his mouth close to Alec's ear. "That plastic," he said, meaning the gloves. "It is also on their tongues."

Alec looked at him. "On their tongues? Are you sure?" Park gave a knowing nod.

On stage, the women were attempting to bring the men to the necessary level of excitement. The overweight man was having obvious difficulties. His face was wet with perspiration. His soft belly stuck out of his shirt where a button had come undone. Finally, he knocked the woman's hand away so he could use his own.

Alec felt himself grow cold. He tapped Park on the shoulder. "What are we doing here?"

Without taking his eyes from the stage, Park said, "It is instead of the Turkish bath. It is also an education, Alec-san. Yes, it is very important."

"This isn't an education, it's sick," Alec said. At the sound of his voice, a couple of men in the audience turned around to stare at him. Alec lowered his voice. "I mean, look at the women, Park-san. They don't show any emotion. It's like they're dead."

"You are near to right, Alec-san," Park said. "These women, they are mostly from the Philippines. They come here very alone, with no money, and soon the Yakuza control their passports. The Yakuza are like the American Mafia. And these women, they make maybe thousand yen in one day. That is not enough to have life."

The glass-bottomed stage glided above their heads. Instinctively Alec looked up, glimpsed the backside of a woman trapped under a man, her flesh obscenely distorted against the glass. On center stage, the other woman had finally given up on the overweight man. Sweaty and dejected, he crawled on his hands and knees, picking up his clothing. As he stepped back down into the audience, several others jumped up from their seats to compete for the vacant spot. Expressionless, the woman moved to the edge of the stage, spread her legs, and bent over.

An elderly man in the front row, not five feet from where she stood, leaned out of his seat to get a closer look. His face was as blank as the woman's.

Alec was afraid he might pass out. Glowing and pulsing, dirty and hot, the room seemed like an interpretation of hell. Two more naked women walked on stage carrying a large trunk. One of the women was bald, with a shiny white scar stretching diagonally across her abdomen. She pulled a leather bullwhip from the trunk and handed it to the elderly man in the front row.

Flushed with excitement, Park said, "Part two is now beginning. It is sure to be action-packed."

Alec closed his eyes and thought again of the neon pulsing over the wet streets above, flashing like an ambiguous beacon from a distant place.

14

STRIPES

It had been a long night—even Mrs. Hasegawa had gone to bed by the time Alec returned home from Kabuki-cho. He walked into the dark silence and the house seemed a different place, each room a capsule of unknown shadows. On the way to his room, he stopped as he often did to listen to the sounds of the family sleeping, soothed by the knowledge that life was continuing as usual. He sat down on the wood floor. He closed his eyes in the darkness, and then he could not move. . . .

He had been thirteen and just beginning to learn basic physics in school. He discovered that there were theories for the forces that bind atoms together and theories for the forces that break them apart. He saw a film in science class that showed how individual parts of a whole are physically driven away from each other. The film was in color, and at first Alec thought the molecule self-destructing up on the screen looked like a flower blooming, its tight bud bursting open. But then it went too far. Atoms scattered, pulling the flower apart, creating a formless mass.

The teacher poked the screen with a yardstick. He talked about theory, about how it could be used to explain the chemical behavior of all matter. Sitting in the back of the classroom, Alec shook his head to himself, because he knew the teacher was wrong. He felt sure that he could watch the breaking apart of a hundred different things a hundred different times and it would never once happen in just the same way. There were too many separate parts and too many different directions in which to go.

There was a scientific name for the process by which molecules break apart, but Alec could never remember what it was. He gave it his own name, destruction theory, and that was how he came to think of it. It seemed that science was all about the world's breaking apart, piece by piece, right in front of everyone. And he thought that there was little left to wonder about after that, except whether theory spoke not just about cold matter, but about families, too.

Perhaps it was then that he first realized that things had already begun to come apart at home. That mothers and fathers and brothers were all not so different from atoms, really, the way they bounced off one another and into their own private places, where there was no room for anyone else.

As long as he could remember, his father had belonged to an all-male club. Alec had never seen the club before, but he knew of it because Mark had gone the year before, when he had been thirteen and Alec twelve. Alec had lain awake that night for what seemed like hours waiting for them to return. He listened through his closed door while Mark put on his pajamas, brushed his teeth, and got into bed. And then, quietly, he went into Mark's room and asked him what the club was like, whether it was dusty and cold and cobwebbed the way he had always suspected it was, even though their father almost never talked about it. Mark didn't answer for a minute. He rolled over, turning his face toward the wall, which was streaked with shadows, and said that he hadn't liked it, that it had been strange and quiet. He wouldn't say any more after that, except that he was tired and wanted to go to sleep. And Alec didn't push him for more, because Mark seemed afraid to him then, and that made him afraid, too. He went back to his room and crawled into bed, thinking about the club, wondering what his father did while he was there, whether he talked and laughed more than he did while he was at home. He knew it would be his turn to go the next year, when he would be thirteen. He fell asleep waiting for it to happen.

A year later, the two of them stood alone in the cool, musty billiard room. The room was dark except for a rectangular light suspended above their table. Rows of other tables shrouded in dust cloths surrounded them, reminding Alec of a graveyard. He took a deep breath and smelled the staleness of the room. His father bent low over the long stretch of green felt and drove the cue ball hard into the multicolored rack.

"No luck tonight," his father said, checking to make sure none of the balls had gone into the pockets. "Your go."

Alec stared at the table until the colored spheres blurred together, until he had to shake his head to make any sense of it. He lifted his pool cue, feeling its weight. Off to the side, where his father stood in the dim light, he heard a brief clipping sound, and then the sudden flare of a match. Thick clouds of cigar smoke began to drift under the overhanging light.

"Dad?"

His father was looking at the end of his cigar. "Hmm?"

"What are we playing?"

"Eight ball. You know how."

"I don't think I remember."

"Sure you do. I taught you and Mark a long time ago. Mark and I played only last year. He was good."

The cue was too long for him, and Alec settled it as best he could on the rest made by his thumb and forefinger. The wood was smooth, and it slid easily back and forth. He lined up behind the cue ball.

"Keep your head down low over the ball, Alec," his father said. "That's the only way you'll really know where it's going."

Alec bent his head so that he was looking almost straight down the length of the cue.

"And don't forget about your legs. That's where the balance comes from."

Alec spread his legs a little wider. He was having trouble keeping his hands still. The movement of the cue against his skin was no longer smooth, but awkward, uneven. He took a deep breath to calm himself. It was full of dust and smoke. He made his shot. The five ball missed the pocket by about half a foot.

His father stepped up to the table and sank the three ball with a quick shot into the side pocket.

"Looks like you're stripes, Alec."

Alec nodded. "Stripes."

"See the way I'm lined up behind the cue ball here? Where my head's pointing, the spread of my feet? All of it's important. And your breathing. Don't forget to stay relaxed."

"It's not that easy."

"You just have to concentrate, that's all. Don't think about anything else."

Alec watched the cue ball hit the dark green six ball and send it rolling softly down the table and into the far corner pocket.

"Do you come here a lot, Dad? I mean, to the club."

His father was chalking the tip of his cue. "I used to play a lot of pool when I was your age. Did you know that, Alec? Almost every day. Your grandpa bought a beautiful table so he and I could play together. And we did."

"So you come here to play pool."

"Sometimes."

"You mean you play pool here sometimes?"

"I come here sometimes after work, perhaps a couple times a week. And sometimes when I'm here I play pool."

Alec noticed that his father still held the lit cigar between his fingers as they gripped the cue. He wondered whether some of the ash might fall onto the felt and burn a hole through it. He watched his father attempt an impossible bank shot. The dark yellow one ball hit off the edge of the corner bumper, just in front of the pocket, and bounced back out to the middle of the table. His father muttered, Shit, and took a couple of steps back from the table, so that he now stood partly under the blanket of darkness that covered the rest of the room. The red tip of his cigar glowed through it like an eye.

"In the library at home, Dad," Alec said. "There's that space. It's big, isn't it? I mean, there's nothing there except that rug. We could've put a table there, don't you think? We really could've put it there. At home."

He waited, but his father didn't say anything. Alec couldn't see his face, but he wasn't even trying to anymore. "If we'd had a table at home, you could've taught Mom to play."

"Your mother never liked the whole idea of pool. She wouldn't have enjoyed it."

Alec bent down quickly and took a shot. The cue ball bounced aimlessly off the bumpers, hitting nothing.

"Your go," he said.

His father stepped back into the light of the table. "You're not concentrating, Alec. Keep your head down and watch the ball. Remember what I told you."

"You don't understand, Dad."

His father lined up for another shot. "No," he said. "*You* don't understand."

There was little conversation after that. The air had turned heavy with cigar smoke. Alec looked through it at the darkened, unused tables, standing stiff as tombstones all around. His father stood always on the other side of the table, the jacket of his soft gray suit still buttoned, his concentration focused on the game. He seemed very far away then, and Alec remembered what Mark had said about his visit to the club, how strange and quiet it had been. And he thought that what Mark must have really meant was that it had been lonely.

The game ended. Alec wanted to go home, but once again his father was bending low over the table and breaking the rack. Sound pierced the room for an instant. The balls scattered, some careening sharply off the bumpers. Alec watched their movement and thought again of the science film he had seen, of destruction theory, of how the flower had split apart into millions of particles. The table seemed to grow brighter as he stood there looking at it, as if it too might burst apart at any second. And he felt suddenly as though it was happening all around him, this coming apart of things. As if his father standing at the end of the long table, pool cue in hand, was at that moment no different from the science teacher with his yardstick raised toward the screen, pointing and explaining while the picture in front of him was being broken down into unrecognizable pieces.

15

PROMISE

Alec held the namecard in front of him with both hands. He ceremoniously studied it, first in English, then, turning it over, in Japanese. He was speaking to the supreme adviser to the Oyama Chemical and Construction Company. Bowing as smoothly as he could, he made the appropriate murmurings in Japanese about the great honor it was to meet such an exalted official from such an exalted company. That done, he waited eagerly for anything the supreme adviser might say in regard to his own lowly position of assistant manager. As usual, nothing was forthcoming. Alec thought he saw Boon hide a smile.

It was later, somewhere around eleven o'clock. They were in the hallway of a building in Ginza. Dinner had been a feast of Kobe beef and fresh vegetables, washed down with warmed sake. Alec had sat next to another Oyama executive and talked

American baseball statistics for most of the meal. He was pleased that he was finally getting a handle on doing business in Japan.

A bare wooden door opened at the end of the corridor, and the four of them walked into a dimly lit room. Inside, there was just enough space for a short bar and a piano with stools around it. Everything was close at hand, intimate, luxurious. The carpet felt like cushions under his feet; the curtains were made of velvet.

The mama-san of the establishment made a huge fuss at their arrival, grabbing Boon's arm to lead him to a seat at the piano and chiding the supreme adviser for having forsaken her for so many weeks. "Tomorrow, I was going to close," she announced, then grabbed his hand, too.

Three other hostesses, all attractive young women, rushed over to the guests, taking their coats and exclaiming at the rugged good looks of the foreigners. Alec translated the compliments to Boon, who quietly warned him not to pay any attention. They sat around the piano. Bottles of imported Scotch appeared. The women expertly mixed drinks.

Alec was sitting at one end of the piano, an empty seat between himself and the keyboard. To his left, the supreme adviser sat as though in meditation, his eyes glazed and hands on his thighs. Prospects for conversation seemed a bit dim. Alec felt a light hand on his wrist. The empty seat had been filled by one of the hostesses. Things seemed to be looking up.

"You are from America?" she asked in Japanese.

Alec grunted, was pleased with the way it sounded. He took a big swallow of Scotch. "Yes. From New York."

Her fingers closed around his arm again and squeezed; a little of his drink spilled on the piano.

"Eh! I love New York! The Biggu Aperru."

Alec looked at her more closely. "The what?"

"Biggu Aperru," she repeated.

"Oh. Yes. Have you been to New York?"

"Me?" She touched the tip of her nose with her forefinger. "No, not yet. But I want very much to go. Yes, I want to go. I am an actress and singer, so I love New York."

He smiled. "I love New York, too. Where do you perform in Tokyo?"

Her lower lip jutted out a little. Alec felt a wave of physical interest. He took another long drink.

"Work is very difficult," she said. "I work every night, so there is not much time. In one month, I will stop working here. I want to be on television."

Alec said, "You are very pretty."

She stood up, moved around to the piano stool. "I will sing now. Do you like American music?" Alec nodded. "Yes? Good. I will sing Barry Manilow." She started to play.

Alec stifled a groan. Why was everything always so difficult? The way Nobi had described it, all a person had to do was behave according to established social guidelines and everything would work out. Why was she playing Barry Manilow instead of sitting next to him?

She began to sing "I Write the Songs," mispronouncing most of the words. With the music, signs of life began to emerge around the piano. The supreme adviser drummed his fingers on the piano top. In between remarks to the other Oyama man, Boon hummed a few notes of the song, noticeably off tune. Seated at the bar by the entrance, four Japanese businessmen sang along word for word, pausing only to take quick gulps of Scotch. The mama-san bustled back and forth between bar and piano, serving, chatting, finally coming to rest on a seat next to the now exuberant supreme adviser, who allowed his hand to rub lightly over her thighs. She gave his fingers a playful slap, eyeing him with feigned innocence. Alec watched with interest as the mama-san, herself in her fifties, brought the supreme adviser to life with lively, flirtatious conversation. She seemed to know exactly when to speak and what to say, when to laugh or touch his arm. As though awakening from a deep sleep, the supreme adviser appeared to shake himself and sit taller on his stool; he laughed loudly several times and dabbed perspiration from his forehead with a handkerchief.

The song was over, and the hostess came back to sit beside Alec.

"I enjoyed that very much," he said. "You have a good voice. Better than Barry Manilow."

She looked pleased but shook her head. "Thank you, but I do not practice enough."

The sounds of conversation filled the small room. Boon and the other Oyama man were the only ones speaking English. A hostess brought a cordless microphone to the back bar, where one of the young businessmen waited, jacket off and sleeves rolled up. Accompanied by a different hostess at the piano, he began to sing a Japanese love ballad that Alec had difficulty understanding. Something about love being just another form of pain. The phrase reminded Alec of the sex club he had visited with Park.

"My name is Masako," whispered the woman beside him.

Alec introduced himself, nodding his head as a way of bowing without actually standing up. Now that he knew her name, she seemed more real, distinct from the other hostesses. Her hair was short, her face wonderfully Japanese, he thought, with almond-shaped eyes set above wide cheekbones and a full mouth. Her nose was tiny and would have been too small for her face if she herself were not barely over five feet tall.

As she mixed him another drink, Alec watched her cross her legs, the beige skirt rising up to expose smooth, stockinged skin. And he watched her hands, putting in more ice, pouring more Scotch with a touch of water. Her movements were precise, economical, as though she kept much of herself in reserve.

Smiling shyly, she put the new drink in front of him. "Please excuse me for not knowing English. I never learned."

He smiled back at her. "If you speak slowly, there is no problem. Please do not worry."

"Yes. I will speak slowly," she said, looking relieved. "How long will you be in Tokyo, and what do you do here?"

"I will be in Tokyo for the rest of the summer. But perhaps I will stay much longer. I am working for an American computer company." He used the Japanese version of the English word for computer, pronouncing it "computa." He felt very Japanese.

"*Sugoi,*" she said, the word indicating that she was impressed.

Alec looked around at the rest of his party, seeing them as though for the first time. The supreme adviser seemed to function at two extreme levels of activity: virile, almost youthful, when in conversation with the mama-san; sullen and aged when she was busy with other patrons. Across the piano, Boon appeared to be having a fine time, his face red and unusually animated. Unable to communicate with him in Japanese, the hostess beside Boon was spending most of her time topping off his drink.

The first man had finished his song. Time was racing by, measured only in music and drinks. Alec was finding it difficult to keep himself from grinning all the time. Masako remained next to him, speaking slowly and simply, laughing at his attempted jokes. Talking to her, feeling her hand on his arm now and then, he felt very sure of himself. The anxious times he had known since coming to Japan fell away under her spell. Once, she reached over and brushed his hair back in place with her fingers.

Word began to circulate in the room that it was time for one of the foreigners to sing. Boon was looking at the microphone, his lips pursed in worry. Then he pointed across the piano at Alec, who watched wide-eyed as a book of popular American songs was placed in front of him. Masako had stopped talking. The businessmen at the bar were clapping in unison. Boon just shrugged sheepishly at him. The supreme adviser turned slowly and squinted at him with the meaty, shining face of a retired boxer. The woman at the piano said she knew how to play "Johnny B. Goode."

Alec was giddy enough to sing. He thought he might even get up and dance on the piano, gyrate his hips like Chuck Berry. But Masako touched him then. Hidden by the piano, she trailed her fingers up the inside of his thigh and took him in her hand.

16

WHEEL
OF FORTUNE

The conference room was windowless, long and sleek as a cabin cruiser. A black oval table reached almost from end to end, surrounded by a ring of black chairs, their backs contoured to fit the natural shape of the seated human body. Alec was alone in the room, waiting for his first solo business meeting to begin. His palms were sweating.

A Japanese secretary knocked once and came into the room with a cup of coffee. Alec said hello and she blushed, then disappeared without a sound. The nondairy creamer was in a thin paper tube, sealed at both ends. There were no perforation marks or arrows indicating where to tear open the package. The yellowish powder spilled all over his lap when he ripped it across the middle.

For days now he had been working on a report about Japan's commitment to liberalize its high-technology markets. He had found what English research materials he could and was finally ready to sit down to write the report when Park hurried over to his desk, blinking and pointing wildly to a small advertisement in a Japanese-language business magazine. The advertisement was for a new encyclopedia of Japan's high-tech industry, written by members of a prestigious Japanese economic research institute. Over sushi, it was decided that a meeting with a member of the institute should be arranged. Magnanimous as ever, Park had made the arrangements, assuring Alec that the people at the institute would all be able to speak English.

There was another knock on the door. The secretary entered, followed by two men dressed in identical navy blue suits, white shirts, and wide, striped ties. Alec put the cup and saucer down on the table, stood up.

"Please excuse me," the secretary said in Japanese. "This is Ichikawa-san and Yasufuku-san."

Alec introduced himself, put both palms on his thighs, and bowed. He thanked them for taking the time from their busy schedules to meet with him. Both men bowed in return. Not at all, they said. Apart from their clothing, they looked completely different from each other. Where Ichikawa was thick-set, with a ruddy face, salt-and-pepper hair, and a confident, bow-legged stance, Yasufuku reminded Alec more of a mortician: thin, stooping, and hollow-cheeked, his jet-black hair parted straight down the middle.

They exchanged business cards, Alec trying to receive theirs and give his all at the same time. The secretary glided out the door. They sat down, the two men facing Alec, nodding and smiling expectantly at him. He nodded and smiled in return, thanked them again for meeting with him. Ichikawa glanced quickly at Yasufuku, then both men nodded. The room was still. Alec decided that he would say a few introductory words in Japanese before switching to English for the more serious parts of the meeting.

"I am writing a report for my head office about Japan's high-technology markets," he began slowly. "So, I am looking for information about this subject." Both men grunted and nodded. "I saw the advertisement for your encyclopedia and thought that you might be able to answer some of my questions. . . ."

Both men smiled. As the older of the two, Ichikawa spoke first. "Of course, Stern-san, we will help you in any way we can."

"Thank you," Alec said clearly in English. "Now, my first question concerns the effective attitude of the Japanese government in general, and of MITI officials in particular, toward future tariff regulation of high-technology imports from the United States."

Ichikawa and Yasufuku looked openly at each other and then at him, their faces molded into expressions of total incomprehension.

"Is the phrase 'effective attitude' giving you trouble?" Alec finally asked in English.

The two men just stared at him.

" 'Future tariff regulation'?"

Nothing.

Finally, Ichikawa politely shook his head. In Japanese, he said, "Please excuse me, Stern-san, but we do not understand English."

"Please excuse me, I did not know," Alec said in Japanese.

There was more nodding followed by more silence. Alec thought he could hear himself sweat. As calmly as he could manage, he took his handkerchief from his back pocket, unfolded it, and mopped his forehead. Park had done this to him. Alec wanted to wring his neck.

The secretary returned to clear away his empty coffee cup. I love you, Alec thought, don't leave. The door closed solidly behind her. He heard one of the men quietly clear his throat, realized they weren't going to go away. He had to get control of himself, had to focus.

"Well, my first question is about tariffs," he said in Japanese. There was a joint sigh of relief from across the table. "And about the Japanese government and American high-technology products." The last part of the sentence came out in little bursts.

Ichikawa said, "Yes. . . ."

"About their future," Alec emphasized.

Yasufuku nodded vigorously. "Yes. The future of tariffs in Japan."

"For high-technology products," Alec said, suddenly excited.

Ichikawa looked like a contestant on "Wheel of Fortune." "You want to know about the future of Japanese tariffs on American high-technology products."

"Yes, that is exactly right," Alec said.

Everybody smiled.

Yasufuku had moved to the edge of his seat. "The future," he said, glancing quickly at Ichikawa to make sure it was all right to speak. "The future is very bright for Americans."

Alec said, "I am very glad to hear that, Yasufuku-san."

"Yes," Yasufuku said.

Alec waited.

Yasufuku smiled at him. A mortician's smile.

Alec said, "And why is the future very bright?"

The two men looked at each other. Ichikawa cleared his throat. "Because of trade friction between the two countries, the American government has put a great deal of pressure on Japan to open its high-technology markets. Yes?"

Alec nodded.

"So," Ichikawa continued, "Japan must lower its tariffs to allow more high-technology imports from the United States."

"But is that really going to happen?" Alec asked.

"It must happen," Ichikawa said.

"And is this problem discussed in your encyclopedia?"

"Yes," Yasufuku said. He stood up and disappeared through the door.

Alec wondered if he had said something to offend him. He studied Ichikawa's face for a sign.

Ichikawa smiled uncomfortably. "Very soon the rainy season will end."

"Yes." There was nothing else to say.

"And it will become hotter."

Alec nodded.

Yasufuku entered, bowed, and handed him a thickly bound volume. "Here is our encyclopedia," he said. "I think that you will find all the necessary information inside. If you have any further questions, please contact us."

Alec stood up and bowed to both men. On his way out, he passed the secretary who had brought him coffee. This time it was he who blushed.

Out on the street, he walked for a while, not really sure where he was going. It was only three o'clock, and they would be expecting him back at the office. He glanced up at the darkening sky, thinking about the rainy season.

17

THE FORCE
OF NATURE

Masako appeared before him wearing a flowered summer yukata, loosely tied. Setting down red-and-black lacquer trays of sushi and sashimi, she knelt beside him. The sliding fusuma were open, and a light breeze stirred the hem of her robe. She poured tea for him. With his chopsticks, he lifted a piece of raw yellowtail, glided it through the soy sauce and into his mouth. He chewed slowly, savoring its oily, sensual taste. She asked him if he liked it. In answer, he put his mouth to hers. His hand moved inside her robe. . . .

Alec's head snapped upward, jarring him from his thoughts. The knock came again; three successive raps, confirming his suspicion that it had not been a part of his daydream. Turning around on the swivel chair, he said, "Come in."

Park closed the door behind him. "Good afternoon, Alec-san. I am surprised to find you in Boon-san's office."

"Hi, Park-san. Mr. Boon's at a meeting. He said it was all right if I used his computer to make some graphs for my report."

Park's mouth tightened in disapproval. Alec realized that the computer wasn't even turned on. He patted the terminal as if it were an old friend.

"These machines tend to heat up pretty quickly," he said. "I turned it off for a minute to give it a rest." Alec squirmed in silence for a few seconds before Park grunted and handed him a sheet of paper with several lines of Japanese written on it.

"As we have discussed, I have prepared for you a message of love for Masako-san," Park said. "I would say that it is impossible for her to hear these words and not desire with all her heart to please you."

"This sounds a little strong, Park-san. It's only the second date."

"The second meeting." Park nodded his head gravely. "The second meeting is where Nature becomes the strongest force."

Alec burst out laughing.

Park's blinking quickened. "Alec-san, you should not laugh. Much has been practiced over the last two thousand years. Now, please listen." In a throaty voice, he began to recite by memory what was written on the sheet of paper Alec held in his hand. "I am at the office, but I cannot work. The only thing I can do is think about seeing you. The first meeting brought me to ecstasy, but even it was not enough. I need to see you again. Tonight. You are very beautiful."

"You want me to tell her this?"

"It would be the best thing."

Alec read the message aloud. "Was that okay?"

Park's eyes bulged like those of a tree frog. He handed Alec the phone.

He had buzzed up from below, and she was waiting for him in the doorway, wearing gym shorts and a T-shirt that said "Mickey's Gym" under a picture of a boxer being knocked out of a ring. There was not a yukata anywhere in sight. Alec took off his shoes before going inside, thinking that his fantasy was already being altered. Masako helped him take off his jacket and tie. There was one chair in the tiny apartment; she made him sit in it.

"Are you tired?" she asked.

It was nine-thirty, and he had just come from the office. "A little," he said. He pointed to her T-shirt. "Who's Mickey?"

She giggled. "I do not know. Would you like something to eat?"

He nodded, she started the electric hotplate. From where he sat, he could see the only other room in the apartment. The floor was hidden beneath an enormous futon.

In a few minutes, Masako brought him a warm plate of miniature hot dogs and a can of beer. She sat down on the floor beside him and began reading the newspaper. He ate quickly, not really tasting the food, wanting to be finished.

When his plate was empty, she said, "You did not like it." She pushed out her lower lip, pouting.

Still in the chair, Alec reached down and stroked her cheek. "It was delicious."

She smiled. "Good." She went back to reading the newspaper.

A little disconcerted, he took a sip of beer. What was in the paper that could be so interesting? What about the force of Nature? Putting the beer down, he began to massage the back of her neck with both hands. Her breathing quickened, but she kept reading. After a little while, he bent down and kissed the spot he had been rubbing. The newspaper shook a little but didn't go down. He gave her a peck on the cheek.

"Dame," she said.

Her voice lilted when she said it, reaching a schoolgirl's high note on the second syllable. But Alec was too shocked to enjoy the sound: *dame* meant "bad," "wrong," or "don't do that." He sat back in his chair. Had he imagined the events of that evening in the Ginza club? Was it possible that she had been teasing when she took hold of him beneath the piano?

Tentatively, he let his hand dangle over the arm of the chair to ruffle her hair. She giggled, a response that he wasn't quite sure how to interpret. Deciding to take it as a form of encouragement, he leaned over to kiss her. She didn't turn her head away, but the moment his lips touched hers, he realized that he had made another mistake.

"Dame," she said, her eyes still focused on the newspaper, which stood, raised vertically in her hands, as impenetrable as the Great Wall of China.

Alec leaned back to think some more. It was now almost ten-thirty. Ignoring Masako, he got up and walked the short distance to the bedroom, where he waited behind a wall. He heard his heart beating fast. Over it came the sound of a newspaper crackling as it was folded and set down.

And then she stood in front of him, looking at him inquisitively. He had the vague sense that he wasn't behaving as she expected him to. Placing a hand on each of her hips, he ran them up the full length of her torso, drawing her to him. Her lips parted and touched his, then skirted over them, teasing. He felt her tongue in his ear and reached his hand under her T-shirt.

"Dame," she said, her voice singsong on the last syllable.

Panting, Alec said, "What?"

"Let's take a shower."

He stopped trying to kiss her. "What?"

"A shower," she repeated.

"Together?"

"No. Me first."

She walked to a narrow closet, brought out two towels. Handing one to him, she disappeared into the bathroom and closed the door behind her. Soon, he heard the shower running.

Alec rubbed both hands over his face, still radiating the warmth from her body. He sat down on the bed, tried to laugh but couldn't. *"Dame,"* he said softly to the empty room, then paused as if waiting for a reply. Then he said it again. And again, until he was laughing.

He hurried out of his clothes, saw at least one button fly off his shirt. Naked, he opened the door to the bathroom and walked in. Another door, this one of frosted glass, led to the shower. For a moment he stood outside it, focusing on the blurred outlines of her body, imagining for himself the slight curve of her hips, the black wetness of her hair. And then he was inside.

"*Dame,*" she said, and giggled.

The water from the shower was hot, and the steam rose around them like a fog. Legs around his waist, arms around his neck, she hung on to him, a hand buried in his hair. He held on to the shower head for support. His other hand was digging into her buttocks, lifting her into him. Her breath came in rapid pants, in gasps, in yells. He could feel in his throat that he was producing sounds of his own but didn't know or care what they were. Their bodies, so different in size, had found a mutual rhythm, and he clung to it, trying to hold off just a little longer. He counted silently to himself backward from ten in Japanese. She cried out and pushed herself even harder against him. He came then, wrenching the shower handle from its bracket on the wall. The handle fell, hanging by its metal coil, writhing like a snake, shooting water in every direction. He stood holding her, still inside her. She was kissing him all over his face, in his ears, on his eyelids. She refused to let him unwrap himself from her limbs. He carried her out of the bathroom that way.

18

GIFTS

The Mercedes hurtled down the street. People who saw it coming stepped quickly back into the shops from which they had emerged. Old women pressed their frail bodies against those houses farthest from the danger.

One young man, dressed in the deep-pocketed pale blue smock of a pachinko parlor employee, wasn't paying attention. He was crossing the street while reading a comic book. He looked up to find the Mercedes about fifty feet away and closing fast, an indigo streak of death. His mouth began to open and close rapidly. His smock, caught by a sudden breeze, billowed about his narrow-hipped body. He froze where he was.

"Mother . . ." Alec whispered from the passenger seat of the Mercedes.

Mrs. Hasegawa didn't seem to hear him. She slapped her hand against the steering wheel and held it there. The horn blared loudly. Alec noticed the man's mouth had stopped opening and closing. The car was now less than thirty feet away.

"Mother!"

"That man is crazy!" Mrs. Hasegawa hissed.

Fifteen feet away.

"Mother!" Alec shouted.

Almost casually, she turned the wheel to the right. The man's mouth opened again, this time to scream, as he dived to the other side of the street, the car missing him by only a yard.

Mrs. Hasegawa straightened the wheel. "See? It was not even close." She shook her head in disbelief. "Stupid man. Eh, Alec? Stupid man!"

The kids, all three of them, were in the backseat, hysterical with laughter.

"She drives like a New Yorker," Yoshi said. "All New Yorkers are crazy."

Alec covered his face with his arms, trying to calm himself. He felt Hiroshi's diminutive hands on his head, scratching his scalp.

"Don't be scared, Little Monkey," Hiroshi said, reaching over the seat. "Little Monkey, your hair is still very short."

Yukiko grabbed Hiroshi by the arm, yanked him back in his seat. "Eh! Hiroshi! Leave Alec alone. You're being a baby."

Hiroshi hit her on the leg. "I'm twelve," he said.

"You're short." She smacked him on the back of the head.

Yoshi said, "That's enough." The bickering stopped immediately.

Satisfied, Mrs. Hasegawa grunted. "We are going first to Mitsukoshi Department Store," she said. "It is the best department store in the world. Did you know that, Alec? The best for shopping."

Alec cleared his throat. "I brought many things with me to Japan, Mother. Perhaps I should not do any more shopping."

She dismissed his words with her clucking noise. "We are going shopping," she said. "And Mitsukoshi is the best in the world for shopping."

* * *

Alec was right behind her as she led the way into Mitsukoshi. Her boxy pink skirt made her appear even more stocky than usual, and the uniformed women who greeted them at the entrance actually took small steps backward in fright. Mrs. Hasegawa paid no attention: she brushed by them without looking and, reaching past Alec to grab hold of Hiroshi's arm, pushed and pulled her way toward the escalators.

She didn't walk through the aisles of jewelry and cosmetics, of perfume sprayers and mud maskers, but stalked them, a predator. Full-waisted, low-set, with fleshy fingers and ears, fleshy nose and a wide mouth, she was the sort of woman from the provinces who might be found one evening dragging an uncooperative bull into its stall by the horns or wading through the murky waters of a rice field. Watching her, Alec thought that her short legs were designed not for strolling or shopping, but for hiking somewhere far from the city, moving with the sure, uphill lean of the farmers of the north. It seemed to him as if she had been picked up and set down in the wrong place for her, a foreign place. She rarely went out now. Her legs, probably strong once, had grown veined and heavy.

Today she looked formidable, though, and Alec followed her through the store. Single file with the rest of her children, past counters and counters of the most expensive beauty products from Milan and Paris and New York, past filmed demonstrations of the latest techniques in eye-liner application. The uniformed Mitsukoshi women were everywhere, an army of Mickey Mouse Club fanatics, appearing like genies from behind cardboard advertisements, rapid sales pitches flowing from their mouths in the high-pitched, cartoon octaves of people who have just inhaled helium. But they were no match for Mrs. Hasegawa. She bulled down the aisle and through them, scattering them without a thought. Her face set in a ferocious scowl, she put the threat of menace behind her bulk and stampeded across the great Mitsukoshi plains. She reached a single thick arm behind her and hauled her children to the safety of the escalator, where the moving steps led steeply upward to the men's clothing department.

"Alec! Do you like them?"

Mrs. Hasegawa's words reached him through the dressing room curtains. He was looking at his reflection in the floor-length mirror, absorbing inch by inch the full effect of the black stretch pants she had made him try on. The pants hugged his legs like a wetsuit, pulled upward at his buttocks and crotch. The leather knee patches rubbed uncomfortably against his bare skin. Alec stared at himself and thought that his body had never looked so awkward, so knobby-kneed and gangly. He wondered briefly whether puberty might not be a single stage of development after all, but something he would have to go through over and over again until death.

"Alec!"

"Yes."

"He likes them!" It was Yukiko's voice.

Alec sighed. "No. I said 'Yes, I'm here.' Not 'Yes, I like them.'"

"He doesn't like them," Yukiko said, softly this time.

Mrs. Hasegawa was clucking. "Alec! Come, stand here. So we can see."

Alec looked at the price tag, converting the yen into dollars. The total was somewhere around three hundred. He added this to the rest of the clothes they had already picked out for him: another pair of pants, two shirts, socks. Hundreds of dollars. "I think the pants are too small, Mother."

"Hiroshi," she commanded. "Bring Alec here."

"Okay. I'm coming." He stepped through the curtains.

There was a moment of silence while they studied him.

"Alec looks very smart," Yoshi said finally. "Issey Miyake is the best in Japanese fashion."

Mrs. Hasegawa looked at Yoshi. "Smart?"

Yoshi nodded. "The best. I have the same pants."

"Very handsome," she agreed. She looked at the rest of her family. "Alec looks smart in Yoshi's pants. Eh? Very handsome."

"Handsome *and* smart," Yukiko whispered.

Hiroshi said, "Alec is a movie star. A big American movie star."

"Okay. Good," Mrs. Hasegawa said, and pointed to a wizened man with a tape measure coiled around his wrist. The tailor stepped forward, gesturing with his hands for Alec to turn around.

Alec ignored him, turned to Mrs. Hasegawa. "About these pants . . ."

She looked surprised. "You don't like them?"

"They are expensive."

"Not expensive," she said firmly. "It is a gift. This is a Japanese custom."

"Please, Mother. It is too much."

Yukiko said, "I like them. I think they are very smart."

"Maybe Alec likes Italian clothes better," Yoshi suggested.

"Both," Mrs. Hasegawa declared. "Alec will have both Japanese and Italian clothes."

Yoshi pointed to a nearby rack of clothes. "These pants go with that jacket over there. Hiroshi, bring that jacket here."

Hiroshi returned with the jacket.

"Why are the shoulders so big?" Mrs. Hasegawa said, her lips pursed.

"Big shoulders are very smart," Yukiko explained. "All the rock stars wear jackets with big shoulders."

Yoshi held the jacket out to Alec. "Try it on."

Alec shook his head. They were crowding around him, getting closer. The tailor already had his hand on the hem of the stretch pants.

Yoshi said: "The pants and jacket are also in brown."

"I think black is better," Yukiko said.

Yoshi nodded. "Yes, black is better."

"Please turn this way," the tailor said.

*   *   *

"Mother," Alec said. "Come and look at this."

It was almost an hour later. They were on the ground floor again, slowly making their way toward the exit. Alec stood beside a glass-enclosed jewelry counter, marking the place of something inside it with an extended finger.

Mrs. Hasegawa had stopped a few feet ahead of him. She glanced quickly over her shoulder to check on the children, who had continued walking.

"Eh! Yoshi!" she called. "Wait at the exit! And hold on to Hiroshi!" She turned to glare at several women who were looking at her with expressions of disapproval and mild horror. They quickly went about their business.

"Come and look," Alec said. "It is very beautiful."

She came up beside him, peered into the display case. "Do you like jewelry?"

"Not for me. But look, that thing there. What do you call that in Japanese?"

"A ring."

"No. To the left."

"A brooch. It is made from jade. Perhaps it is Chinese."

"Yes. Do you like it?"

Mrs. Hasegawa fogged up the display case with her breath. She laughed loudly and wiped it clean with the sleeve of her blouse. "Eh! There it is! Yes, it is very beautiful. I will buy it for you, and you will give it to your girlfriend." She looked at him. "Do you have a girlfriend yet?"

"No," Alec said, thinking of Kiyoko. "Not a girlfriend. There is someone I like, but I am not with her."

"When you give her this present, she will want to marry you. And then you will move away and leave me all alone. I will be very sad, Alec." She laughed again. "And all because of Mitsukoshi!"

A saleswoman with her hair in a bun walked toward them, but Mrs. Hasegawa waved her away.

Alec lowered his voice. "But Mother, you do not understand. I want to give it to *you*. As a gift."

He saw her glance toward the exit, looking for her children.

"That is impossible," she said finally.

"You don't like it," Alec said, thinking that it was the sort of thing she would say.

She studied it through the glass. "It is beautiful."

"So, a gift."

"I give *you* gifts. That is the custom. When I am in New York, you give me gifts. But this is Tokyo."

The saleswoman was still hovering nearby. Alec asked to see the brooch. Looking relieved, she unlocked the display case and brought it out.

"He speaks such fine Japanese," she said to Mrs. Hasegawa.

"I *am* Japanese," Alec said.

Mrs. Hasegawa let out a guffaw.

For a moment, the saleswoman looked as if she might fall down. Then her mouth tightened up like a clam and she went away to another counter.

"That is bad, Alec," Mrs. Hasegawa said, trying to be serious. "Very bad. You should not do that. You are American."

Alec looked down. "Yes, you are right. Please excuse me."

"But it is also very funny. She is a stupid woman, that one."

"About the gift . . ."

She picked up the brooch, weighing it in her hand. It was a miniature frog made of jade, with eyes of black onyx.

"It is very heavy," she said.

Alec touched it with the tip of his finger. "I do not know why, but I like it very much."

"Yes, I like it, too."

"I want to give it to you, Mother."

"You should give it to a young woman. So you can get married."

"It is a frog," Alec said.

"Women love frogs."

"Please, Mother. Will you accept this gift? It is important to me."

"Yes, it is important to me, too," she said softly. "Thank you."

And then she laughed and grew merry again. She waved the beleaguered saleswoman over and, watching her come, whispered to Alec: "You told her that *you* are Japanese. You are very funny, Alec. What a good day of shopping!"

19

LOVE

Alec had never bathed so much in his life. It was the first thing he and Masako did when he went over to her apartment after work. It was the last thing they did before he left to go home. Bathing had become as important a part of their evenings as anything else, even taking precedence over the ritual snack of miniature hot dogs.

They had just bathed again, and he lay on her enormous futon, his head propped on a pillow. Above the sounds of the television, he could hear Masako blow-drying her hair, the noise fading in and out. They had been together just over a week.

Naked, she jumped on the bed, sprawled out across him. "Does Alec really want to watch television?" She was batting her eyelids up and down.

Alec found it hard to look at her. He wanted to tell her that she didn't have to act flirtatious all the time, like some bad Japanese idea of how an American woman would behave with a man. But he didn't say anything.

She lay back beside him, resting her head against his shoulder. They were quiet for a while, watching a dubbed episode of "Dynasty," her fingers gently moving over his body.

When a commercial came on, she said in English, "I rubbu you."

Alec sat up, looked down at her. "What?"

She giggled, pointing at him. "I rubbu you. Rubbu you."

Alec wanted to shake her. "Love is complicated," he said in Japanese.

"I rubbu you," she repeated.

"No, you don't. I know you don't." He was getting up, practically pushing her away from him.

She said it one more time, I rubbu you, but her expression was already changing, collapsing. She looked as if she might cry.

"I have to go, Masako."

Alec turned away from her. He watched himself in the mirror, noticing how quickly he dressed, as if this were the way he always dressed, running like a thief from a woman's apartment. She was crying softly on the futon behind him. He angled his body so that he couldn't see her. He could see only his own reflection now. And the television. Both of them lifeless images that moved. The commercial had ended, and another had taken its place. A blond-haired American woman in a high-cut leather skirt stroked the hood of a red Toyota sports car. She didn't say anything about love.

20

BLIND SPOT

What Alec remembered most about learning to drive was the blind spot. Three mirrors properly positioned, the car in gear, and, suddenly, a sense of shadow, a feeling that some dangerous element was gaining on him fast and hidden and dark. Don't turn your head, his father would say, you have to learn to use the mirrors. So he wouldn't turn his head, knowing all along that his father was wrong, that terrible things were waiting to happen. Things he couldn't see. He would feel a car behind him somewhere, usually off to the left and a little behind, but the mirrors never showed the truth when he looked at their bright surfaces. In the blank clarity of their frames was the presence of a world unseen and unknown, a world chasing him as he drove with stiff arms and an aching neck, even as he privately mourned its absence.

Perhaps it was crazy, but Tokyo seemed darker after the night he left Masako for good, as if he were learning to drive all over again and had lost parts of the world around him in a blind spot that had descended without warning. The car was still moving, the mirrors still in place, and most things appeared as they normally would. There was just that one area, filled to overflowing with mirrored nothingness and the sense of shadow all over again.

The feeling seemed to come and go as it pleased, as if it didn't care what he thought. So he tried not to think about it. That didn't change things, though. Days continued, and he was often surprised to find himself an active participant in each one. He half wondered who it was going to the office each day, sitting there for hours just so he could return home again. Who it was that had taken to drinking whiskey like the old men in movies. Who it was that could have treated anyone the way he had treated Masako that night, the numbness he had felt looking at his reflection in the mirror, the absence he had seen in it.

21

TAKING LEAVE

The rain was heavy, summer-warm even at five-thirty in the morning. Fog rose lethargically from the surface of the bay, hovering and then settling over the fishing boats webbed with netting, over the fish market that hugged the waterfront like an ancient village. The fish sellers paid no attention to the weather. They had mapped out this territory years before and knew their business. The ground between the rows of stalls was paved with cobblestones to facilitate drainage, and tarpaulins were stretched taut above the wooden shelves and crates of fish. Clad in waterproof aprons, the sellers meticulously rearranged their wares, adding more crushed ice, slicing thin strips of sashimi for customers to sample. Around them the rainwater ran in streams down the tarpaulins. It ran between the cobblestones and through newfangled plastic gutters. It made a kind of music as it beat against the canopy of brightly colored umbrellas that progressed purposefully, like a single, living creature, from stall to stall. Beneath this canopy walked a busy crowd of people, women mostly, the intensity and pitch of their voices rising and falling as they changed from the low murmur of salutation to the polite, determined fierceness of price haggling.

Alec stood beside Nobi at one end of the central row of stalls, taking in the scene. They were both dressed in suits, Nobi's navy blue with pinstripes, Alec's solid gray. Their black umbrellas stood out like bruises against the moving background of lilac, green, blue, and red ones.

Alec indicated the entire market with a wave of his hand. "Not many black umbrellas."

"There are not so many men here," Nobi explained. "This is mostly a woman's place. Of course, the fish is caught and sold by men."

"It's certainly crowded." Alec was having second thoughts about being rained on so early in the day. The expedition had been Mrs. Hasegawa's idea in the first place—she had billed it as "the best fish market in the world." To Alec it had seemed like a good excuse to call Nobi. Now he wasn't so sure.

"It is crowded, yes," Nobi said thoughtfully. "But also we are late: the best time for this market is about four-thirty in the morning. That is because it is now very famous in Tokyo. And so to buy the best fish, you must arrive early. Of course, we are here only to look, yes?" Alec nodded. "Good, because I understand fish only when I eat them."

They moved with the crowd, lurching now and then on the irregular cobblestones. A metallic clicking was clearly audible above the beating of the rain and the cries of the fish sellers. After a minute, Alec realized that it was caused by the umbrellas bumping against one another, the tips of the spines briefly colliding, tapping out urgent messages in code.

An old woman silently pushed her way in front of them. Her face was so wrinkled that the deep lines themselves appeared more prominent than her nose, eyes, or mouth. She could not have been much above four feet tall, dressed in a blue-and-white kimono tied at her waist with an obi of dark green. Her geta, traditional wooden sandals, clacked sharply against the wet cobblestones.

Watching her, Nobi said, "Alec, this market is good for old women. They like to come here because it is a safe place. They remember things when they are here. My grandmother often comes here. She would say that this fish market is not so different from the markets in old Tokyo, before the war. Of course, some things have changed. Like that—" Nobi pointed to one of the plastic gutters. "And clothes have changed. But the purpose is still the same. Women come here to buy fish and to discuss the price of that fish. That discussion is very important: you must have energy to get a good price. So it can be like exercise to these women. One morning every week, they come here to push the younger women and buy fish, to have energy and tell stories. Then they go home before the new Tokyo is awake, and again they are safe. It is why I enjoy this market. Its spirit is old."

They stopped in front of a stall that was less crowded than most. Hanging from the wooden stanchions, lanterns cast white light. Beneath them the fish glistened in their coffins of crushed ice. The seller was a sturdy man with a neatly trimmed mustache and the beginnings of a beard. His faded green cotton pants were rolled up to his knees. A woman wearing a red silk scarf stood beside him, pointing at a fish Alec didn't recognize. The seller hooked two fingers into the gills of the fish and raised it at arm's length for inspection. A brief silence fell over the women gathered in front of the stall as they collectively paused to assess the fish. Then, with an expectant nod from the seller, the haggling between him and the woman with the scarf began in earnest. Alec felt a tug on his elbow and reluctantly followed Nobi back out into the rain, which had lightened somewhat.

"The rain is less," Nobi said.

Alec was looking at the cobblestones, not really listening, trying to get a question out. "Have you talked to Kiyoko recently?"

"Probably you have talked to her more recently than I have," Nobi said. "At work, perhaps."

"We don't talk much at work," Alec said. "And I haven't seen her outside of work since that time at your place."

Nobi didn't say anything.

"Is she angry with me?"

"I do not know."

"Wouldn't she tell you?"

Nobi stopped to peer into a crate filled with enormous live spider crabs. He shrugged as he stood up. "Japanese women and men do not tell many things to each other, Alec. And Kiyoko is a very complicated Japanese woman. It is true she is like a sister to me, but I do not always understand her. Sometimes she can be strange. That is the way things are. In Japan, you should not try to hurry any kind of relationship."

"What about the advice you gave me when we first met, Nobi? Remember? About how to meet women. That was all about how to hurry relationships." Alec listened to himself and thought he sounded like a child.

Nobi stiffened visibly. "I think there are some things that you are not seeing. This is different because you know who Kiyoko is. She is not someone you see at a bar. And it is different because I know her. Perhaps that is enough."

That was the last they talked of it. They walked without speaking for a few minutes. All at once the rain stopped, as though a tap had been turned off. The brightly colored umbrellas were closed and furled up, wilted like flowers. Alec and Nobi made their way to the end of the main row of stalls and down to the edge of the pier. Several fishermen sat nearby mending a section of netting. The fog began to lift, gradually unveiling a hazy, indistinct sun. The unfocused light reflected off the still wet, colorless waterfront and turned sharp, making Alec squint. He noticed Nobi looking at his watch. He waited.

"It is almost time to be at work," Nobi said.

"I have a breakfast meeting with Boon at eight," Alec lied.

"It's nearby, so I guess I'll just stay here until it's time to go. It makes more sense."

Nobi appeared confused for a moment. But then his round face settled. "Yes, it makes more sense. I will catch the train, then."

"Okay. See you." He held out his hand.

Nobi took it, saying, "Soon we will have lunch." Then he left.

Alec stayed where he was at the edge of the pier and watched him go, noticing for the first time what a sharp figure Nobi cut in his pin-striped suit, how cleanly it fit his back and shoulders. Finally, he turned and walked back along the pier, past the fishermen, who looked up from their work without interest, and over to a weathered bench that faced inland toward the market. He sat down to wait until it was time to go to work.

An hour passed that way. The women who had for hours pushed and poked, who had so fiercely fought for the lowest prices, began to disappear. They left quietly, singly and in small groups, without a trace of the determination they had shown. They carried their neat packages in string-net bags and walked carefully toward the train station and home, old women once again. The fish sellers remained, left with their unsold catch. Some of them stood in front of their stalls, sucking on their teeth while the sun dried their wet feet. Others began to pack up. They took down and folded the tarpaulins, stacked the crates of yellowtail and eel and squid. They swept the crushed ice into wooden barrels, whistling as they worked. They would move to another location now, a more permanent place to sell the remainder of their goods. Alec got to his feet and walked back down the row of partly dismantled stalls. He felt their eyes on him as he made his way unsteadily along the cobblestones and walked more quickly. It seemed to him as if the day were beginning and ending at the same time, the morning's raw light exposing the emptiness that always lies in the wake of a hurried leavetaking.

22

GODZILLA VS. THE SMOG MONSTER

It was more of a stayover than a slumber party. The two boys, Alec and Boon, staying up late, drinking booze and watching dirty shows on television. They removed their jackets and ties and shoes. They sat on the hard chairs in Boon's study with the lights dimmed, a half-empty bottle of single malt Scotch whiskey on the table between them. A late night talk show flickered into the room from a television in the wall. The guests on the show were all female and topless. Boon said the name of the program was "Boobs," pronounced "Boo-boos." He poured more whiskey for both of them.

They had been at the office until midnight, caught in the final negotiations for a joint venture with a small Japanese computer company. Alec had done some research on the deal, and Boon said he wanted him there for the finish. Alec had sat dully through the meeting, watching five Japanese executives smoke thirteen and a half packs of cigarettes. The trains had stopped running by the time everyone left. The stayover was Boon's idea.

It would be nice to have a chance to talk, he said. They rode through the near empty streets in his chauffeur-driven car.

There was the sense in Boon's modern, sprawling house of the furniture and carpets and prints not belonging to him. The colors were not his colors: earth tones and pastels in shades like off-salmon. Chairs and sofas and even desks were all chrome and glass, hard and gleaming under halogen light cast by Italian lamps. Alec looked but could not find Boon in this house. There were no old reading chairs to give the rooms Boon's sense of being comfortable with himself. It was as if someone else had one day set the house just as it was and then left, and Boon had not wanted to, or not been able to, change it. Alec thought as he watched him that Boon walked like a guest in his own house, not quite tiptoeing, but almost, having taken his shoes off at the door so as not to disturb his invisible hosts.

But those thoughts had already come and gone. Things seemed less complicated to Alec now as he sat in Boon's study drinking whiskey. He compared the breasts of the different talk show guests and felt a warm contentment settle somewhere in his chest. He looked over at Boon.

"Joe?"

Boon turned his face so that he could keep one eye on the television and the other on Alec. "Yeah?"

"I just remembered this dream I had a few nights ago. Okay if I tell it? It's funny."

Boon put his full attention on Alec. "Sure."

"Okay. It's very vivid. Ready? It opens and I'm standing alone in a field somewhere in the Midwest, probably Kansas. The land is flat and green and endless. I can see for miles, as far as you can imagine. There's a wind blowing, ruffling my hair. It's coming in gusts, sweeping through the long grass in these wild, pulsing patterns. And I'm standing right in the middle of it. There's just this huge open space—no other people." Alec laughed. "So I spread my arms and dance across the country like Julie Andrews in *The Sound of Music*. That's it."

Boon was laughing. "That's it? The whole dream?"

"You want more?"

Boon held up his hands like a traffic cop. "That's enough. You started like a poet and finished as Julie Andrews."

"I've already got the interpretation," Alec said. "It's all about the lack of open space in this country. Did you know that within a thirty-mile radius of where I'm living there are more people than in all of California? Think about that. No surprise I'm dreaming about dancing across Kansas."

"So what about me?"

"You don't have to because you live in this huge house. Your living room could easily be Kansas. Your dining room's Idaho. The bathroom off the kitchen would have to be Delaware or Rhode Island. I've got it all figured out."

Boon was shaking his head. "I can't believe I hired you."

Alec grinned, took another belt of whiskey. Warm contentment had turned into loquacity. Boo-boos, he thought.

They were quiet for a while. Watching television, drinking. Boon looked almost asleep, his eyes heavy-lidded and bloodshot.

"Um, Joe?" Alec said finally.

Boon nodded imperceptibly.

"I was just thinking this house isn't what I expected. It doesn't seem like you."

Boon gave a wry smile. "It's hard for me to imagine what a place that *seemed* like me would look like. And I doubt I'd live there if I knew."

Alec shrugged. "I don't know. More lived in, maybe. And wiser, if that makes any sense. Some old leather reading chairs and a beat-up sofa. An antique desk. A pool table. Those sorts of things."

"You mean a real home?"

"I suppose so."

"I don't spend enough time here for that," Boon said. "It seems there are business dinners almost every night. Or just work to do, like tonight. Then up every morning at six. Anna makes me breakfast, and I'm off to work again. That's my routine."

"Anna?"

Boon had a peculiar expression on his long face. "Anna cooks for me. She's lived here since Diane left—in the room off the kitchen. She's probably asleep now."

Alec didn't say anything.

"She's half Filipino," Boon said quickly, as if he felt he had to say something. "Her father's American. He was an old friend of mine."

"So she's pretty young," Alec ventured. It seemed safer than asking a question.

"Yes," Boon said.

The topless talk show was ending. As the credits were moving up the screen, pop music began to play. The host and his guests got up and started dancing. The topless women looked pale and young beneath the bright stage lights. Their movements were jerky, their smiles uninspired and unchanging. Alec wondered if they would dance across Kansas with him. Then the credits ended, the women disappeared. An old monster movie took their place. *Godzilla vs. the Smog Monster.*

After a couple of minutes, Boon muted the volume with the remote control. "About work . . ." he began.

"I know," Alec said gloomily. "The high-tech report. I'm working on it. It's coming along. I just need a couple more weeks. Sorry."

Boon waved his words away. "Relax, Alec. I know you'll get it done. That's not what I'm talking about. I was really pleased with the way the meeting went today. That's a good-sized deal for us, and you were a big help with it. I was impressed by the way you handled yourself."

"I hardly did anything, Joe. I basically sat there counting cigarette butts. I've never seen people smoke so much. It was Guinness book material."

Boon's thin mouth turned up at the corners. "How about

being just a little serious for a couple of minutes? Okay? I've been watching you at work the last few weeks—probably more closely than you think. And I've been reading over some of your reports. They're good: you have an eye for the kinds of things that make products and companies successful. More than that, you're good with people. They seem to like you, to feel comfortable around you in both English and Japanese. That's how to establish a good business environment in this country." Boon took a swallow of whiskey. "What I'm saying, Alec, is that so far the job is a success—that *you* are a success at the job—and you ought to stay on. One summer is nowhere near enough time. You're younger than I was when I started here, and you probably know a lot more than I did. My guess is you'll be a successful businessman with or without my help. But as long as I can help and advise you, I'm glad to do it. That's the nice part of being in my position."

Alec noticed that Godzilla and the Smog Monster were engaged in mortal combat over the miniature cardboard city of Tokyo. Godzilla was visibly choking on the dark clouds of soot and toxic fumes. He was stumbling backward, trying to cover his mouth with his useless, reptilian forelegs. And then he was collapsing, crushing an entire neighborhood beneath his gargantuan frame. Even with the sound muted, Alec imagined he could hear the cries of woe rise up from the rubble. He helped himself to more whiskey. The bottle was nearly empty.

"I don't know, Joe. Business to me has always been what my father does, the big part of *his* life, not mine. I don't think I know enough about anything to make plans right now."

Boon didn't appear to be listening. "The important thing is that you stay on. You'll do very well here. But it's good to think about things, too. So I thought this might not be a bad time for you to take a weekend away from Tokyo. I've arranged for you to spend the next few days with Kawashima's grandparents up north in Yamagata Prefecture, in a small village called Yamadera. They don't speak any English, but Kawashima assured me they'll be happy to have you. Unfortunately, she has too much work to go with you. But I'm sure it will be fine anyway."

Alec was on the edge of his chair. "You've *arranged* with *Kawashima* for me to go away this weekend? Alone with people I've never met? Joe, that's crazy. It really is. I can't go."

"Why not?"

"A lot of reasons. I don't know these people. Kiyoko's not even speaking to me these days. This wasn't my idea. Things like that."

"You *can* go, Alec," Boon said, and he was already getting unsteadily to his feet. "You should get out of the city. Everything's arranged. I'm giving you tomorrow off to catch the twelve-thirty train. I've booked you first class." He was moving slowly toward the door of the study. "And as for Kawashima, if you want to talk to her, you ought to make the effort. Or if you want me to talk to her for you, that's fine, too. Okay? Right. Well, we've settled a few things, then. That's good. I'd say it's time for me to get some sleep. If I don't see you in the morning, have Anna make you some breakfast. Good night, Alec." He disappeared out the door.

"Good night," Alec mouthed. He gave his chair an open-handed smack and felt the whiskey rear up and come down on his head with a numbing thud.

Godzilla was back with a vengeance, scorching the Smog Monster with breaths of fire. There was a mad chase, more cardboard rubble flying everywhere, more silent screams of woe. But Godzilla was winning: gradually the Smog Monster was melting, his body turning shapeless and then liquid, running through the war-torn streets like sewage. People held their noses and ran for cover.

23

YAMADERA

The bullet train took him north from Tokyo to the coast city of Sendai. He managed to sleep most of the way; curled in his seat, he was only vaguely aware of the train's speed. At Sendai, he switched to the Yamagata line, took the express train for the one-hour leg to Yamadera. He was fully awake now, his initial resistance to the trip already eclipsed by the unnerving thought of staying with Kiyoko's grandparents. Turning away from the old man sitting beside him, he pressed his face against the window and stared through his own breath at the unfolding countryside.

The land was lush and green, rising as it pleased, now into sloping hills, now into steep mountains and rocky gorges. Scattered along the ridges, pine trees grew in clusters like people gathered in the afternoon to talk. Between its valleys and ridges, though, the land had been given over to the growing of rice, the flat, geometric uniformity of the paddies contrasting with the sharpness of the surrounding landscape. Looking at them, Alec thought he could feel the soothing coolness of the paddies, the way the thin, pointed shoots rose like needles from the fields of murky water. They flashed past him and changed shape, cresting again into razor-edged peaks, descending again into hidden pockets of foliage and pin-pricked envelopes of dark water. Had he been asked, Alec would have sworn that he had seen this land before. It was like a collage of familiar images, each one akin in some way to a sister image in his memory: hills he had climbed somewhere else in his life and woods he had walked through; the mottled green of an orchard he had once visited in Massachusetts; the cool darkness of a brook where he had fished with his father as a small boy. This was not just one place he knew, but many.

Its wheels screeching and clacking against the iron rails of an old bridge, the train passed over a narrow river. Alec could see a few men fishing, waist-deep in the fast-flowing water, their bodies still. Only the long, thin rods moved, worked as though by some invisible hand. Stretched out across the far bank of the river, grapevines crawled up their latticework supports. Alec craned his neck to watch the fishermen until they had disappeared from sight. The train moved deeper into the countryside. Small farms appeared only to be obscured by groves of cherry trees. The old man in the seat next to him said that this was the growing season, the time to watch the land as though it were your own child. His Japanese was gritty, full of the country, and Alec could only catch a word here and there.

As the train slowed, the conductor called out Yamadera Station. Alec jumped to his feet to gather his belongings. Stepping off the train and into the crowded station, he sensed immediately that he was the only foreigner in the building, perhaps in the town. People gathered around him as if he were a museum piece. They pointed and stared, unhurried and unashamed. They touched and prodded him with their eyes. He walked out to the front of the station and looked around. People of all ages continued to mill around him. Giggling and saucer-eyed, the young children tended to dawdle the longest, eventually dragged away by their mothers. He stood there for a while, the center of activity. And he thought of Kiyoko, wondered how he would feel if she were with him.

A piece of clothing was poking out from the top of his duffel bag; he bent down to stuff it back in. As he was getting up, he almost knocked heads with a silver-haired man. Excusing himself, Alec stood up, but the man remained bent over at the waist, head down and eyes closed. His ears were large and curved sharply out from his head. He was dressed in a summer yukata the color of wet hay and wore wooden geta on his feet.

Alec bowed, too, trying to exactly match the angle of the man's torso. Just when he thought he had gotten it, the man bowed lower.

"I am called Kawashima," he said in Japanese.

Still bent over, Alec stretched his neck upward to look at the man, but all he could see was the back of his head. "I am called Alec."

They both stood up. The man was shorter than Alec had originally thought. Even with the geta, the top of his head barely reached Alec's chin. He had the rough, tanned face of someone who spent much of his time outdoors, with deep lines around his eyes and forehead. In Kawashima's strong cheekbones and chin, Alec was sure he detected a resemblance to Kiyoko. Though their color was dark, Kawashima's eyes were alive with light— actually gleaming, Alec thought.

Picking up the duffel bag, Kawashima led the way to a sparkling white Honda sedan. His geta click-clacked against the pavement. Alec stared at the car, then back at the old man, trying to put the two images together. Kawashima started up the car like an old pro, opening the moon roof with the flick of a switch.

They drove through the main part of town in silence, Kawashima hardly seeming aware that there was another person in the car. They moved slowly through the narrow streets, past modest shops and markets. In their midst, rising above the low roofline of the houses, wooden torii marked the entrance to Shinto shrines.

And then, suddenly, the town was left behind, the Honda winding its way through one cluster of trees and then another. They were pines, most of them, but thinner and sharper than the ones Alec knew from home. They grew wherever they could, huddling in small groups along either side of the road, raising their pointed heads to the vertical landscape with an air of fierce pride. Beneath them in the valley, a house would occasionally show itself, the overhanging eaves of its roof appearing as purely horizontal as the rice paddies that belonged to it.

They turned off onto a dirt road that meandered upward through the pine trees. The car hit a bump and Kawashima let out a grunt; Alec realized they had been riding in silence since leaving the station. Now they were on another dirt road, heading down into the valley. Gradually the land leveled out, turning into a series of rice paddies that led almost to the edge of a narrow river. Like others he had seen along the way, the house popped into sudden view, a gift. It sat nestled among a grove of cherry trees at one end of the valley. The plain wood of the frame and worn, green roof tiles seemed themselves to be a part of the earth, and Alec had to look closely to make out the exact boundaries of the house.

They headed down another road, this one more rocks than dirt, until the car was under a cherry tree that marked the edge of a small orchard. In silence, Kawashima stopped the car, got out, and started walking. Alec followed him through the trees.

Kawashima's wife was waiting for them at the entrance to the house, her yukata fluttering in the wind. Her hand pressed the hem against her legs to keep it from rising. She was shorter than her husband, but broader. There was a natural steadfastness to her bearing that made Alec think she had no fear of hardship. Her tiny feet were covered in white ankle socks, which had a separate toe so they could be worn with thonged sandals.

She bowed low, but Alec was prepared this time and moved along with her; he thought he heard the old man chuckle. She welcomed him, told him that he could call them Grandmother and Grandfather, since they were the grandparents of his friend. Alec bowed even lower. As he straightened up, there was a clarity to the scene—to the old couple, their house and land— that made him suddenly aware of the day's end. The light had changed, grown at once less strong and more crystalline, imparting everything with a greater sense of depth. The three of them stood still and watched the sun, already a fiery orange, as it gradually drew its colors in ever-deepening hues across the horizon.

The house was two stories, but small. The top floor was a bare, open space that could be divided into separate rooms by pulling closed a sliding screen of wood and rice paper. One side of the room was where the old couple slept on their white cotton futon. The other side was to be Alec's. With his elbow, Grandfather indicated that, when the time came to go to sleep, Alec could fetch his own futon from the cupboard in the wall.

A navy blue yukata lay folded on the tatami. Grandfather said, "Yukata," and watched with amusement while Alec put it on. When the belt had been tied, the old man grabbed the knot and pulled; it held. With a grunt, he turned around.

Together, in silence, they walked down the rickety stairs.

It was strange at first, sleeping in an open space with Kiyoko's grandparents. Alec lay awake for a long time, the sounds of the old couple's snoring and coughing making him feel as though he were listening to passengers on a night train; their noises had the steady sense of routine about them. Openmouthed, head cocked to one side, Alec strained and listened, and gradually, reluctantly, the old man and woman began to identify themselves to him until he knew for certain which noises belonged to whom. And once he could read the rhythms of their sleep, it was only a matter of time before he started to remember things he thought he had forgotten long ago. They came to him as they had from his first day in Japan, as images and scenes, each one belonging to something larger and unidentifiable. It was as if he had lost control somehow, as if his memory did as it pleased, mocking him by playing his childhood back to him in bits and pieces. He watched them as he would someone else's home movies, and felt the foreignness of his own life. Like thick rope, it coiled around him and held him where he was.

A month had passed since Alec's visit to the men's club with his father. He had just begun eighth grade the week before. People were already starting to talk about high school. It was Saturday, the tenth anniversary, Alec's father told him, of their renting the house in upstate New York. They made the three-hour drive so that they would be there to celebrate.

The house was Colonial style, painted white. It was old and at one time had been a schoolhouse. A cracked school bell still sat in one corner of the attic, its surface long since covered with dust and cobwebs. A back porch had been added on to the second story of the house. Maple trees bordered the property on two sides, sheltering it from neighbors. A rope swing hung from the tallest tree. A long field began at the edge of the house and sloped down to the steep bank of the river.

That same Saturday the head of the town's historical association arrived to hang a wooden plaque on the front of the house. He was portly, all tweed and wide-wale corduroy, and he peered at the house and its occupants through round, gold-rimmed spectacles. He took his coffee with milk, he said, and sat down heavily in the Victorian chair by the Ben Franklin stove. He spoke of the history that had occurred on the site, of the famous people who had learned their childhood lessons within the walls of the old building. There were pages and pages of records, he said—dusty old books filled with important facts and schoolboy stories. Alec didn't recognize any of the famous names the man mentioned and spent the rest of the day looking them up in his father's 1952 edition of the *Encyclopedia Britannica*.

It was late that night when he awoke, perhaps two or three in the morning. The sound of Mark's uneasy, openmouthed sleep reached him from the other side of the room. Alec's bladder ached, and he thought that he should probably go to the bathroom. He climbed carefully out of bed and walked into the playroom, where he paused for a moment to get his bearings in the darkness. The corner of the Ping-Pong table felt splintery against his outstretched hand. To his right, his fingers brushed over the wall of shelves that held his and Mark's natural history museum. Alec could picture in his mind the placement of each bird's nest, of each animal skeleton and jagged piece of quartz. A hollow robin's egg, he knew, rested in a tightly woven nest on the second shelf from the top. He moved slowly through the room, feeling his way. He closed the door behind him and shuffled down the long hallway to the bathroom, which was just to one side of the staircase leading up to the second floor. But he never went inside. He heard his parents fighting upstairs in their bedroom. They were shouting at each other, over each other, and Alec could tell from the wildness in their voices that they were both drunk. He turned from the bathroom and sat down on the bottom step.

Alec couldn't remember his mother ever having been drunk before or shouting the way she was doing now. Shouting, then sobbing, then shouting again. He wasn't even listening to what she was saying. It seemed to him that it was all about sounds now, not words. Terrible, animal sounds that raced down the wooden stairs and pounded into him like a fist as he sat in the darkness. A door slammed. Something made of glass shattered against a wall. The noise was brutal, too clear to believe, and Alec cringed as if the object had been thrown at him. He felt again the ache in his bladder, and then the sudden loss of it, like an exhale, as the warm urine flowed out of him and into his flannel pajamas.

Things were quiet after that. Alec didn't move. Already he could smell his own sour-sweet odor. He held his breath and waited for Mark to appear. But no one came. For some reason Alec thought of the plaque hanging on the front of the house, of how the head of the historical association was so sure that he knew everything there was to know about the house and who had lived in it. And he realized that no one understood the history of the house the way he did now. He had sat on the stairs and pissed in his pants and no one would ever know a thing about it. He had listened to his parents rage and battle against each other, while Mark had slept through it all. The historical record would show that nothing had changed.

It must have been then that Alec understood for the first time that he had to get away from that history, from the house, from the sounds he had heard that night. He had seen and heard too much. He would go away to school the next year and leave it all behind him, leave Mark sleeping soundly in his bed. He would find something of his own and never once remember any of what had happened here. He would never look back.

The next morning, it was dark when Alec woke, shivering. The air through the open window still tasted of night, cool and moist. He kicked the crumpled sheet back on top of him but knew he wouldn't be able to go back to sleep.

Reaching for his yukata, he stood up and put it on. The cotton felt harsh against his skin. He groped his way to the stairs; they groaned loudly under his weight. Then he was down and out the door to the porch. The dew-laden air clung to his skin, raising goose bumps on his chest and arms. Out in the open, it was a different kind of darkness from that of the interior of the house—it seemed to Alec somehow more complicated, filled with things beyond his imagination—and it took him a minute to recover his vision. Slowly, as though emerging from a tunnel, things became clear: the cherry trees standing like soldiers around the house; the bare outlines of a rectangle of garden off to one side; Grandfather sitting motionless on the porch, staring across the darkness of the valley.

Alec felt his heart jump upward, bounce against something, then fall back into place. Before he could stop himself, his mouth made a loud sucking noise.

"Sit," Grandfather said without moving.

Alec stared at him openmouthed. The sky seemed suddenly to have grown lighter, exposing him like a spotlight.

"Sit," Grandfather repeated.

Alec sat down next to him, his knees cracking. "I am sorry for disturbing you."

The old man didn't respond. Alec tried to figure out what he could be looking at for so long. The sky was fully waking up now, the light spreading through it with a surprising gentleness.

"Do you like to fish?" Grandfather still hadn't moved.

"What?" Alec said, not understanding the word for fishing.

"Fish. In the river."

"In the river? Yes, I like to fish."

Grandfather stood up, started walking briskly down the slope in the direction of the river. Without looking at Alec, he pointed to where the fishing equipment lay, the bamboo rods resting against the side of the house.

"Good," he said. "I like to fish, too."

Barely able to carry everything, Alec rushed after him.

They walked for a while. When they reached the river, Grandfather turned downstream along the bank. Finally, he stopped. Alec stood beside him at the edge of the river, studying the strength of the current. A twinge of fear rocked his stomach; he had once tipped his canoe and almost drowned in the river that ran behind his family's country house.

"It is a very pretty river," he said.

Grandfather grunted, began threading the fishing line through the eye of a small lure. When he was finished, he reached into one of the bags Alec had been carrying and brought out a pair of rubber fisherman's waders. Alec extended his hand, thinking they were for him. But the old man put them on himself, tucking the edges of his yukata into the chest-high waders. Picking up his rod, he walked carefully into the water, planted his feet, and began fishing.

Alec stared after him, too shocked to even laugh. He wondered if he had been brought along simply to carry the equipment. He picked up a lure.

Five minutes later, he was still trying to thread the line through it. Grandfather hadn't even turned around to check on him. Sweaty and humiliated, Alec cleared his throat loudly.

Grandfather didn't turn his head.

"I can't do this," Alec mumbled.

"You said you like to fish."

"I do."

With a loud sigh, Grandfather reeled in and, dripping wet, came up beside him. Feeling like a little boy, Alec handed him the line and lure.

"Watch," Grandfather said.

Slowly, so that Alec could see exactly what he was doing, he threaded the line through the eyehole and tied it off with a tiny, secure knot. He looked at Alec for a moment, then cut away the knot with a sharp pocketknife. Holding the lure and line, Alec stared after him as he walked back into the river. On the third attempt, he threaded the lure, then secured it with the same knot he had seen Grandfather tie. There was a second pair of waders in the bag. They were too small, just barely reaching his waist.

He paused again at the edge of the water, thinking that it was a very strong current for such a small river. The problem didn't seem to bother Grandfather, who was so still in the water that he didn't even appear to be fishing. But with the first step, Alec felt the water rushing under his foot, taking his balance with it. Letting out a yell, he began to go over, his waders filling with water. Grandfather reached out with one hand, grabbed hold of the top of Alec's waders, and hauled him to a standing position.

"Thanks," Alec said, feeling very wet.

Grandfather said, "You move too much." And went back to fishing.

After about an hour, Grandfather brought out a small snack of dried seaweed, rice, and Japanese pickles. They sat on the bank and ate in silence. Alec had already wolfed down his portion and was looking around for more food when Grandfather grunted and stood up to resume fishing.

By midafternoon, Grandfather's bag was almost full of trout, a few scaly tails poking through the opening. Every so often, Alec would look at them enviously, wondering how the old man could be so lucky. Sometimes it seemed to him as if he, Alec, were fishing for both of them, reeling in and then casting in a long, sweeping arc that sent the lure almost to the other side of the river. A few feet away, Grandfather looked practically asleep, the rod held loosely between his fingers, swaying back and forth just enough to keep the lure from sinking. He never reeled in unless there was a fish on the line. Alec thought he looked as if he could go on fishing that way forever. Like a bird, perhaps an egret, hunting for its supper.

Finally, Grandfather's bag couldn't hold any more trout. He reeled in. Alec watched him walk to the bank, thinking how sure of himself the old man looked. The thought was still in his mind when Grandfather suddenly stopped moving and clutched his head. His face had turned ashen.

Alec took a careful sidestep toward him. "Grandfather? Are you all right?"

Grandfather didn't respond. He was only a step from the bank, but he made no attempt to move. Alec hurriedly reeled in and, throwing his rod onto dry land, maneuvered himself beside the old man.

"Let me help you, Grandfather. Are you sick?" He took Grandfather's fishing rod and threw it on the bank near his own.

"It is nothing," Grandfather said, but Alec could hardly hear him.

Holding him by the elbow, Alec walked him to the bank and helped him to sit down with his back against a smooth rock. Grandfather was no longer clutching his head, but his face was still pale. His breathing was strained and sharp, clearly audible above the hushed gurgle and hiss of the fast-flowing river.

"I will take you home," Alec said, trying to sound confident.

Grandfather waved him away. "No, Alec. The pain has already gone. It was nothing. A headache."

"Grandmother will worry."

"You will not tell her," Grandfather said. "Do you understand? Now, go back to the river and fish. I will watch you while I rest."

Alec studied the old man for a few seconds, finally deciding that he was probably right, that it was just a headache. He picked up his rod and waded back out into the river. It seemed no time at all before he was cold and wet again, wanting nothing more than to throw his rod into the river. But he felt the eyes on his back and kept going, trying to make each successive cast longer than the one before it. While casting, he would shift his feet around to get more leverage, often fighting to regain his balance in the strong current.

After another twenty minutes without any sign of a fish, he returned to the bank. Grandfather was still resting against the rock, but already his face had regained some of its color. Removing the water-filled waders, Alec found a minnow in one of the legs. Sore and soggy, he sat down next to Grandfather.

"You said you like to fish," Grandfather said.

"I like to fish."

Grandfather shook his head. "You move too much. The fish are not stupid. They know you do not have patience."

Alec thought it over in his head, made sure that he hadn't misunderstood. He had just spent five hours in the water without getting a single bite, and he was being told that even the fish knew he had no patience.

"I am a terrible fisherman," he said.

To his surprise, Grandfather shook his head again. "No."

Alec waited for more, but there was none. The old man stooped down, gathered up all of the equipment in his arms. From across the water, Alec heard the call of a lone bird looking for its mate. He stared at the river, feeling the power behind its motion.

While they walked, Grandfather sang an ancient Japanese

farming song. Carried by the rhythm of men working in the fields, the words lifting and pushing into the darkening valley, Alec felt his tired feet light against the ground.

He woke gradually to the sound, a distant *thwack* coming from behind the house. He had learned already to sleep through the dark glow of early morning, rising instead with the sun already up.

Again he heard the *thwack,* coming now at regular intervals. He put on his yukata, rolled up the futon, and stored it in the cupboard. Downstairs, he said good morning to Grandmother and sat down to breakfast. He mixed a raw egg in a small bowl with a little soy sauce and poured it over a bowl of rice. Grandmother poured tea for him.

After breakfast, he walked outside. Grandfather stood just beyond the porch, legs spread to shoulder width, an axe raised straight above his head, the blade gleaming like silver in the sun. Shirtless, he wore white cotton workpants rolled up to his thighs and a large white headcloth that covered most of his silver hair. His eyes appeared to be closed; his face was pure concentration. And then the axe swung down in a single, fluid arc, the blade landing with a *thwack* in the top of a log of wood. For a second Alec thought he could see the blade hesitate as it made contact, before accelerating through to split the wood exactly in half. The two pieces flew apart, each landing in separate piles, which looked neat enough to have been stacked by hand.

Grandfather bent down to pick up another log, placed it vertically on a small wooden block in front of him. He balanced himself and raised the axe.

Alec cleared his throat. "Good morning, Grandfather."

Slowly, the axe came down. "Good morning, Alec."

"Would you like some help?"

Alec wasn't sure but thought he saw a subtle change of

expression in the weathered face; the line of the mouth softening around the edges, the eyes again showing a look of amused approval.

After a while, Grandfather said, "Yes. Come here." He offered the axe, handle first, in Alec's direction.

Alec walked over, paused, then took the axe in his hands. The handle was made of beautiful, light-colored wood, worn smooth where the hands would be placed. But the blade was magical. Like a samurai sword Alec had once seen, the shining steel had been crafted in layers, perhaps hundreds of them. Feeling its weight, he ran his thumbnail lightly along the sharpness of its edge.

Grandfather stepped back and Alec took his place in front of the splitting block. He tried to concentrate on the log but kept thinking about the sharp pine needles that had worked their way into his sandals. He knew as the blade started its downward arc that the angle was off; he had rushed his preparation. The metal barely caught the wood at all, splintering the edge and sending the rest of the log tumbling off the platform. Alec didn't move for a few seconds, waiting for his arms to stop vibrating from the shock. He kept his head down, counting the splinters, afraid to look at the old man.

Finally Grandfather walked over to him, took the axe from his hands. "You do not think," he said.

"I know."

"You do not know, Alec. You expect too many things."

As if proving the old man's statement, Alec couldn't think of a single thing to say. He nodded dumbly.

Grandfather hoisted the axe above his head, testing the weight. The blade hovered, then began to dance in the sunlight. He brought it down in one clean motion, splitting the log. Alec bent down, picked up one of the halves. It was split perfectly, the grooves of the wood clean and precise. He put out his hand. Gently, Grandfather placed the axe in it.

"Until dinner," he said, and walked into the house.

Alec watched his small form disappear into the shadows. And then he started to work.

The next day was Alec's last at the farm. It had been raining all afternoon, and he had already finished the one novel he had brought with him. Grandfather had been resting upstairs since lunch. Alec guessed he had another headache and had briefly considered telling Grandmother about it. But then he remembered his promise to the old man.

He sat now at the low table, looking out through the porch at the cherry trees. In a few weeks, the blossoms would emerge, showering the land with color. But for now, the green leaves held their place, soaking up the rain. Dark thunder clouds sat on top of the valley like a hat. Behind him, sounds of cooking came from the kitchen. Something heavy was set down hard on the counter. And then the staccato clack-clack of a chopping knife against a wooden block. In the background, something was frying.

Grandmother's yukata was gray, the cotton soft and worn. She looked up when Alec entered the kitchen, nodding her head as though she had been expecting him. Alec stayed where he was for a moment, watching her while she chopped and diced vegetables. Her head was bent low over the chopping block, the blade of the long knife rising and falling in steady passes by her ear. The motion was precise, restricted, yet her expression remained free and relaxed, her mouth slightly open. The knowledge that he was there seemed to satisfy her; she didn't look at him again, just continued chopping. Occasionally she would throw a handful of the diced vegetables into a big iron casserole sitting on the stove.

Alec cleared his throat. "Excuse me, Grandmother, but what are you making?"

The blade of the knife stopped suddenly, poised somewhere above her right ear. *"Nabe."*

Alec nodded his head, realized he hadn't thought of what he was going to say next. "That's nice. I like *nabe*."

Acknowledging his comment with a brief smile, she went back to the vegetables. She was slicing onions now, the translucent rings falling in a neat row.

"When I was small, I used to help my mother cook," Alec said.

The sound of the knife against the chopping block continued uninterrupted.

Alec tried again. "Excuse me, Grandmother, but would you like some help?"

This time she looked up. "Alec, you want to help me cook?" She laughed.

"Excuse me, but yes." He wasn't sure if she was making fun of him.

"Come here." She handed him the knife, handle first. "You can do this, yes?" She walked over to the sink, began rinsing a colander full of long, white noodles.

His first cut was tentative; afraid of making a mistake, he slowly pushed the blade through the onion, as if it might break from too much pressure. There was no sound. He kept an eye on Grandmother, whose back was turned. She turned off the water after a while, cocking her head to one side. Alec struggled with the onion, his arm feeling tense, the knife unwieldy in his hand. He squinted against the sting.

"It is okay if it is not just right," Grandmother said after a while, still turned toward the sink, head tilted in the air.

"Thank you," Alec said.

She gave a quick nod of satisfaction. Alec relaxed his grip on the knife, tested it against the crisp flesh of the onion. After a few minutes, the translucent rings began to dance and hop to the beat of the knife as it struck the chopping block. They fell in a row that was not as neat as Grandmother's had been, though it was neat enough—as orderly as the piles of split logs he had made the day before. Ignoring the sting in his eyes, Alec bent low over his work. The blade passed swiftly by his right ear.

Grandmother laughed. "So. Alec is a cook."

Alec looked over at her, then put down the knife so he wouldn't hurt himself. "I need practice. I always need practice."

"Yamadera is a good place to practice," she said. "With Grandfather, you can practice fishing and chopping wood—do you understand 'chopping wood'?" She walked over to where he was, picked up his knife, and wielded it over her head like a heavy axe. "Chopping wood, yes? And with Grandmother, you can practice cooking. If it stops raining, you can also practice gardening. In Yamadera, these are the important things, Alec. In Tokyo, in the cities, these things are no longer important. But we have always lived here. Always, and we will never leave."

"Kiyoko talks about Yamadera often," Alec said, thankful for the chance to finally mention her. "Sometimes I think she likes Yamadera more than Tokyo. She would like to live in the country, I think. Here in Yamadera, with you and Grandfather."

"This is Kiyoko's home," Grandmother said softly. "In Tokyo, people do not understand what is important. But Kiyoko is different. She understands these things, and perhaps Tokyo people do not understand her."

"When Kiyoko was young, Grandmother—when she was a baby—what was she like?"

"Kiyoko was always very beautiful. And she was quiet. But sometimes she liked to talk to Grandfather. She would help me cook, but she would sit on Grandfather's lap—*here*." She patted the front of her thighs. "She would sit and listen to him talk."

She scooped up the onion he had sliced and carried it over to the casserole on the stove. Using her hands, she mixed it together with the other vegetables already in the pot. Then she wiped her hands on her yukata.

"It is sad that Kiyoko has not married yet," she said as if talking to herself.

Alec was still wondering how he should reply when he heard the creak and groan of the stairs.

He said, "Grandfather is coming."

She turned to wait for her husband, and Alec thought he saw a look of worried expectation on her face, like a girl waiting to catch her first glimpse of a blind date.

Grandfather's sleeping yukata was black and as soft and worn as the gray one Grandmother liked to wear while she cooked. It was oddly creased and wrinkled from having been slept in. The belt knot had slipped round his waist so that it now pointed out from his hip. His hair, usually slicked back with tonic, was disheveled, tufting at the back of his head. Like his robe, his face had taken on bed lines. They merged with his own wrinkles, which had grown deeper from sleep, and pulled the tightness from his face.

The expression of concern had not left Grandmother's face, though now it had changed, grown softer. She walked up to her husband and gently tugged his belt knot back to the center of his waist. Her gaze was fixed on his face.

"Tea," Grandfather said.

She prepared tea for him. He sipped it loudly in appreciation. After a moment, she turned back to the sink and began rinsing the noodles again.

"Grandfather rested all afternoon," she said to no one in particular.

Grandfather was looking at her back. "It has been raining all afternoon."

"Perhaps Grandfather is sick," she said to the noodles.

"No," Grandfather said firmly. He went and stood behind her at the sink, peering over her shoulder. "Alec, what is Grandmother making for dinner?"

"Nabe," Alec said.

Grandfather touched his chin to her shoulder. "That is

good, Alec. Grandmother makes the best *nabe* in Japan. The best."

Grandmother gently shook him off her shoulder. When she turned around, Alec saw that she was blushing.

"It is not true, Alec. My husband is only teasing me." She reached back, wet her hand under the faucet. Then she smoothed down the hair on the back of Grandfather's head. "Besides," she said to Grandfather, "Alec is helping me. He is a very good cook."

Grandfather's face had regained some of its life. He scrunched up his eyes as if he was chuckling to himself. "It does not require patience to be a good cook. Eh, Alec? Not like fishing."

"I don't know, Grandfather." Alec picked up a whole onion from the chopping block. The old couple watched him while he peeled off the outer skin, put the onion back on the block, and handed Grandfather the knife, handle first. "It is a very big onion."

Slowly, the valley was awakening. Alec felt the thrill of being there to watch it happen on his last morning. The early light seemed to have nothing to do with the sun. It moved from the darkness without a trace of where it came from.

He walked for a while, feeling the dew soak into his feet and ankles. Life was changing around him, stretching, shaking off a night of sleep. Still roosting in the trees and bushes, birds gave their first hesitant calls of the morning, as if afraid they might have lost their voices during the night. Alec heard the river before he saw it. When he was close enough to see the dark ripples in its surface, he veered right, walked along the bank a ways, and stopped in front of the smooth rock where Grandfather had rested.

He set down the canvas bag and bamboo fishing rod. It only took a minute to thread and secure the lure. He laughed when he put on Grandfather's child-size waders. The coldness of the water touched him through the green rubber, making him shiver. But he held his place, gradually digging his feet into the soft bottom. It was an easy cast, the lure making it only halfway across the river. Striped and triple-hooked, it hovered on the surface, kept afloat by the slightest lateral movements of his hands. Alec watched the outlines of its form grow more and more distinct in the light. Except for his hands, his body was motionless, settled in. He studied the moving water.

24

BROTHERS

When he returned to Tokyo that night, Alec found a letter on his pillow. He recognized the handwriting on the front of the envelope immediately. He turned it over. The return address was his mother's apartment in New York. Above it, written in a large, wild script, was the name: *M. Stern*. Mark.

Alec's fifteenth year had run over him like a truck. He grew taller and his voice changed from a sweet soprano to a painful squawk. He went away to boarding school, leaving home to surround himself with people he had never seen before, scared and homesick and wondering why he had ever wanted to go away in the first place. Just before Thanksgiving break, his parents called to tell him they were getting a divorce. They asked him if he wanted to come home. He said that he had to go, someone wanted to use the phone. They asked him if he wanted them to visit. He said that he really couldn't talk right then, people were waiting. They told him that Mark was on his way up to the school, that it had been his idea to see if he could help his brother.

Alec hung up and walked through the faculty adviser's living room, where some of his classmates were sprawled across sofas and on the floor, eating popcorn and laughing uproariously at Laurel and Hardy on television. He continued out into the hallway, where a couple of other boys were kicking a soccer ball back and forth. And he moved around them and down the hall, away from his room, where he knew his roommate was studying, and into the enormous bathroom. The tile was cold and damp. He closed himself up in one of the stalls and sat down on the lidded toilet with his knees held tightly against his chest. And with his face buried in the warm pocket formed by his own body, he cried.

It was Mark, tall and gangly and wild-haired, who found him there. He had come alone from New York on the train. He told Alec that things would be okay. Family would still be family, just different. Divorce didn't mean they weren't your parents anymore. He suggested they go get a pizza before curfew. So Alec washed his red face in cold water, and they walked to the Greek pizza parlor in town. It was a large pizza, pepperoni and mushroom. They ate the whole thing, then felt sick afterward. And Mark put his arm around Alec's shoulders and told him that he should never be ashamed to cry in front of anyone, especially his older brother.

In bed that night, Alec tried to remember if any of this had ever happened before. He tried to think back to when he and Mark had been babies lying next to each other in the crib, whether they had been close then; whether they had laughed and cried and held each other the way innocent children were supposed to, the way brothers were supposed to. But he could not remember Mark ever once putting an arm around his shoulders, ever supporting him the way he had that night. He could not recall in their life together the quiet comfort of a walk to town and a shared pizza. There were only the endless mad dashes through the apartment, the hot fury and tears, atoms bouncing, deflecting, bouncing, too far apart to see each other. But Mark was there in his room that night. That night they were brothers. And it seemed too strange, that sudden closeness. Alec fell asleep wondering what would come of it.

And now, as he read the letter and discovered that Mark would soon be coming to Tokyo for a visit, Alec leaned his back against the wall, brought his knees up to be hugged fiercely by his arms, and once again buried his face in the warmth of his own body. But it didn't work this time. Slowly he rocked back and forth, felt a chill come to him in the heat of the little room. He shivered to himself.

25

A HOME
FOR ECHOES

The view was from a prone position on the hardwood floor of the Tokyo University gymnasium. The ceiling was distant, spotted with yellow lights shining weakly from within little domes of wire grating. The space beneath the lights was empty, boundless, a home for echoes. Alec turned his head and saw people standing around him, looking down at him. Sweaty men in gym clothes, stolid and unmoving, like a bizarre Stonehenge impersonation. Park was closest among them, nervously peering at him through foggy lenses. Alec felt the familiar, comfortable urge to reach out and strangle him. It was Park who had talked him into joining his team in a Sunday basketball league; the same Park who had arranged for him to guard Miyaki, the biggest and ugliest Japanese Alec had ever seen outside of the national sumo championships.

Alec peered through Park's legs and saw the three Hasegawa children sitting on the uppermost row of the otherwise empty

aluminum grandstand. They were whispering among themselves, their expressions caught somewhere between concern
and laughter. They had insisted on coming to watch him play.
Americans are the best at basketball, Hiroshi had said. Filled
with visions of slam dunks and game-winning corner jump
shots, Alec had agreed. Now, having just been knocked flat by
Miyaki, he silently cursed himself.

Park extended his hand. "You are all right, Alec-san?"

Alec grabbed his wrist, pulled himself to his feet. "I guess so."
He rubbed his throat where Miyaki had caught him with a sharp
elbow.

"You are not in pain?"

Park was whispering as if his words contained secret information. Alec decided not to remind him that no one else on the
court understood English.

"A little, but I'm all right. I thought you said this was a
basketball league."

Park looked confused. "Basketball, yes."

"Then how is it Miyaki's allowed to knock me to the ground
every time I touch the ball? That's football, not basketball."

"Ah, yes, football," Park said, showing his teeth. "You are
making an amusing joke, Alec-san."

"Jesus Christ," Alec muttered, and turned away. He waved
and smiled at the Hasegawa children. Yoshi and Hiroshi waved
back, Yukiko jumped to her feet and clapped her hands.

"What score is it?" Alec asked Park.

"Already we are behind by three baskets," Park said, still
whispering.

A dull clapping echoed through the gym. Alec saw Miyaki
dribbling the ball back and forth between his legs. They made
eye contact for a moment before Alec looked away.

The game continued. Taller than Alec, and heavier by about
twenty pounds, Miyaki played a physical game, using chest,
hips, and elbows to achieve dominant position under the boards.
There were no referees, and the fouls had begun in the very first

minute of play, increasing in frequency until Alec was barely able to regain possession of the ball without being knocked to the ground. Each time he sat for a moment on the hard floor, staring up at Miyaki's pug, sweaty face, at the feigned expression of surprise. Then Park came hurriedly to give him a hand up, whispering that Miyaki hadn't meant anything personal by it. And each time Alec nodded slowly, absorbing the words, afraid of the consequences of not believing them. He waved and smiled at the Hasegawa children to show them everything was all right. Then the ball was put into play, and he was back in it. The goal was simply to run through to the end, accepting the images as they unfolded.

It was almost ten years since Billy Bevins had challenged him to a fight in front of the entire seventh-grade class. They had met after school in Central Park, in the center of the meadow off Ninety-sixth street. A few classmates, willing spectators, lingered expectantly nearby. Alec could hear them whispering. A light rain was falling, making the ground soft and slick. Above, the sky pressed down on them like an oily-dark iron griddle.

Alec could not decide whether this was the worst moment of his life. His stomach seemed to think so. It groaned and bubbled like an orchestra until he was sure everyone in the park— especially Billy Bevins—could hear it. Billy moved forward a few steps, his eyes locked in an angry, intimidating stare. His fists swirled out in front of his chest like the blades of a threshing machine. Alec studied those fists as they came toward him. He could not get over how confident they looked.

He tripped Billy Bevins because it was the only thing he could think to do. And then, suddenly, he was on top, in control, cocking his fist back the way he had seen other kids do. Billy looked up at him, as surprised as he was, expecting for one brief second to be hit.

When it was over, and Billy Bevins had gone home, Alec lay still in the meadow, bleeding from his nose and lip, mud smeared in his ears. The rain was coming down harder now, and he could hear around him the splatter of puddles. Already he found that he couldn't remember the fight. He could remember only that brief second, his knee on Billy Bevins's chest, his fist coiled tight and ready, and then the sudden moment after, the impotence of it, as he realized he could not throw the punch.

Alec backed his way closer to the basket, a couple of inches at a time, putting his full weight against Miyaki's chest. The contact was all body, too close for elbows. Miyaki was pushing him, soaking him with his sweat. Alec worked his way down to the low post, just to the right of the basket, and extended his arm in a silent call for the ball. Behind him, he could hear Miyaki's stuttering breath. Standing just above the top of the key, Park was directing the offense, showing more poise and assurance than Alec had ever seen him exhibit in the office. Dribbling to his right, Park spotted him and fired a perfect over-the-shoulder pass. The moment the ball touched his outstretched hand, Alec felt himself slammed from behind. His head snapped back, his arms flailed as he was sent sprawling to the ground. His shoulder hit first, the pain was immediate.

Only Park was there to give him a hand. When he looked up, Alec noticed that the Hasegawa children had moved to the bottom row of the grandstand, nearer to courtside. They were watching him closely. Around him his teammates stood as they had every time Miyaki had knocked him down, staring at the floor in awkward silence. But in his mind, Alec was hardly aware of any of them. They had become background.

He let Park pull him to his feet.

"Are you in pain, Alec-san?"

"That was a foul."

"Yes. I think you are right. But soon the game will be over."

"I want the ball. One-on-one with Miyaki."

Park seemed to wince. "Perhaps that would not be a good idea, Alec-san. Soon the game will be over. Perhaps you are injured and should no longer play."

Alec brought his face close to Park's and spoke in a harsh whisper. "I need the ball, Park-san. Do you understand? Now."

Park studied him for a moment, then turned and quickly huddled the team together, giving quiet directions. When he finished, he threw the ball out to Alec at midcourt.

Alec brought the ball into play, interchanging hands on the dribble, deliberately feeling the grooves on the ball. Much of the movement on the court was taking place in his peripheral vision, the players reduced to abstract shapes and blotches of color. It was as if a channel between him and Miyaki had formed within the court, the two points intense and focused, pushing toward a confrontation.

Miyaki was coming out to meet him at the foul line, knees slightly bent, arms spread as if he were trying to fly. Alec paused in front of him, showing him the ball. He took in Miyaki's liquid eyes as they watched him dribble. And then he saw Miyaki take a quick step forward, his hand darting out toward the ball. But Alec was already ahead of him, dribbling the ball between his own legs to the other hand. His weight too far forward, Miyaki tried to correct his balance by taking a large step backward. Space opened up between them and Alec stepped into it, pulling up as though to shoot. Miyaki jumped, arms raised, hoping to block the shot. But it never came. Alec stood still for a moment below the airborne body, lumbering even as it floated, and watched it begin to descend.

It was hardly noticeable when he leaned his hip into Miyaki's thick legs, bumping them sideways and out. He barely heard the crash as Miyaki landed on the hardwood floor in a heap, his body all thickness and sweat and smell. Alec's concentration was focused entirely on the ball as it left his hands, the easy lightness of its flight, its soft spin off the glass blackboard, the sudden tick as it brushed the inside of the net.

He caught the ball as it came through. He spun it round on his palm and felt the release of frustration lift him like a drug. He turned and saw the other players gathered around Miyaki, who lay on the floor clutching his hip. Alec didn't go to him. Instead he walked toward Park, meaning to thank him for the pass. But Park turned away and busied himself with the water cooler. Miyaki was helped slowly to his feet. The Hasegawa children didn't respond when Alec waved to them. They stood quietly by the exit without looking at him. The game was over. There were no sounds strong enough to echo.

26

O-MIAI

Nobi called a few days later. His voice sounded surprised and then remote on the phone, as if he had dialed Alec's number by mistake. He was calling to arrange a meeting, he said.

The bar where they met was crowded with men who had stopped for a drink on their way home from work. Some of them stood in a line along the wooden counter with their jackets off, their white shirts appearing woven together in the dim light, a canvas stretching the entire length of the room. Alec and Nobi sat at a table near the back. A waiter wearing a black T-shirt beneath his white jacket brought them a large bottle of Sapporo and two small glasses. Nobi poured first for Alec and then for himself. The foam rose quickly to the rim of the glass before halting as though upon command.

They drank in uneasy silence for a couple of minutes, draining and refilling their glasses at regular intervals. Alec thought back to their morning together at the fish market, how tense it had been, almost eerie; the thick blanket of fog, the water gushing everywhere, the old women pushing and poking, how little he and Nobi had actually said to each other. But then it seemed as if it had always been that way between them. The afternoon when he and Kiyoko had made sushi together, when he touched her and she fled, Nobi had never even said that he knew—if he knew—what had taken place. Instead there had been the reticence, the distance, the voice of wrong numbers, as he suggested they go out for lunch.

Nobi signaled to the waiter for another bottle of beer, though they had not yet finished the first one. When it arrived, he cleared his throat and began to talk, his eyes fixed firmly on the beads of moisture as they merged and trickled down the side of the translucent brown bottle.

"Two days ago, I telephoned Kiyoko," he said. "It had been some time since I had last talked to her. She has been very unhappy since the afternoon when we all met for lunch in my apartment. I did not know this. She had not told me exactly what happened when I went to buy sake that afternoon, the reason why she left so quickly. So, when you and I met at the fish market, I was not speaking of those things I knew. Do you understand, Alec? I saw only her anger that day when she left, and because I did not speak closely with her afterward, I did not see her sadness. She says that she has not been able to talk to you, that it is too difficult, and that she is afraid of embarrassing you and making you angry with her. She is no longer angry, only sad. I can see now that she is missing you."

"I miss her too, Nobi."

"I have arranged for her to come here tonight. It will be easier for her if I am here at first, and then I will leave."

"She's coming *here?* Now?"

Nobi glanced at his watch. "Yes. Soon."

Alec poured more beer.

"She will be very nervous, I think. But then she will be fine. I will try not to be so protective of her. I do not have a sister, you understand."

"Yes."

They waited for her arrival in silence. Nobi looked continually at his watch, then at the entrance, then back at the watch. Alec drank several more glasses of beer and thought of how certain he was growing that things would never turn out as expected. Almost two months before, he had left his first meeting with Nobi full of the confidence that they would become close friends. He had not thought of Kiyoko that day, not once. He had not even known her first name.

It seemed a long time before he heard Nobi's sigh of relief.

"Alec," Nobi announced, "Kiyoko is here."

Alec stood up and turned around sharply, almost bumping into Kiyoko. Above the red silk of her blouse, her face had a frightened paleness. She opened her mouth to speak, but nothing came out. Afraid that she was going to fall, Alec reached over and pulled out a chair for her at the table. She sat down, stared at the floor.

Nobi's expression was serious. "If this was a traditional O-miai meeting, I would stay to help with the conversation. But these are modern times, yes? And you already know each other. Besides, I must return to work." He put on his jacket, laid a tentative hand on Alec's shoulder. "Perhaps sometime we can have lunch? I will call you at the office."

Alec waved at him weakly, watched him leave. A heavy silence formed around the table like a Ziplock bag. He kept thinking of possible things to say, then ruling them out. The waiter replaced the empty bottle of beer with a fresh one Nobi had ordered on his way out.

Alec held up the bottle. "Beer?"

Kiyoko looked up from the floor. "Yes. Thank you."

She lifted her glass slightly, he poured for her. She took a tiny sip, her left hand delicately folded under the glass to catch any drops.

"You changed," he said.

She didn't answer immediately. Finally, she shook her head. "I do not understand."

"Your clothes from work. You changed them. Before, you were wearing that blue dress."

"Yes. First I returned home."

"Your blouse is beautiful."

"No, it is nothing."

"I feel as though I haven't seen you for a long time."

"Yes," she said, "I know that feeling."

The people at the next table got up to leave. A waiter appeared immediately to take away the glasses and wipe the table. Alec watched him, admiring the efficiency of his movements. It was all done in a few seconds.

"What exactly is O-miai?"

Her eyes covered him for an instant. "O-miai? It is a traditional Japanese custom."

Alec waited, but she was silent. "Yes. And what happens?"

"A person is brought together with another person by a relative or friend of the family." She paused, took a deep breath. "Usually, it is to see if they might be suitable for marriage."

"Have you been involved in many O-miai?"

She frowned slightly. "When I was younger, there were many O-miai. But they were not successful. My family could not understand why I did not like something that often leaves a woman without feeling or decision. It was difficult for many years. But now that I am old, my family no longer arranges O-miai for me."

"Nobi does," Alec said.

"Please do not be angry with Nobi. We have been friends a long time. But already you know that."

"Yes."

"It is not so easy for him as it sometimes appears," she said. "It is true that in Japan Nobi is the very top of society, because of his job with the ministry. But there are many pressures. He is encouraged to be international, but he must also be more Japanese than anyone else. You have seen both these sides of him, I think. When he first met you, he was very excited. He remembers his time in America very clearly, and he could be that side of himself with you. But I am like family to Nobi, and with family he is always a Japanese man, he is always protective, and he does not easily give trust to . . ." She didn't finish.

"A foreigner."

"Yes."

"Is that how you see me? As a foreigner?"

"You should not ask that question. I see you as Alec. When I have thoughts of you, they are of you, not of where you come from. I say it now, and maybe it sounds silly. But it is all that matters to me."

"I'm sorry. And I'm sorry for the afternoon at Nobi's. I couldn't think straight." It came out in a rush.

She shook her head. "No. I was also confused. You surprised me too much."

"When I came back and you had already left . . . I don't know. I thought, that's it."

She looked at him with her dark eyes, but only for a second. Another silence set in; Alec noticed they seemed to come at regular intervals, like the rising of the tide. He felt heat rise up in him as he looked at her face, her features at once strong and soft, and at the graceful sweep of her neck. There was a trace of loneliness in her eyes that made him want to lean forward across the table and touch her all over again.

Finally she said, "It made me very happy for you to go to Yamadera. My grandparents also were very happy."

Alec smiled, remembering. "They are wonderful people—just being with them those few days made me feel different, as if I had never even looked at things before. I only wish I had paid more attention. Suddenly I woke up and I was back in Tokyo."

"Yamadera is not like any other place in the world," she said. "And so when a person goes there he is faced with many new things, many new ways of seeing. It can take a great deal of time to change. Because my grandparents have lived in Yamadera since they were born, these are the things that they understand."

"I wish you had gone with me." His chest felt hollow.

"Perhaps next time we will go together," she said.

Alec looked straight into her eyes, and this time she didn't turn away. Time seemed to slow down, the seconds dragging across the space between them. And then something in the way she looked at him changed. He felt as though he was touching her.

27

HANDS

Mark's face came first. Just the face, wild and angry, staring at him from across the room. His lips were moving and wet with saliva, his teeth flashing. Alec sat on a stool in the opposite corner of the room, like a little boy who had been bad at school. He could see that Mark was shouting at him, but he couldn't hear anything. He leaned forward. Not a thing. He just sat there, staring at the angry face, the silence gradually putting him to sleep. And he knew that he would be dead if his eyes closed, though he was helpless to do anything about it. Not without sound, anyway. Or a touch, something human to bring him back. He felt so alone. And then it was getting darker, and he could hardly see the face anymore. His eyes were all he had left. But they were almost closed now, he could feel it. All he wanted to do was to tell someone what was happening to him. But there was no one there to listen. And then there was only darkness. Eyes closed. No eyes. It was too late. . . .

Alec's eyes snapped open, he awoke in the heat, to the heat. Sweat had soaked the heavy cotton of the futon and comforter. The window was open to the night, but the darkness itself seemed a wall, blocking any movement of air in or out of the small room. For a moment it was still a dream, a nightmare, something to wake up from. He was trapped in nothingness and heat, unable to breathe. But then he felt the damp cotton against his skin.

He stood quickly, opened the sliding screen, but the hallway was just as stifling. Ten feet away, the door to Yoshi's room was closed. Alec could hear the constant hum of an air conditioner from inside. He considered waking Yoshi, perhaps sleeping on the floor of his room. But it would be too unusual a thing to do, and trying to explain would be too difficult. Instead, he reached across and slid open the glass door, stepped onto the narrow balcony. His mouth gaped open and he inhaled deeply, pushing his face into the blanket of air like a burrowing animal. He couldn't get enough.

Thirst finally moved him. Grabbing his yukata from his room, he put it on and headed downstairs. The house cooled by degrees as he followed the stairs. Each stair was a pocket of shadow, the darkness gradually lifting as he neared the second floor.

A light was on. Mrs. Hasegawa lay sprawled face up on the tatami, snoring. Her flowered house dress was rumpled, her thick, veined legs emerging awkwardly from under the hem. The fluorescent light gave her skin a pallor. Alec smiled when he saw her. Quietly, he stepped around her legs.

The account books lay open on the low table, the numbers exactingly drawn in black ink, the miniature yen signs in red. There were no ink smudges, nothing was crossed out. Everything was perfectly aligned. Checking to make sure she was still asleep, Alec flipped back a couple of pages. He was surprised by how consistent the numbers were, how orderly and machinelike. Just about to turn the page, he noticed several light marks at the bottom, almost off the edge. Looking more closely, he realized that they were tiny Japanese characters written in pencil:

"Yukiko's dress by Monday." He smiled, turned to another page and, in the upper right-hand corner, read: "Shirt for Alec." He thought of the shirt she had bought for him at Mitsukoshi.

Another page and then another and another, each one holding another reminder or message. He turned back to the first page he had seen and read the most recent note, a single word, practically illegible: "Tired." Intermingled with the lifeless numbers and columns, he realized, was a journal of sorts, a mind expressing itself in bits and pieces, expanding and contracting, afraid to take for itself an entire sheet of blank paper. He looked from the book to her and knew that he must not wake her.

Tiptoeing into the dark kitchen, he took a bottle of *mugi-cha* from the refrigerator, poured himself a glass. It was a physical process—opening, grabbing, lifting, pouring, replacing, closing—by now completely instinctive, yet the moment he heard the heel of the bottle touch the lip of another one, he knew that it had gone wrong.

A bottle of milk crashed to the floor, painting it in uneven patches of white. "Damn," he hissed.

"Eh?" Mrs. Hasegawa's sleep-filled voice came from the other room.

"Damn."

"What's that?" she asked, and he knew that she was sitting up now.

"Nothing," he said, now in Japanese. "Everything is fine." He was trying to pick up the larger pieces of glass from the floor but having difficulty in the dark. He felt one piece slice his fingers.

He heard her labored breathing as she stood up. "Alec! Is that you?"

"No. Yes. Please go back to sleep, Mother. There is no problem." He groped on his knees in the wetness.

"What are you doing?" She walked into the kitchen.

"Wait!" Alec shouted. But it was already too late; he saw her take a step, her broad face twisting as a piece of glass pierced her bare foot.

"Please don't move, Mother," he said. "Let me help you."

Carefully he stepped around the puddles of milk, moving on the outer edges of his feet to avoid the splinters of glass. He grabbed the roll of paper towel from its plastic holder above the sink. She watched him walk awkwardly into the eating room.

"Don't get blood on the tatami," she said.

Alec nodded and spread several sheets of paper towel, already bloodstained from his own hands, on the tatami. Then, slowly, he helped her hop on one foot to the covered area and sit down. Droplets of sweat formed an intricate pattern on her upper lip. They were both silent as he brought out the first-aid kit from the top drawer of the Western-style bureau, leaving a light smear of blood on everything he touched.

He gently took her cut foot in his hands. Using a cotton swab, he probed inside the wound, looking for the glint of glass. She didn't speak, but he heard the sharpness of her breathing. When he had finished, he cleaned the cut, taped on a gauze bandage.

She had been silently watching him work, her face an intense mixture of interest and pain. Now she looked quickly from her bandaged foot to Alec's face, and nodded her head in satisfaction.

"Good job," she said. "I was afraid you were drunk."

"I did not drink tonight. But I was afraid, too."

"Hands," she said.

Alec gave her his hands. She cleaned the cuts and put Band-Aids of varying sizes and shapes on them. Her thick fingers were surprisingly agile.

He looked around the small room, at the bloodied paper towel, at the gauze and Band-Aid wrappers. He shook his head. "It looks as if we were attacked by samurai."

Mrs. Hasegawa let out a belly laugh and slapped her thigh. But as she looked at him, he saw her features tighten in concern.

"Are you sick?" she asked.

"Me? No." And then he realized what he must look like, hair still matted down with sweat, face pale.

"You look sick."

"It was very hot in my room. I could not sleep. I thought perhaps some *mugi-cha* . . ." He stopped. She was looking at him as though she didn't believe what he was saying. "It is difficult to explain."

"It was hot," she offered.

"Yes," he said. "And I had a bad dream. And I could not breathe when I woke up. I became scared. It was very strange. I do not really understand what happened."

"You have a fever." She looked adamant.

He shook his head gently. "When I was small, sometimes I had this same feeling of being . . ." He paused, hanging, trying to think of the Japanese word for "trapped." Nothing came to him, he closed his mouth. In frustration, he slapped his hand on the tatami, felt the sting from his cuts. It was always so difficult. So exhausting. Just to talk. Even when things were going smoothly, they never really got any easier. Now, right now, he needed it to be easy, needed the words and feelings to flow from his mouth like water, constant and strong and clear. So he could relax, close his eyes, and when he opened them again, he would already have told her everything in his mind. He would be free of his thoughts—free, just for a moment. They would belong to her then. She could do what she wanted with them.

Mrs. Hasegawa grunted softly, encouraging him. Alec looked at her. She reached over, brought out the bottle of Scotch and two glasses. Neither one of them wanted to go back into the kitchen for ice and water; they drank it straight.

"My family had a house in the country." He said it slowly, concentrating on the Japanese, forcing the words to be right, to be what he wanted. "And every Friday night we would drive to this house, about three hours. I was very small, and I would become tired. My parents always sat in the first seat, the front seat. And my older brother was in the backseat. But I always moved down to the small space between the two seats—on the floor of the car. Yes?"

Mrs. Hasegawa nodded.

"I liked it because it was warm," Alec said, staring at a spot on the floor, "and I would sleep for a while. But sometimes when I woke up I would be too hot, and unable to move because the space was so small. And breathing would be difficult, there was not much air. But I would not say anything, or try to move to a different place. Instead, I would listen to the noise of the car and the voices of my family, and realize that they did not understand what was happening to me. Do you understand, Mother? They always thought that I was okay. So I would lie there and wait for someone to mention my name. As long as it took, I would wait. Then I would move up, next to my brother, and allow myself to be . . ." He hesitated, wondering if the word was too abstract to convey his feelings in translation.

She grunted, hardly more than a breath.

"To be free," he said finally.

Silence. Alec thought how inadequate words were sometimes, the way they all possessed the same basic acoustical properties. As if no one word could ever be more important than any other. He couldn't stand the thought that she might not have really grasped what he had said. He searched her face for some kind of confirmation.

Mrs. Hasegawa hadn't moved for some time. She stared at a spot on the tatami, the light horizontal lines of her forehead intersected by deep grooves of concentration that curled up from between her eyebrows. The movement of her eyes as they traveled along the floor to his face was indirect, unsure. When she spoke, it was a question.

"And tonight, in your room, it was the same feeling?"

Alec nodded, feeling as though he had just finished a race of some kind. And then he lay back, feeling the give of the woven fibers under his weight. Eyes closed, he heard her get slowly to her feet and leave the room. When she returned, she slipped a thin pillow under his head.

"Sleep," she said.

He heard his own voice. "Mark is coming."

"Sleep," she whispered, lightly stroking his hair.

His head felt warm under her gentle touch. He smiled without knowing it.

He fell asleep that way.

28

SECOND PLACE

Alec waited for Mark outside the restaurant, unsure of where to stand. If he had been in New York, he might have leaned against a streetlight or a parked car with his hands dangling from his front pockets. But he wasn't sure that image would go in Tokyo, so he stood stiffly at the curb with his arms folded across his chest. He watched the masses of people move along the sidewalk and tried to think about nothing. But Mark's face—the angry face he had lost sight of in his dream—kept coming back to him, fading in and out. Long minutes passed by, though he didn't look at his watch; not once. And then he heard a familiar voice, and the picture in his mind was no longer lost in shadow, but brightly lit, and he felt for an instant as though he were falling. Then the voice again, so clear in a city full of people.

"Alec?"

He turned around. "Jesus. Mark."

Mark laughed nervously and hugged him. They went inside.

The restaurant was noisy, the small tables spaced only a few feet apart. In one corner, a group of about ten people was busy toasting a grinning, red-faced man dressed in a polo shirt and sweatpants. Alec led Mark away from their shouts of *"Kampai!"* and raucous laughter, to a table near the entrance to the kitchen. Through hanging curtains, a grill could be heard sizzling and popping, filling the room with the greasy odor of frying meat.

Alec realized that he had grown accustomed to feeling big in Japan and was a little disconcerted to find how much smaller he was than Mark, whose chest and arms seemed even more muscular than they had during his football-playing days. Otherwise, Mark looked much the same, his strong cheekbones and nose framed by the heavy line of his dark eyebrows. His hair had grown longer, the brown curls playfully flopping down over the collar of his white button-down shirt and across his broad forehead, giving him, Alec thought, a look both wild and innocent.

A waiter arrived with beer and small dishes of yakitori. Alec poured for both of them:

"Kampai," he said.

"Cheers," Mark said. They clinked glasses. "So. You look pretty good."

Alec smiled. "Do I? I haven't been getting much exercise. But thanks. You look good, too."

"Thanks."

"How do you like the beer?"

"It's okay," Mark said, taking a sip. "Yeah, it's pretty good."

"The Japanese make good beer," Alec said, wondering why he was even bothering to say it.

"Yeah."

"So what have you been up to? I got your letter, but I couldn't really tell what was going on. I mean with the job and stuff."

Mark shrugged, looking away. "There's not a whole lot going on right now. I've been offered a couple of things, but nothing that's any good. So about all I can say is that I'm still looking."

"You still living at home?"

"Yeah. Where else? No job means no money, which means that Mom and I are still roommates. It's starting to get me down—I'm going to be twenty-four in a month."

"I know when your birthday is," Alec said. "What about Dad and the business? I thought he said he'd start you off as a manager or something."

Mark looked at him. "That's what he said."

"So?"

"So whose career would that be, Alec? It'd be his, not mine. That's just the way he wants it. I don't see you rushing to join up."

Alec looked down at his beer.

Mark cleared his throat. "Anyway, Dad gave me the money for the trip."

"You asked him for it?"

"Not exactly. I just kind of mentioned it, and he encouraged me. I think he hopes I'll become interested in international finance."

Alec smiled. "Have you seen him much?"

"No. He and Janice have been in Florida since about the time you left. They're talking about maybe moving down there permanently."

"Florida?"

"You should know about that."

"What's that mean?"

"It means that maybe you should've written a letter or called or something. Then you might know a little about what's going on with the family. Mom's going crazy. She says she hasn't heard from you even once."

Alec felt suddenly tired. "No, she hasn't. I've been meaning to write to both of you. But things have been incredibly busy. It's no excuse. I just haven't thought about much outside of what I'm doing."

Mark didn't say anything.

"I've been working a lot," Alec said. "More than ten hours a day. The deadline's coming up on this report I'm writing on high-tech trade. It's for the head office in New York, so I'm feeling some pressure."

"And what else?"

"What else have I been doing? I don't know. A lot, I guess."

"It might help if you made at least some attempt to explain it."

"What do you mean, *help?* Help what?"

"Nothing," Mark said. "Forget it."

They were quiet after that, eating and drinking. Alec hated the way Mark ate his food, the way he pulled the small pieces of grilled chicken and vegetable off the wooden skewers with his fingers. When the yakitori was almost gone, Alec took a long swallow of beer and cleared his throat.

"Maybe a lot of what I'm doing here has to do with having a clean slate," he said. "I mean, you get here and no one knows who you are or what you've done, except that you have a college degree and a job. That's all they really care about at first, you know, like a stamp of approval of some sort. But after that it's up to you. You move in with a family and start your job. You meet people. You speak another language. And then you wake up one morning a few weeks later and realize that you've made some friends and that you know your way around a little bit, and it seems almost like a natural occurrence. It's as if you suddenly realize that your slate's not clean anymore, that it's covered with new people and places, new ideas that belong to you and nobody else. I guess it's all about making things your own."

Mark deliberately finished his beer. "And you feel like you've done that—made things your own?"

"Yeah, I guess I do. Some things, at least."

"You still haven't told me what those things are."

"Not things, really. People and places. Like the family I live with—I feel like they belong to me in a way, especially the mother. We understand each other. And sometimes even my boss, Joe. And my girlfriend. The house I live in. My neighborhood."

"You have a girlfriend?"

Alec grinned. "Yeah."

"American?"

"No, Japanese. She's thirty-three."

"That's old," Mark said.

"I don't think so," Alec said. "How about you? You have a girlfriend these days?"

Mark shook his head. "I told you, there's really not a whole lot going on at home."

"Things will pick up."

"Glad to hear it."

"They will."

"Who are you to tell me that?"

Abruptly, Mark spotted a waiter and waved him over with a sweeping gesture of his arm. Alec saw several people at a nearby table look over. He felt his stomach tighten, looked down at his plate. The waiter appeared but wouldn't look at either of them. Mark pointed to the skewer in his hand.

"More chicken teriyaki," he said loudly in English.

"Mark, let me do it," Alec said quietly.

Mark ignored him. "More chicken teriyaki," he repeated to the waiter.

Alec coughed. "Yakitori."

Jabbing the skewer into the air, Mark said, "Fine. I don't care. More chicken yakitori, then. And more beer."

The waiter didn't move or acknowledge the comment. His face was expressionless. Alec let the silence sit for a few seconds before repeating Mark's words, this time in Japanese.

The waiter turned and left. Noise seemed to become a part of the room again, though Alec wasn't positive it had ever really stopped. He and Mark were quiet for a while, cautious, pausing like two blind men at opposite corners of an intersection, sensing between them the presence of something foreign and hidden and dangerous. A man walked by the table. Alec watched him, glad to have something to do. Tight and uncomfortable, his body felt as if it belonged to someone else. He sat back, took a paper napkin from the tabletop dispenser, and touched it to his forehead. It came away wet.

Mark gestured toward the soaked napkin. "Muggy as hell in Tokyo, huh?"

"Worse than the city," Alec said.

"That reminds me. You get a 'Hi' from Jake."

"Yeah? When did you see him?"

"Couple of weeks ago. He's an investment banker now, working ninety-hour weeks. I ran into him in a midtown coffee shop. We had barely talked five minutes when he said he had to rush back to the office. He said he'd give me a call."

"Are a lot of your friends doing that kind of work?"

"Yeah. Just about all of them."

"Mine, too," Alec said.

Mark looked away. "Jake was my best friend at school, Alec. For four years he always had time. Now he doesn't even know what the hell I'm doing. When I ran into him, he asked me how I liked my job at the bank, started talking to me about bond issues. Can you believe that? More than a year after graduation and he just assumes that I'm working at a bank like he is. He doesn't know anything about me. None of those guys do."

"Then to hell with them."

Mark laughed, but it was bitter. "Right: to hell with them. So then what? I sit at home and play backgammon with Mom."

"You never wanted a job in business anyway. Remember a couple of years ago? You told me you wanted to be a writer. I read one of your stories. You were good, Mark. Everyone thought so."

"I thought so, too," Mark said. "And I was wrong. I sent off a few stories to magazines. That was three months ago. You know what I've heard? Nothing. Not even from Mom's friend at *The New Yorker*."

Mark cut the air with his hands, as if to wipe away what he

had just said. "But that's not even the point. The point is that things change after graduation, practically overnight. People change. They get busy and go off to wherever to do their own thing. And I'm left hanging, watching all of them, with time on my hands to run into them in coffee shops and ask them questions about themselves, about how it is they're so brilliantly focused and motivated in their careers."

A different waiter arrived with fish yakitori and beer. Alec felt a wave of anger and frustration; he knew he had ordered chicken. He silently watched the waiter leave, hoping he would see him smile. Mark removed a bite-size piece from one of the skewers and chewed it but didn't seem as though he cared very much what it was.

Alec touched him on the arm. "Have you talked to Mom and Dad about any of this?"

"Are you kidding?" Mark sat back, looking weary, and rubbed his eyes with his hand. Alec saw him take three deep breaths before speaking. "There's really nothing for me at home right now. I mean nothing. Mom and I don't seem to have much to say to each other anymore. She and Jerry go out to their dinner parties and come back and I'm still up watching "Letterman" or something. But that's it, you know? Hi, how are you, good night. And that's not enough. It's like my life—or whatever you want to call it—isn't even my own. The apartment isn't mine. The TV isn't mine. I don't work. I hang around like an ape. And as long as I won't work for him, Dad's not even in the picture. He's out of there, doing his own thing like everyone else."

"At least he gave you the money for the trip," Alec said, and hated the way it sounded.

"Yeah, you're right," Mark said. "So I get two weeks away from all the crap. Two weeks. That's all I kept thinking before I left: two weeks and then I'd have to go back. And after thinking about it, I realized that there wasn't much point to going back. I mean, no job, and all the guys from school are spread out all over the place. There's just you, and you're over here. And as for the job, I suspect I'd have as good a chance of getting one here as at home." He paused, looked intently at his hands. "So, I've decided to stay here for a while."

The last sentence came out as an exhale, frantic and uncontrolled. For once, Alec forgot to worry about small talk and silences. He wasn't bothered when Mark closed his mouth and leaned back in his chair with his arms folded. And it hardly concerned him that he was expected to say something in return, something warm, sympathetic, inviting. He fingered the rim of his glass and stared at the table without seeing it. Something bad was happening. That was all.

"You're not going home?" He was surprised to hear his own voice.

Mark was sitting up on the edge of his chair now, searching Alec's face. "That's what I said."

"For how long?"

"I don't know yet," Mark said impatiently. "Not the rest of my life or anything. But a while."

"So where are you going to stay?"

"Actually, I thought we might live together. You know, find an apartment somewhere." Mark paused. "It's not like we haven't lived together before."

"No, it's not," Alec said.

"So what do you think?"

"I can't think right now, Mark. Okay? Not right now."

"Tomorrow night, then."

"Can't tomorrow. I promised my girlfriend I'd see her."

The smell and sound of food cooking on the grill had faded away; the room was almost empty. Alec's face felt flushed, as if he had been walking for a long time in the sun. He closed his eyes. Yet, in his thoughts, it wasn't the sun he felt but the night, its darkness resting just beyond the window. For the moment, it seemed too much. Everything did.

"So how are the Mets doing?" It was on his mind when he opened his eyes; it was the only thing he could think to say.

"Second place, five behind the Cardinals." Mark's voice had gone flat, dead.

"Shit," Alec said.

The restaurant was closing. Finally, Mark shuffled on his seat, as if to get up. He put both hands palm down on the table. "Alec," he said quietly. "I think it's been a long day for both of us. Why don't we get out of here?"

Alec nodded his head. In silence, they paid the check.

And then the door was open and they were in the street. They watched the cars speed by, their movement straight and free. Holding hands, young couples walked unhurried along the sidewalk. Life moved with them.

29

SLOW DANCING

The next night Kiyoko was waiting for him in the doorway of the apartment she shared with her aunt. He reached out to kiss her. She brushed her hair against his cheek.

"I am happy to see you," she said.

"Me too," he said.

It was hard to speak, she looked so beautiful. Her white kimono was printed with wildflowers, a garden of color spreading the full length of her body. An obi ran the course of her waist like a deep red river of silk. Her black hair hung in a shining band to her shoulder blades.

She knelt down, began unlacing his shoes.

"I can do that," Alec said.

She handled his feet as if they were delicate animals. "Tonight I will do it for you."

"You disappeared from the office after lunch."

"I had meetings," she said. "And today I went home early to try to become beautiful. I have been nervous."

"You *are* beautiful."

"No." She was removing his jacket, his tie, putting them on hangers.

He said, "I guess this means we're eating in."

"Yes."

"And your aunt?"

"She is with my parents."

"That's wonderful." He reached for her.

Kiyoko smiled but shook her head. "You must be patient, Alec. I am an older woman, and tonight I would like to do something for you. But you must let me. You must wait. Now, please come."

She led him by the hand down the hallway and to the right, through the eating room, and into another small room that was bare of furniture. Alec breathed in the fresh, reedy scent of new tatami. In the center of the room, an iron kettle was warming inside a brazier of unpainted clay. An alcove of rusticated bamboo shelves stood off in one corner. The wood had been stained so that the knots and holes in its surface appeared like dark eyes looking out from the white plaster wall behind. A single iris arched upward from a painted bowl filled with white pebbles, reaching and then dipping, like the lovely, flowing neck of a swan.

"The iris is my mother's favorite flower," Alec said.

"It is also my favorite," Kiyoko said. "At the Meiji shrine here in Tokyo there is a beautiful iris garden with forty thousand flowers. Sometime I would like to take you there."

"I would like that."

Kiyoko went out and returned carrying a thin cushion and a black yukata. She placed the cushion on the tatami at one end of the room and handed him the yukata.

"I will be some minutes in preparing," she said. "And so you must wait for me here, Alec. It is proper to wear a yukata. It is proper also to kneel. With the cushion, it will not be so painful." Then she left the room.

Alec changed into the yukata, which fit him perfectly. He

settled down to wait for her, squatting at first the way he had seen Toshiro Mifune do in *The Seven Samurai*. When that grew too uncomfortable, he knelt down on the cushion, resting his hands on his knees.

She appeared a few minutes later, carrying a round lacquer tray of bowls and containers and odd-looking implements. A napkin the color of her obi was tucked in at her hip. Putting down the tray, she knelt at the entrance of the room and made a single bow. Then she rose and entered, set down the tray in front of the kettle and brazier, and knelt again.

"Tea ceremony is about beauty and waiting," she said. "And there can be great pleasure in waiting. Tonight, I would like to do that for you, Alec. To make you wait and give you pleasure."

Kiyoko picked up a ceramic bowl from the tray and placed it by her knee. She took the red napkin from her hip and folded it, then used it to wipe a lacquer caddy and a thin bamboo tea scoop. When she was finished, she moved the napkin to her other hand and fitted the lid on the kettle, which was steaming. Her hair fell over her shoulder as she leaned forward. Lifting the kettle, she filled a shallow tea bowl with hot water. She picked up a wooden tea whisk, dipped its head in the water and lightly knocked its handle against the edge of the bowl three times. Her hair fell back into place. . . .

Alec remembered watching her in Nobi's kitchen, the way her hands had danced over his chest. They were dancing now, but the rhythm was different. Slow dancing. Seconds falling like raindrops from her fingers. Hot water being emptied out, tea bowl being wiped. Three and a half rotations for the outside, four for the inside. Seconds draining into minutes, tiny oceans of anticipation washing over him as he looked on.

She did not have to speak. The careful attention paid by her hands to whatever they touched told him everything. Objects were wiped to purify, not to clean. The tea scoop was rested against one side of the tray, and the napkin hung over the other because that was the way it had always been done. Forever. Her hands said so. To each object they gave promise, picking up in one place, setting down in another, slow dancing and leading, in tune with the ceremony and the passing of time. They whispered to him, her hands. After every movement, every second and minute, they said pay attention, hold on, wait. Wait for pleasure. Already his heart was beating through him like a drum, filling his ears. Already he was missing things, gestures too subtle for him to understand. How long had he been waiting?

And then Kiyoko made tea for him. Alec watched her whisk it into a green froth. He watched her move on her knees around the brazier and toward him, carrying the half-full tea bowl in front of her like an offering. She smelled of freshly washed hair and cotton and faintly bitter tea. Turning the bowl round on her palm, she handed it to him. He had seen this part of the ceremony in a movie and knew what to do. He turned the bowl round to study its simple beauty. But he did not see it. He saw beyond it to the line of her neck, the fullness of her mouth. He drank the tea in one gulp and thought it tasted as thick and gritty and green as it looked. She took the tea bowl from him and set it aside.

Her eyes were fixed on his as she began to unwrap the obi at her waist. There was no rush. As if a dam were slowly crumbling, the red river of silk began to flow around her kneeling form, around and around, until it seemed there was neither beginning nor end to it. Like a warm tide, it lapped against his knees and thighs, rose higher and grew stronger, stirring him until he thought he might go under. The obi ran itself out then and, spent, dropped to the tatami. Kiyoko arched her back and let the kimono slide off her shoulders. It fell to rest beneath her like a trampled bed of wildflowers. On her knees she moved until her naked body was full against him. Dizzy, waiting, slow dancing, Alec felt her hands loosen his belt and the yukata fall away, felt the shiver-shock of her burning skin against his own, her dark nipples reaching into him, her wetness spreading over him like warm milk. He lay back and heard her whisper: "It has been a long time."

30

FOREIGNER

Twenty-four hours later Alec and Mark stepped quickly from the dance club into the heavy night air, Alec in the lead, refusing to stop until he could no longer hear the music pulsing up from below. They had been in the crowded basement almost four hours, drinking gin and tonics and dancing with two seventeen-year-old models from New Jersey. Alec had been there only once before and in fact had vowed never to return. But he had been reluctant to take Mark to any of the places he went with Japanese friends or business acquaintances, afraid that people would take them for some kind of American tourist package. Though it occurred to him now that being trapped in a basement with two vapid teenagers from New Jersey was not much better than being labeled a tourist.

He had had too much to drink. They both had, really, although Alec's certainty that he was involved in a social ordeal had prevented him from ever feeling very giddy. Now all he felt was a light-headedness that made him think he might still be able to laugh. He thought it would be nice to be able to laugh just then, a real belly laugh. It seemed a long time since he had laughed like that, and for a moment he hungered for it, as if not having laughed deeply was the same as not having eaten a full meal. But dizziness rose over his head like a dark hood, and no solutions came to him.

They reached the corner and stopped, neither one of them quite sure what to say. It was one-thirty in the morning, but in Roppongi the sidewalks were still filled with people. Across the street, eager young men and women stood as always in front of the Almond coffee shop, checking their watches, still waiting for their boyfriends or girlfriends to show up. It was never too late to hope in Tokyo, Alec thought as he watched them. Time never ran out, people never stayed away too long, just put themselves to bed for a little while before the neon turned off at daybreak. They came back to wait again, and their lithe figures seemed always to be hovering by the chrome entrance of the Almond, beneath the pink-and-blue canopy, cool in their linen suits and silk dresses. It was all chrome and neon and youth and energy and waiting. Tonight it made him sad.

"How about if I walk you to the hotel?" Alec said after a while. "It's not that far."

They turned left down the main avenue, heading in the direction of the business district. Within two blocks, most of the people had been left behind. The street itself became a kind of stranger, and it seemed to Alec to offer only strangeness to those who walked its shadowy, rough line. He looked over at Mark, who was smiling to himself.

"What's so funny?"

"The Plotzner girls. Remember?"

"Julie and Katie."

"Identical twins."

"Right. I was with Julie."

Mark shook his head. "Katie. Her hair was shorter."

"It was one of those weekends you came up to see me at school," Alec said. "What was it, my junior year? We were in that beige-and-gray hotel room with those huge orange beds. Jesus. What a place."

"The New Haven Concord," Mark said.

Alec laughed at the name, remembering how he had lied to Katie Plotzner, telling her he was far from a virgin. And then how scared he had been when she tore off her clothes and sat down on the bed.

He said, "It's still hard to believe it really happened that way. You've got to wonder what the hell we were thinking about."

He had thought Mark would be laughing with him—after all, they had been through the same thing at the same time, on different beds in the same hotel room, with girls whose looks were so similar they might have been the same person—but when he looked over again his brother's face looked tight and unhappy.

"You know," Mark said finally, "I bet you no one else in the world knows that about you—about exactly what the hotel looked like, about who was with Julie and who was with Katie. Any of that stuff."

Unsure of how to respond, Alec turned away from Mark, as if he had suddenly recognized the building across the street as an architectural treasure. When he turned back, Mark was walking with his head down in intense concentration, like a little boy trying not to step on the cracks in the sidewalk.

Mark cleared his throat, a low rasping sound with a hitch in the middle of it. "You know, I've been thinking a lot about when Mom and Dad split up."

Alec stared at him for a few seconds before speaking. "Why?"

"What do you mean, *why?*"

"I mean, I don't really want to talk about it. Just let it go."

"Let what go?"

"The divorce. Everything. It happened a long time ago."

"It wasn't that long ago," Mark said. "You remember the actual night it happened—when I went up to school to see you?"

"Of course I remember."

"The way you're talking, I'm not so sure."

"People don't forget things like that," Alec said.

"Some do."

"Maybe they do. I don't."

"You were crying in the stall of the bathroom on the third floor of your dorm," Mark said quietly, as if to himself. "I had looked for you in your room, but no one knew where you were. And I didn't know where else to look. Finally, I just went into the bathroom to take a leak. So I was standing there at the urinal, staring at the wall or whatever, and I heard you sniffle. You must've been trying really hard to be quiet, because that was all I heard for a little while, not even any breathing. But then I heard it a couple more times, and I knew someone was crying in there. It made me feel strange, like I was spying on someone I didn't even know. But I would've felt worse just leaving, knowing someone was crying alone in the bathroom. So I said something. Right?"

"Yeah."

"What'd I say?"

"You said my name."

"And then what?"

"What're you getting at?"

"Just tell me what I said next."

Alec made a show of peering around the area in which they were walking. "What, is there an audience around here I should know about? Or how about a huge applause sign that lights up when we speak our memories out loud? I guess I'm just missing the point."

"Just act like I'm telling a story, okay? And tell me what I said. That's all. It's not much to ask, is it?"

Alec gave a loud sigh. "I came out of the stall after a while. You asked me if I wanted to go get a pizza before curfew."

"Right," Mark said. "So we went and got a pizza. I stayed with you then. I cut two days of classes to be with you."

Alec looked out of the corner of his eye, saw Mark staring right at him. "We're brothers."

"Yeah, we're brothers. And we counted on each other."

"That'll never change. You know that."

"Then maybe you at least owe me an answer. Maybe you at least owe me that."

A white car drove by. Two kids stuck their heads out the back window and yelled something in Japanese. Alec heard the word *gaijin*, foreigner, but that was all. Mark seemed oblivious of the whole episode.

They were close to Mark's hotel now. Alec could see the neon characters extended in a vertical line out over the sidewalk, about a block and a half away. He thought about the first time he had seen the movie *Jaws*, with the little boy swimming happily on the raft, and the huge killer shark going after him. If he could just make it to shore before it was too late. . . .

Mark stopped walking. Alec was two steps past him before he stopped and turned around. Things had turned serious quickly, though that had been happening a lot lately, now that he thought about it. He was supposed to say something, there was no doubt about it.

"I don't think your living here is a good idea, Mark."

Mark's entire face appeared to contract as he listened, a grimace that began with the eyes and spread outward; the look of a person who could just as easily hit someone as cry. When he spoke, his voice was barely audible. "Tell me why not."

"Because right now being alone is too important to me," Alec said. He saw Mark start to shake his head. "No. Listen. Remember what you were saying about living at home—how nothing belongs to you, not the apartment, not the TV, nothing? Well, I always felt like that. Like I was there just to *watch* things happen. It's like you're empty, because nothing's yours. You have no control over anything. All those afternoons when you were out playing football and Mom and Dad were working—for a while then I tried to make things my own. Isn't that strange for a kid? I took tours of the apartment. I went through Mom and Dad's closets. I found old clothes you wouldn't believe: Dad's old prom suit, Mom's miniskirt from the sixties. I found Grandpa's gold pocketwatch, an old stadium coat, your old baby blanket. Everything. Rings, shoes, broken pieces of china, loose buttons, letters. The whole family history. No one else recorded it the way I did then, tried to understand it the way I did. I guess I thought that if I knew every single thing that our family owned and touched, our history would become mine in some way. But I was wrong. I didn't know anything. And then I tried to get away from what was going on at home. The thing is, I couldn't. Not really. Then you came up to school when it happened—the whole scene in the bathroom and the pizza and the two days of talking. And you did help. You really did. But it was as if you had caught up with me, too. As if I knew then for the first time that I couldn't really get away from home, as if even my problems weren't my own anymore, but yours, and you were going to deal with them for both of us. I couldn't stand that. Not even when we were both at different colleges, when you didn't come up to see me so much, when Mom and Dad finally stopped calling every other day to make sure I hadn't gone crazy. I guess I should've been able to handle it by then. But I couldn't. No matter where I went, I couldn't get far enough away. And now I'm here and I've got hold of this feeling that I'm finally starting to belong to something, to some people. I need that feeling—the way you need something you've never been able to get your hands on. I'm sorry, but I need it."

They were standing under a street sign. Mark jumped up, swatted it with his palm. The street exploded in sound, before fading to a metallic echo that clung to Alec's ears as though it would last forever.

Mark said, "That's just great. Sounds like you've really mapped out your place in the world: your own personal needs and wants. Congratulations."

"You're not even listening to what I'm saying."

"Oh no? But you, of course, understand exactly what *I'm* saying. Every goddamn thing I'm feeling. Is that it?"

"Mark," Alec said, but that was all, because it was the only safe thing he could think of to say.

"Mark *what?* Huh? There's got to be more from you than

that, because you're leaving me hanging, with nothing. Not a goddamn thing."

Mark turned away, rubbing his hands over his face. Three men walked between them along the sidewalk, making derisive comments, obviously assuming that the foreigners wouldn't be able to understand. Alec screamed at them in Japanese, telling them to mind their own business. For lack of anything better, he called the shortest of the three "Radish Legs." The men walked away laughing. When he turned back, Mark was staring at him.

"Do you know what it's like to live at home after a divorce?" Mark said. "I mean, have you ever even thought about what it might be like to be someone different from yourself? I didn't go away to school the way you did. You never mention that, do you? There was no one calling me up to ask if I wanted to come home *for a weekend.* And there was no one but me around to take care of Mom after Dad moved out. Did you even know that Mom needed to be taken care of then, that for three goddamn months she was so upset she couldn't get out of bed? That I made her breakfast every morning before I went to school? No. You never knew. You never asked. You always had your goddamn back turned, running in the other direction. You still do."

Alec felt his head shaking back and forth like a rattle. "That's not fair. That's not goddamn fair. And you know it."

"Do I?" Mark said, his voice hardly there. "Maybe there's not a whole lot left to be fair about anymore."

"What the hell kind of comment is that?"

Mark stared at him for a moment, then turned and started walking down the block toward the hotel. The neon signs above their heads continued as always to spatter the street with patches of color, a collage of light that seemed cold, indifferent. Alec wondered if the warmth had gone underground, harbored like gold in the subway tunnels and basement shopping centers, kept during the night hours from those who so badly needed it. Or was it hidden among the throng in front of the Almond, not ten blocks back, waiting to be identified and absorbed? Wherever it was, it had left them all for the time being.

He walked after Mark. "Hey."

Mark kept walking. "You don't belong here," he said. "Not the way you think you do, anyway."

"That's not for you to decide," Alec said quietly.

Now they were facing each other in front of the entrance to the hotel. A pigeon-toed doorman in a sky blue uniform opened the glass doors when he saw them. Mark waved him away, the glass doors closed.

"Then what is there for me to do here? Can you tell me that?"

Alec slowly shook his head. "I don't know." A minute of silence passed between them.

Mark swung his left arm outward, but the sleeve of his shirt didn't rise far enough to expose the watch underneath. He shrugged his shoulders. "It's pretty late. You probably ought to be getting back." He waved at the doorman again, this time to call him. The glass doors parted, the sky blue hat dipped down in a bow.

"Work tomorrow," Alec mumbled. "You won't forget about dinner with my family."

Mark was already moving toward the doors. "Your family," he said. "I won't forget."

Alec couldn't look at him. "Mark . . ."

"I won't forget," Mark said.

And then he was gone. The smiling doorman had disappeared like a magician, leaving only the glass doors in his place, a fan closed up against the night. Alec stared at his distorted reflection until he was able to move himself toward home.

31

TIME APART

Mrs. Hasegawa went to the salon to have her hair done. She came back with three times more hair than she had before. It floated out from her head in an oblong shape. Her dress was new, too—pink chiffon with puffed shoulders and sleeves.

Wearing a stiff suit, a gold watch, and a diamond ring, Mr. Hasegawa looked as sleek as a gangster. Privately, he told Alec that he had been to the barber that day for a tonic treatment. Alec examined his bristles, told him that he had never seen anything quite like it. Mr. Hasegawa gave a toothy grin and reminded Alec that the tonic was used exclusively by company presidents.

The children looked straight from the pages of the youth fashion magazines Alec had seen lying around the house. Yoshi wore an oversize linen jacket and pants that tapered to his ankles. The toes of his black shoes appeared razor sharp. Like her mother, Yukiko brought out her best dress, this one white with bold black stripes. It was strapless, and Alec noticed Mrs. Hasegawa checking to make sure her daughter's breasts were properly covered. Meanwhile, Hiroshi seemed the most uncomfortable of everyone, constantly pulling at his starched collar.

They all stood, stiff and formal, in a row along one side of the low table. As he led Mark into the room and made introductions, Alec wondered whether he was in fact watching a reenactment of his first night in Japan, everything hazy, not quite clear or real: people bowing, tea being poured; Mr. Hasegawa grunting like a wild boar; Mrs. Hasegawa getting slowly to her feet and going into the kitchen to fetch another platter of squid; Yoshi leaning forward over the table, brows slightly creased, earnest and friendly; a secret giggle from the younger children.

But then, as his eyes traveled more carefully around the room, and as he studied Mark sitting sullenly beside him, Alec had the feeling that things were going to be different. Now as he looked, he saw the Hasegawas arranged in a receiving line on one side of the table, their backs straight and their eyes upon the two American visitors.

"Alec," Mark whispered. "Wake up and say something. It's too quiet in here."

"What? Sorry. I wasn't paying attention."

Alec turned to the Hasegawas and spoke in Japanese. "My brother says that it is a great honor to see a real Japanese home and meet a real Japanese family. He thanks you very much."

In unison, the whole family nodded their heads in approval. Mr. Hasegawa grunted forcefully and said that Alec was the best American he had ever met, and so Mark must be, too. This statement elicited further exclamations of approval from the family. Yukiko let out a loud *"Sugoi,"* then covered her face with her hands when people looked at her.

"But Mark and I are different," Alec said.

"Yes. Mark-san is taller," Mrs. Hasegawa said. The entire family laughed.

Mr. Hasegawa said, "Mark-san looks like an athlete. He could be a football player."

"Yes, Mark is big," Alec agreed.

"Is Mark-san as smart as you, Alec?" Yukiko asked.

Alec nodded. "He is smarter than me."

"Mark-san eats a lot of meat," Mr. Hasegawa announced.

"All Americans eat meat at every meal," Yoshi told his father. "Every meal, every day. Hamburgers, steaks, cows."

"No," Hiroshi said in his high voice. "Not cows. That is not possible."

Mrs. Hasegawa shot him a disapproving look. "Eh? What did you say, Hiroshi? Now be quiet and let Alec speak."

Mark nudged Alec's foot. "What's everybody saying?"

Alec ignored him. "I don't eat a lot meat," Alec told the Hasegawas. "Americans are all different. They eat different things and understand different things."

Mr. Hasegawa chuckled. "Alec is joking. It is all as I said: all Americans are like other Americans. And Alec, he is the best American. Mark-san is his brother, so he is also the best."

Mark jabbed Alec in the back with his finger. "Tell me what's going on."

Alec took a deep breath. "Mr. Hasegawa said that he thinks you're one of the best Americans he's ever met. Everyone agreed."

"That's it?"

"Yes."

"So what about you?"

"What about me, what?"

"They don't think you're such a great American?"

"I think they see me a little differently. I mean, I live here." Alec said the last words slowly, emphasizing each one.

"You think so? Just becau—"

Alec cut him off. "Listen. We can talk about this later. Okay? Right now we're being rude." He turned to the Hasegawas, said in Japanese how much Mark liked the house. Mrs. Hasegawa was on her way into the kitchen but turned to give Alec a beaming smile.

Hiroshi tugged on Alec's foot. "Do you and Mark-san fight?"

"Hiroshi!" Yukiko elbowed him.

"No, it is okay," Alec said. "At your age, Hiroshi, we fought almost every day."

"I think Mark-san always won," Hiroshi said.

Alec nodded slowly. "Yes. Mark always won."

"Enough, Hiroshi," Yoshi warned.

Mark exhaled sharply through his nose. "Are you going to tell me what they're saying?"

"They asked if we fought a lot. I said yes. They guessed that you killed me every time. I said yes, you always won." Alec looked quickly at his brother. "You see, Mark? I'm impartial. That makes me a hell of a good translator."

Mr. Hasegawa said, "It is surprising to have two American brothers with us at the same time. If our house had another room, we would invite Mark-san to stay with us, too. Eh, Alec? Then there would be two Americans in one Japanese house. Of course, Mark-san would come to my barber. After Alec's visit, my barber is honored to cut the hair of Americans."

Before Alec could translate for Mark, Mrs. Hasegawa returned from the kitchen with steaming bowls of pale green tea.

Mark leaned over toward Alec. "To tell you the truth, I'd really prefer a beer."

"No beer. Tea," Alec said without looking at him. "Now, how about saying something interesting to the group?"

"Okay. Ask them if you're the first foreigner they've ever had stay with them?"

"I'm not," Alec said quickly. "There have been two before me."

"Okay, then," Mark said. "Why don't you ask your family why they like to have foreigners stay with them in the first place."

Alec felt the frustration rising inside him. He fought back the urge to say something on his own.

Mrs. Hasegawa listened to the translation, then waited for her husband's nod of approval before answering. "We have only been to America once, and that was for a very short time. Of course, Yoshi was there for longer, so he knows more about it than his parents. But we are very interested in Americans and how they live. New York is a very exciting place. Every day, we learn new things about America from Alec—he is very funny." She laughed. "He has brown hair, and so now we know that all Americans do not have blond hair."

The other family members nodded in agreement. Alec nodded along with them, his mouth smiled; he may have even produced sounds of laughter. Feeling very far away from himself, he translated word for word to Mark.

Beside him, Mark pursed his lips and gave a quick nod, as if Mrs. Hasegawa had simply confirmed a suspicion. He took a small sip of tea, raised his eyebrows. It was okay, he said.

Alec tried to ignore him. He asked Mrs. Hasegawa for more tea, although his bowl was still half-full. She gave him an odd, questioning look. He tried to ignore that, too. He wanted to ignore everything, make it all disappear. Hiroshi was tugging at his foot again, fighting for his attention. Did Mark-san like sushi? he wanted to know. And had he heard of Hulk Hogan?

As he translated, the questions evoked in Alec memories of the time when he had been their recipient, the one being looked to for answers. He saw the dark and bitter side of remembrance. And it seemed cruel beyond belief, and certainly beyond deserving, as though his life within the family were being turned into some kind of game show parody right in front of him. There was a new big-winner contestant on "Ask Your Gaijin," and his name was Mark. Poor Alec simply didn't have the goods anymore. What people wanted was a fresh face, a new look. After all, the perspective was always the same, wasn't it? Only the little things were different: hair color, height, hobbies, things like that. But certainly the basic mold never changed.

Suddenly the room was too small, there were too many things in it. Three television sets, clocks, chandelier, china, home video game console. Not a single inch of free space. And they were all staring at him, expecting him to be the Great Translator, to facilitate the important cross-cultural flow of information. Anger and frustration knitted themselves into a ball in his stomach.

They were already eating dinner. He was amazed to find that, outside himself, he was still functioning, translating sentence after sentence, making inappropriate comments appropriate, adding small jokes to lighten the atmosphere. Almost against his will, he felt the obligation to perform the role that had been chosen for him, to take some satisfaction from his ability to mold himself into the type of person that was expected for the occasion; to act Japanese and somehow remain immune to the irony of it.

Mark took a piece of sushi in his fingers and popped it in his mouth.

"It is unusual that both brothers like sushi," Mr. Hasegawa proclaimed.

Still chewing, Mark shook his head. "Sushi is popular in America. There are many more people just like us." He looked at Alec. "Go ahead. Tell him."

Alec translated. Again, Mrs. Hasegawa smiled at him, saying how pleased she was that his Japanese had improved so much. But no other words followed, only the muted sounds of people eating. Alec waited for more praise without knowing it, his ears transformed into a kind of vacuum, hungry, sucking him in.

Down the stairs and out the door, they walked into the thick blanket of night air. The lit streets and slumbering buildings soundlessly released their accumulation of heat from the past day. There was no breeze to dissipate it, and Alec felt the muggy air cover his skin like a damp cloth as he led Mark on the long walk to the Takadanobaba subway station.

Alec knew the route as he knew no other part of Tokyo. He knew that there, on the opposite corner, the Okunis kept their dry cleaning shop open an hour longer than the others. And he knew, because Mrs. Okuni had told him, that the fish market two blocks down sold the best fish in the neighborhood. And that three shops beyond that, in the front room of their house, a man and his son ran a first-rate bicycle repair business. They opened earlier than most other shops, at six in the morning. The man wore round, bookish glasses, and his head was shaved like a Zen monk's. He always nodded wisely as Alec passed by each morning, and Alec had often found himself wishing for a bicycle just so he could watch the man repair it.

The walk to and from the subway station had become second nature to him. Twice each day, its length and pace provided a time to move and think, telling him by his own step how he felt that morning or night. And gradually the neighborhood absorbed him, one shop and streetlight at a time, painting him with its singular, electric colors.

But tonight things seemed eerily quiet, as if somehow the evening had overstepped itself, grown late too quickly. Fewer people roamed the long, narrow avenue. Like the release of residual heat from the pavement, a hush had risen over the shops and streets of the neighborhood, bringing with it a sense of lifelessness that Alec observed as he might a thundercloud in the distance.

They walked in silence for a while. Mark kept some distance between them, his head down, watching his feet move in long, deliberate strides. Looking upward through the sharp groove of the avenue, Alec saw the formless haze of the moon, wondered if it would be raining when he woke in the morning. When he finally spoke, he was surprised by how calm his voice sounded.

"Why did you do that?"

Mark looked up, his eyebrows arched, as if he had just realized that he wasn't alone. He stopped walking. "Do what?"

Alec stopped a few feet ahead of him, turned around. "Don't do that—play stupid. Not now. You know what I'm talking about. You were rude as hell tonight."

"Yeah? What did I do that was so rude?"

"Your whole goddamn attitude. You were condescending to my family and a pain in the ass to me—trying to manipulate me in front of them. What gives you the right to do that? To stick your nose in my life like that?"

"You don't know what you're saying."

"I don't? Okay. Fine. How about we forget the whole evening? Just forget about everything that happened tonight. How about that? The only thing I ask for in return is that you leave me the hell alone."

Mark took a sudden step toward him, and Alec flinched, thinking he might be hit. But nothing happened, and he hated himself for still being scared of his brother.

"Yeah, just forget it," Mark said. "Sounds good, doesn't it? Seems to me you've become pretty good at forgetting. In fact, it's probably the thing you do best these days. The skill you display when you talk about *your* family and *your* house is really something. I bet most people would never even guess that you're not talking about your real family or your real house— that you managed to forget both those things a long time ago. Not just anyone could pull that off, Alec. You should be proud of yourself."

"Cut it out."

"Why should I? Why bother? I'm only here for two weeks, remember? So why not try to remind you of some things? Why not try to show you that what you have here isn't necessarily what you think it is—that your Japanese family isn't really your family at all and that their house isn't your house? I've got nothing to lose. Not really. When I take off you can forget everything all over again and go back to believing whatever you want."

"Be quiet."

"And stop being so goddamn controlled. That's bullshit like all the rest of it."

"No, this isn't bullshit," Alec shouted. "The way you acted at dinner was bullshit. And your sarcasm is bullshit. You want a goddamn fight? You want a fight so you can beat the shit out of me the way you used to? Is that what you want?"

Mark didn't say anything. Alec looked at him hard for a

moment, then started to turn away. Mark grabbed him by the shoulders. "Maybe I don't know what I want. And maybe you don't, either. Has that ever occurred to you? No, you think you're so goddamn sure what Japan means for you—how it's the one place where you finally feel like you belong, where there's a family that really cares for you. But let me tell you something: you don't know half of what you're so sure you remember about our family—about your real family. Not everything happened just the way you think it did, and not everyone's the same person you remember from before. Things might not be so great at home, but that's not the point. I guess it's my fault for thinking that family still meant something to you. And my fault for thinking you'd be there for me when I needed you. But life's too short to waste time thinking about family, isn't it? And you're too goddamn selfish. Just be careful you don't get the same treatment if you ever try to come back home."

Alec wrenched himself out of Mark's grip. "And who made you arbiter? Huh? Of our family, of my life here. You talk big, but you don't know anything about any of it. Do you?"

"I know *you*," Mark said, his voice suddenly quiet.

"Maybe you think you do, but you don't. Not anymore, anyway." It was too much; he was crying, the tears fighting their way out. "I mean, what do you know about my life here? You sit at a dinner and think you know it all. No, you know nothing. You don't know what I do, what I think, who I am." He pointed to a small shop across the street. "You couldn't give a damn that this is my neighborhood—that I *know* people here. But right now it means everything to me. There isn't a morning that I don't walk by and wave to the shop owners, or go in to talk. They know who I am and where I'm from. What's happened—and this is what you just don't get—what's happened is that they've become a part of my daily existence here and I've become a part of theirs. I'm here, not anywhere else. I *live* here."

A young couple walked by, giving them a wide margin of

space, the man positioning his body between his girlfriend and the commotion. Seeing them, Alec stopped talking. The couple moved on, but the silence remained.

Alec turned, started walking again. Behind, he heard Mark pause and then start to catch up. Some people passed going the other way, and Alec ducked his head to keep them from seeing his face. But they paid him no attention. The street was alive with energy now, as if the lifelessness he had sensed earlier had never been real. Cars flashed by, their bodies all polished muscle. Music escaped through the swinging doors of basement dance clubs. Attractive young couples held hands and kissed. It was brilliant and full and fast-moving, this life, and, head down, Alec felt himself and Mark passed by and stranded together.

In silence, they arrived at the entrance to the subway station. Alec spotted a man carrying an umbrella, felt more sure than ever it was going to rain. Vaguely, he wondered if Mark had brought an umbrella with him to Japan.

They both stood for a moment at the edge of the steep stairs leading underground. Fluorescent light rose up from the tunnel, making them squint. Alec noticed that Mark's eyes were bloodshot.

"Jesus. I don't know. I'm sorry. Maybe if we ..." He stopped, wanting to go on but unable to.

Mark held up his hand, quieting him. "No, don't. Listen. My plane ticket's open. I can leave anytime. There's no sense in, you know, dragging this thing out. I'm going to take off tomorrow."

"Where are you going to go?"

The question hung in the air. "I don't know. Maybe Hong Kong. Or Singapore. I guess I'll figure it out when I get to the airport."

Alec couldn't look at him. "Maybe some time apart will help."

Tears gathered at the corners of Mark's eyes. "Maybe. I don't know. It kind of seems like we've always been apart, and it's not like that's been a whole lot of help." He paused, looking down the avenue. "I didn't handle this right. Did I? I mean, with all the sarcasm and anger and everything. It's not what I'd planned on happening. I'm not sure how else it could've gone, though. All I know is how badly I wanted this trip to work out. I imagined us living together for a while, that we would finally have a chance to be close. But you seem really far away now, more than you ever have. More than when we were young and used to fight all the time, when we almost never said more than a couple words to each other. Maybe it's better to be silent like that, leave things unsaid. Maybe I shouldn't have come here at all—not now, anyway. But I did. You can think whatever you want to about that, but I love you a hell of a lot more than anyone in your neighborhood ever will. There's no substitute for that, not here or anywhere else."

He grabbed Alec's hand, squeezed it hard. And then he was down the stairs. Alec watched him disappear into the tunnel.

He turned around quickly, started to walk back the way he had come. He remembered other nights—nights when he had come back from a dinner or party to walk home along this same stretch of sidewalk. He walked fast those nights, singing his favorite songs to the empty street. Walking, singing, he didn't need or want a single thing more than what took shape in front of him. Everywhere, he could feel the community around him, the neighborhood sleeping four to a room behind the dark, closed shutters. And it was enough.

But he walked differently now and knew that it was no longer enough. From the shadows of the narrow side streets he felt the community pull away from him, withdraw into itself. The houses, boarded up for the night, had lost their warmth. It was as if they existed for no other purpose than to keep him out.

Walking fast, he veered left, past an all-night soba stand. Beyond the light, the street narrowed and became an alley. Head down, teeth clenched, he followed the cracked pavement, turning corners, not knowing where it was leading him. And then space opened up. Aluminum garbage cans stood in a neat row against the side of an unlit building. Light showed itself to him only as shades of darkness. He heard the faint sound of train doors sliding open and knew that he must be somewhere behind the station. A dilapidated chain-link fence stood off to one side. One of the central support poles had been uprooted, and the frame sagged almost to the ground, a weeping willow of rusted metal. Various parts of the fence lay scattered on the pavement, some obviously torn loose by other people who had stumbled into the lot. Among them was a long tube of steel, rusted, with a heavy joint piece at one end. Alec picked it up.

One by one, he destroyed the garbage cans, the club tearing into their metallic skins, turning them all into heaps of scrap. The noise was explosive, inhuman, drowning out his own sounds. None of it took any effort; it was as if his body had been preparing for this all his life. His muscles were tensed and strong, waiting to be released. The weight of the steel was just right, held in two hands like a club over his head. There was no need to analyze, or to think.

His body began to move before his mind caught up. He was running fast, darting through the shadowy side streets. Once, he stumbled and fell, crashing into a bicycle that stood propped against a darkened house. But then he was up again, his shin all pain where it had hit the handlebars. Above the low houses, he saw the electric haze of Waseda Avenue and headed for it.

Once on the street, he stopped running and checked himself over. The bicycle had torn a hole in the leg of his new pants, the fringes of it stained with blood; and his button-down shirt, once white, was now soaked with sweat and streaked with bicycle grease.

As though caught in the current of a river, Alec moved with the flow of pedestrian traffic. He watched people veer away from him on the narrow sidewalk. Some stepped out into the street just to avoid him, staring from the corners of their eyes as if they thought he was drunk or crazy, or both. He wondered what he might tell them: that he was crazy but not drunk; that he didn't know where he was; that he couldn't think of a single song to sing.

And then, suddenly, he felt his face being shoved into the

hood of a parked car, his arm twisted painfully behind his back. Two men were speaking sharply to him in Japanese. It wasn't until they had handcuffed him that he saw their police uniforms, more neatly pressed than any he had ever seen on TV.

"Book 'em, Danno," Alec said in English.

Neither one seemed to hear him.

32

HEARTLAND

The police station was small and well kept, with an air of orderliness that reminded Alec of a suburban kitchen. Formica counters and desks stood throughout the room, bare and sparkling clean, as though waiting for dough to be rolled out on their surfaces. Ceiling fans quietly circulated the night air, casting a net of intricate, moving shadows. Three policemen sat at their desks, smoking and talking quietly. A portable radio was tuned to a ball game.

Alec was sitting in a square, white room, separated from the main area by a wall of clear Plexiglas. After endless misunderstandings with the officers who had brought him in, solitary confinement had been a relief. He could watch the policemen through the Plexiglas, and they wouldn't bother him. There was no other activity in the station other than the lighting and puffing of cigarettes and an occasional trip to the toilet. Alec's right foot fell asleep twice as he waited for the policemen to do their job and arrest some more people. Finally he stopped waiting and turned his chair so that he faced the bare cinder-block wall.

He did not know what time it was. The crystal on his watch was cracked, the hands frozen at twenty-two minutes past eleven. But there was something about the stillness of his room, and the lethargy of the policemen, that made him feel certain it was the middle of the night or later, four or five in the morning, perhaps, the beginning of the day.

Whenever it was, he did not hear the first rap on the wall. The second one was louder, and Alec looked up, saw Boon dressed in jeans, an open shirt, and a checked sport coat. His face was still creased from sleep, his short hair stuck out from the back of his head. A policeman unlocked the door.

Boon stepped into the room. "Okay. Let's go."

Outside, the street was empty of people. It seemed wider because of it, and darker too, as if the street lamps with their dim yellow light were not used to such open space. It reminded Alec of his dream about dancing alone across the American heartland like Julie Andrews in *The Sound of Music*. But then he saw Boon staring fixedly at him, his mouth drawn in a hard line across his face, and he forgot all about the dream. There was something almost familiar in Boon's disapproving look, in the judgment behind it. It pulled and jabbed at Alec until he felt his anger return, stronger this time. He breathed deeply and tried to stuff it back inside himself.

Finally he said, "I'm sorry Joe. I mean, sorry for calling, waking you up, everything. I couldn't have called the Hasegawas. I didn't know what else to do."

Boon shook his head once. "Calling me was the right thing, so forget about it. Let's talk about the rest." He walked over to the curb, sat down on the hood of a parked car.

Alec remained standing; he had been sitting too long. "I guess there's a lot to talk about."

"I would guess the same thing. But that's okay, I've got time—there are at least a few hours before work." Boon smiled thinly, as if he wasn't sure he had meant it as a joke.

"This was my first time in a police station."

"I'm sure it was."

"They handcuffed me. Did I tell you that?"

Boon looked right at him. "Quit dancing around it, Alec."

"I don't know what to tell you."

Boon slapped the palm of his hand on the hood of the car. In the quiet of the street, the sound made them both start. "You're trying my patience, Alec, you know that? It's four in the morning, for chrissake, and I'm getting tired of waiting for you to explain yourself."

Alec ran his hands through his hair, over and over again. He opened his mouth to speak, then closed it again, afraid of what might come out. The silence formed a wall between them. Boon stood up slowly.

"Okay, Alec. You've got your wish. I'm going home. Be in my office at eight-thirty sharp." He turned, started walking down the block.

Alec watched him go, feeling with each step of Boon's as if something, some final bulwark, was collapsing inside him. He jammed his hands into his pockets. Boon was twenty feet away and moving, head down, his clothes all rumpled, looking for the first time like a tired, middle-aged man.

"Don't!" It came out as if by accident, a sudden bark.

Boon stopped, turned around, his arms folded across his chest like a schoolteacher.

"What am I supposed to tell you?" Alec shouted. "That there's some reasonable explanation for my behavior? That all I need is a good night's sleep and everything will be okay—that I'll be standing in your office first thing in the morning? That I won't ruin the goddamn career you have planned for me? Is that what you want to hear?"

Boon's expression didn't change. "I'd change my tone right now, if I were you. *Right* now."

"Maybe you would, but I can't—not now. Now it just sounds like you telling me what to do all over again. *You* deciding when I should take trips, arranging them for me, planning my future.

You telling me when I should talk to my own girlfriend. Organizing me as if I was a goddamn file."

Boon came toward him, and Alec flinched for the second time that night. But Boon brushed past him and sat again on the parked car. Three times he slammed his hand against the polished hood, the noise reverberating through the street like a series of collisions.

"If you were a man, I would've already knocked you on your ass," he said. "But you're not. You're just a selfish, self-absorbed little boy. That's the way you act, that's the way you'll be treated. When you decide it's time to grow up, you'll do it yourself. Because I've had enough of it. Understand? You *will* be in my office at eight-thirty, and you *will* have the high-tech report on my desk in ten days. And then you're free to do whatever the hell you want. I only hope for your sake that you manage to pull your head out of your ass and take a good look at yourself, because you won't grow up until you do. But that's not my business anymore."

Abruptly, Boon got up off the hood and went around to the driver's side. He opened the door and was about to get in, when he stopped.

"It's lonely as hell to think that no one else can feel what you feel—to think that your anger against the world is the only real anger there is. Or to think that you alone have found growing up to be a confusing, painful experience. That's lonely and sad, Alec. And if you ever open your eyes, you'll find that it's no way to live." He ducked into the car.

Alec watched as Boon started the engine and revved it a few times, the white exhaust ghosting around them. The passenger window opened with a quiet hum. Boon's face was in shadow.

"Get in. I'll take you home."

"I'd rather walk," Alec said, and started off down the block as though he knew where he was going.

Behind him, he heard Boon shift into gear and pull away.

33

TEN DAYS

Alec's desk had become a battle zone of empty coffee cups and red-inked computer printouts. Sheets of adhesive yellow notepaper stuck to the monitor of his word processor like tear-away advertisements on a college kiosk. Footnote information was spread through three different drawers when he had planned on it being in only one.

The high-technology report grew from ten pages to thirty, and then to fifty. Alec figured out that he was averaging more than fourteen hours a day at work. He ate lunch in the office, alone in the spare conference room. His takeout *o-bento* was consistently cold, and he liked to think that was the source of the numbness he felt inside.

Every morning he remembered to bathe, shave, and dress. He had taken to skipping breakfast, leaving for the office before anyone else in the family was up. And then the day itself would take control. Most of the time at work, he didn't think about much. Writing was just organizing other people's ideas. There was nothing personal involved.

And for the moment it seemed enough to be like that, uninvolved and unhurt, maneuvering his way through each day as though he were a bumper car. There were times when he almost thought he could reach out and touch the wall of protection around him, the dull weight of it numbing his senses like an anesthetic, giving him solitude in an office full of people.

From his desk he could look through the clear plastic wall of Kiyoko's office and see her face in profile, her finger winding and unwinding the hair by her ear. He had hardly talked to her in the days since they had made love. She had tried at first, asking him questions. What was the matter? Nothing, he said. Nothing was the matter. Work to do. He didn't know what else to tell her. And after a few days, there were no more questions. Instead he received anxious, confused glances when Kiyoko thought he wouldn't notice. She left the office every evening around seven or eight o'clock. She left him alone.

Not everyone seemed so threatening. There were certain people in the office Alec thought he could handle. They didn't look at him too closely, didn't examine him and try to pin him down. He could talk to them without thinking. Like bathing, shaving, dressing. Like writing. Park gave the impression of being one of these people. One afternoon, Alec was almost relieved to hear his uncertain knock on the door of the spare conference room.

"I am not disturbing you, Alec-san?" Park asked, still standing in the doorway.

Alec looked up from his *o-bento*. "No, Park-san. Have a seat."

Blinking rapidly, Park entered carrying his own *o-bento* and sat down across the table from Alec.

"It is my hope that the *o-bento* is delicious today. For, you see, today I am especially hungry."

"It's cold," Alec said.

"You are not perhaps curious, Alec-san, about my sudden appetite?"

Alec checked his watch. "It's not that, Park-san. I've got to finish this report. Maybe another time would be better."

"I will tell you the reason," Park said. "You see, I feel in great health today. Do you remember the club we visited that night in Kabuki-cho? Well, last night I made another visit. When I arrived there, I did not yet know what would happen. But I was a very lucky man, Alec-san. Very lucky. I won the game you call Rock, Paper, Scissors."

Park paused dramatically in his story. At the mention of the game, Alec looked up from his food. "You *won* at Rock, Paper, Scissors? You didn't . . ."

"That is correct," Park said triumphantly. "I performed sex on stage with a woman who was naked."

"Jesus Christ. Not the bald one with the scar?"

"Of course not. She was not the type for me."

Shaking his head, Alec stood up. "You're unbelievable, Park-san."

"You are very kind."

"Listen," Alec said. "Since you're hungry, why don't you have the rest of my lunch. I've got to get back to work. Or else I won't make my deadline. Okay? I'll see you." He waved, began walking out the door.

Park called to him in a stage whisper. "In reality, Alec-san, it was my hope to have a small word with you."

Alec glanced at his watch again, then came back into the room and sat down.

"People are saying that the office has not been functioning properly this past week," Park said. "Boon-san's behavior has been unusual, I would say, even for a man such as himself. He is very quiet, and he does not leave his office to watch over us. Now he goes alone to all his meetings. Yesterday, Takahara-san was greatly upset because Boon-san went alone to a company they were supposed to visit together. This is bad for the office, I think. And bad for Boon-san. He does not look happy."

Alec said, "I don't think there's anything I can do about that."

Park held up his hand. "Please be patient, Alec-san. That is only one part of what I would like to say. People have also worried about *your* behavior, saying that it is strange, even for a person such as yourself. At first, I did not agree with this. But I have watched you. These days, even when you are in the office, it does not seem as if you are here. Your face is always serious, and you do not talk to people. In an office such as ours, this can be a bad thing."

"I've been working hard. You know that. And maybe I have a cold or something. I'll get over it. But right now I've got to finish this report. It's important."

"In the past, you were often in Boon-san's office. Now you are not speaking together. . . ."

"Look, I'm sorry. I'm really sorry. I've got to go."

Alec rushed out, leaving Park alone in the windowless room.

He was alone in the office the night he finally finished the report. After ten straight days of work, he had made the deadline with four hours to spare. The lights hummed and buzzed above his head. He opened a blank envelope given to him by Boon's secretary earlier in the day. The key to Boon's office fell out, along with an unsigned, typed note: "Leave report on my desk when finished."

Alec unlocked the door to Boon's office. He sat in Boon's high-backed swivel chair, behind the glass-topped desk. A band of light jutted into the room from the open door but didn't reach him. The report lay on the desk in front of him, looking foreign and worthless. The venetian blinds were raised, and the part of the room where he sat was bathed in the violet night glow of the city outside.

For a long time, he didn't move. He tilted back in Boon's chair, put his feet up on the desk, and felt the bleakness of the plush, empty office gradually settle on him like silt. Ten days of it, years of it, filling the hollow around him, pushing down on him until he thought he would suffocate. He wondered if this was what his father had felt years before, whether he had stood up from his desk one night after the divorce and realized in a moment the great distance that separated him from the world and how little solace there was to be found in his private office. And he wanted to call and tell him that he thought he understood things a little better now, because he had felt it, too.

Alec got up and went out into the main office. He closed Boon's door, put the key on his secretary's desk. He looked at the telephone, trying to remember his father's number in Florida. But it was no use, and instead he found himself dialing Kiyoko's apartment. Her line was busy. He put his jacket on and walked through the reception room and out into the hallway, locking the door behind him.

Half an hour later, he was staring at the door to the apartment Kiyoko shared with her aunt. He knocked twice and waited for an answer, but heard none. So he knocked again, harder this time. Nothing. Finally, he pushed the door with his finger. It swung open without a sound. Three pairs of Kiyoko's leather shoes were strewn about the entrance. Her raincoat lay crumpled on the floor. Her umbrella was leaning against the wall, a small puddle of water beneath it. Alec left his own umbrella outside. He removed his shoes and stepped inside, thinking that the apartment had not looked like this on his last visit.

There was a single light on at the end of the hallway and a closed door behind it. He called Kiyoko's name, softly at first, then more loudly. No one answered. He thought he could hear sounds coming from the far room and he walked toward it, sliding his stockinged feet along the wood floor. His breath was coming very quickly now, the blood rushing and pounding in his head. He knocked on the door, then turned the knob and walked in.

Kiyoko sat on the bed, holding her knees to her chest and slowly rocking back and forth. Her face was twisted and swollen from crying. She was wearing the same linen clothes she had worn that day at work, though now they were wrinkled.

She stared, unseeing, at the television. Alec whispered her name, took two hesitant steps forward. She turned then, reaching out for him as he moved toward her. He was still standing when he felt her press against his chest, sobbing now, all heat and tears, and he held her as tightly as he could. The shaking of her body gave him his own rhythm, and soon they were swaying back and forth together in the bright light of the room.

Gradually, the heat of her face and body began to cool. Alec let her go gently, turned off the television. He went into the bathroom, brought her back a damp facecloth and a glass of water, which she gulped. He wiped her face with the cloth and made her lie back on the bed with it placed over her red eyes. She groped for his arm and pulled him close.

The worst of the news came out at once, the details more gradually. She spoke in Japanese, which seemed odd to him, since they had always spoken in English. Her eyes were hidden by the facecloth, but he stared at them anyway, as if he could reach her through it.

"Grandfather is dead," she told him. "He died yesterday while he was fishing. Night came and Grandmother waited for him to return. But he did not return, and so she went to look for him. When she found him by the river he was already dead. She could not move him, he was too heavy, and so she stayed with him during the night, and in the morning walked to a neighboring house for help. It was cold at night, and I do not know what will happen to her. My aunt went today to help prepare for the funeral. The entire family will go to Yamadera. I will go tomorrow."

She paused. Alec pushed her tangled bangs away from her face. Her grip tightened on his arm.

"The doctor," she said. "He says Grandfather died because of a growth in his brain, something that had become too big. He says that Grandfather had known about this for a long time. There were tests, but Grandfather never told anyone, not even Grandmother. He died alone, fishing."

She took the cloth from her eyes, raised herself up to face

him. Alec found himself looking at nothing in particular, thinking about the old man and woman and the few days he had spent with them in Yamadera. The strength of his memories surprised him, and he felt them pulling him into sadness. There was something almost embarrassing in this, as if he had no right to feel grief for people he had known so briefly. And so he didn't know what to say to her.

"I want to comfort you, Kiyoko, but I don't know how." She moved closer to him. "Hold me, then."

So he did, the heat of her breath rising around his neck and face. She began to kiss him, and they rolled over on the bed, her body pressing hard against him through her wrinkled clothes, full of a wild need that both frightened and excited him.

Later, in the shadows of the bedroom, he reached over, brushed the hair back from her face. She lay beside him on the futon, her arm draped across his chest. As quietly as he could, he slid out from under her and stood up, his skin prickling in the cold air. He saw her eyes slowly blink open. She reached up and held his hand.

"Will you go to Yamadera with me?"

"Yes," he said.

She smiled faintly, and then her eyes closed. Alec got out of bed, walked through the eating room and into the small kitchen. From the refrigerator, he brought out a bottle of *mugi-cha,* poured himself a glass. He sat down on a stool by the window, its bare frame closed tight against the night, and remembered how Grandfather had clutched his head in the fast-flowing river. The cold liquid tasted fresh and bitter in his mouth.

34

LOSS

The house had already been prepared for the funeral. Black-and-white curtains hung from the entrance, displaying the circular family crest. Paper lanterns perched like birdcages under roofs of reed and bamboo on either side of the steps leading up to the house. A man whom Alec had never seen before was sitting behind a cloth-covered table to the right of the entrance. A short line had formed in front of him as people stopped to sign their names in the guest book. When it was his turn, Alec thought he noticed the man's eyes widen slightly in surprise and guessed that he was the only foreigner at the funeral. He signed his name in Japanese, going over some of the characters twice because his hand was shaking. He thought for a moment about turning around and leaving. But then Kiyoko touched his arm and they were inside.

The main room was crowded with people kneeling in rows behind a Buddhist priest, his long robe blossoming out at his feet. Alec could feel the eyes on him like sticks and the blood rushing into his face. He kept his gaze on the floor in front of him. Kiyoko murmured a word of encouragement that he couldn't quite hear. She led him to an open space among the rows of people, and they knelt amid the sounds of soft crying and prayer. He noticed then that her eyes were wet with tears, brought out his handkerchief and gave it to her.

The priest knelt down at the altar and began to recite what Alec supposed was the Buddhist scripture. His voice was deep and powerful, yet somehow gentle, as if the words were coming from somewhere far away. His hands worked to the rhythms of his voice, burning incense and lighting a large candle. Framed on either side by thick walls of flowers, the altar rose from its base to touch the ceiling of the room. It was a jigsaw puzzle of intricate figures carved from boxwood. Dragon-covered pagodas and candlesticks shaped like scepters fit together with miniature bowls and pillars and ornaments. A framed portrait of Grandfather rested in the center. His silver hair was parted, and the neckline of a formal kimono was visible. He held his head straight and his chin high, as though he thought posing for a picture was a serious matter. But his eyes gave him away. He might have been fishing, the way they were shining, twinkling with quiet amusement, too bright and clear and alive for anything as still as a photograph.

Minutes passed, the voice continued, transforming the room with its presence. It seemed to Alec that the priest was speaking to the old man, bathing the weathered face in a mysterious energy of sound and faith. He closed his eyes and tried to imagine himself as the photograph, staring out through the glass at a world whose texture and meaning had suddenly been altered. For a few seconds he felt as if the priest's voice was actually directed at him. And when he opened his eyes again, each wooden figure of the altar had become a part of something that appeared not dead, but living—the limbs or tentacles of an organism whose nucleus was Grandfather, his eyes shining even more brightly than before.

Alec watched a wisp of incense smoke rise up above Grandfather's photograph, curling up through the sculpted figures, scenting the air with the smell of the earth, rich and full, and the clean, hard smell of wood, until the altar felt more real to him than all the people in the room—a face with two paper lanterns for eyes and the smoke coming out of its nose like breath.

The priest finished his recitation then, and the room was quiet. Alec searched the rows of people for Grandmother, almost passing right over her kneeling form before he recognized her. She looked so small and still that it seemed to him as if she had already left her body in some way, had used her strength and energy to go somewhere where she wouldn't have to be alone. A young man in a black suit helped her get to her feet and walk to the altar. The height of the photograph was equal to that of her own head, and she could not take her eyes from it. Alec wondered what it was about the photograph that made it seem so close to life. It was as if Grandfather were more alive than any of those who knelt down in prayer and mourned for him.

Grandmother knelt in front of the altar. She offered incense and prayed silently to herself. Grandfather stared down at her from the photograph, giving her the warmth of his eyes, as if he were still in the kitchen with her, drinking tea while she prepared dinner. As if his nearness might still make her blush. When she had finished, the young man helped her to her feet and gently led her away.

One by one, the kneeling people rose to their feet and walked the short distance to the altar, only to kneel again. The room had grown hot with grief, and Alec's body felt tight as a fist as he watched the mourners through the scented haze. Each silent prayer, each new private offering and message, pushed Grandfather further away from him, until it seemed he could hardly see the altar anymore, or the weathered face that he remembered, or the brightness of the old man's eyes. He wished that he could hear the priest's deep voice again or even that someone in the room would start to wail, somehow connect him through sound to what was taking place around him.

He looked over at Kiyoko, wanting to talk to her and hear her voice, but she sat motionless next to him, still drying her eyes with his handkerchief. Their eyes met but didn't hold, and he realized that she was in her own place at the moment, grieving among family and friends. And he thought he couldn't really blame her for not wanting to ruin everything with explanations.

There were too many people in the house that night, and Alec woke to confusion in their midst. Futons had been laid out in rows across the top floor. The room was quiet except for the sounds of breathing. Kiyoko was not where she had been when he fell asleep, lying on the futon beside his. Squinting, Alec peered through the darkness but could not recognize any of the sleeping forms around him. He got to his feet and tiptoed slowly to the stairs, and then down them, feeling his way, cringing as they complained under his weight.

He was quiet opening the screen door. Kiyoko was sitting at the end of the porch, her back to him. Alec stood where he was for a moment, looking at her. The sky was spotted with stars. Moonlight reflected off the wet rice paddies, spreading up the valley, licking like a flame at the edge of the cherry orchard. Crickets were in the peak hour of their nightly performance, sounding shrilly from their hidden stages. Kiyoko had brought a comforter from upstairs, and it lay draped across her shoulders and over her legs. Her hair fell down over the bright cotton, and Alec thought that it was the contrast of black and white that made her visible.

Even when she heard him—even when Alec was sure that she knew he was there—she did not turn around. He had already crossed half the distance between them when he whispered her name. But she still wouldn't turn to look at him, and he had to walk the rest of the way. He bent down behind her and put his hands on her shoulders. He buried his face in her hair.

"Kiyoko?" he said. "Are you all right?"

She didn't answer immediately. Then, finally, a nod.

"I woke up and you weren't there," he said. "It was strange with all the people."

"I could not sleep," she said.

Alec wrapped his arms around her, around the comforter, squeezing her to him. He rested his chin on her shoulder. Her cheek was cold against his.

"Are you sure you're okay?"

"I have too many thoughts," she said.

"About Grandfather?"

"When I was young, a girl, I would come here often," she said, her voice quiet and distant. "I would take walks with Grandfather, and he would hold my hand and tell me so many different things about this land and about our family. About life. He said to me once that life moves like a river, and that to have happiness a person must find balance in it. Because of Yamadera, because I understood this river, he said that I would find this balance. And always I listened to him. And so I felt, I think, that it would not be hard to grow older—to grow up, as you say. But I was so foolish. I never thought how hard it would be to live like this. To have my years, my work, to live as a woman in Tokyo. Do you understand, Alec? Sometimes it is hard just to . . . to balance these things in my life. I thought I had learned how to make them balance, but now I am forgetting. Because of you, I am forgetting. I did not think that I would care about you so much; that I would think about you so much. But as it is, I do, and it is too difficult. Sometimes you are like me, I think, in too many directions, wanting to find balance. It was too hard for me when you did not pay attention to me after we made love. I could not work. I could not live my life. But then today, at the funeral, it was too much the other way. Today you wanted me to be with you. But I could not do that today. And perhaps not tomorrow. To be a confused person in Japan, not to have balance, is dangerous. There is no one to help. And you are confused. Because of you, I am confused again. The way it is now, it is too difficult. Perhaps as friends it will be better."

Alec didn't say anything. He realized that she had not moved since his arrival on the porch, that her face was still turned away from his, looking out into the darkness. And he felt her slipping away from him even as he held her, the pieces coming apart. He wanted to shout at her, shake her, tell her that this was the one thing that couldn't happen right now, because there was nothing else to count on.

He stood up. When he spoke, his voice sounded foreign to him, weak and pleading. "Maybe we ought to go away from here, take a few days off and go somewhere else. Anywhere you want. You can get the time off work. I know you can."

"I can't."

"You can."

"I am sad, too," she said, and from her voice he thought she might be crying.

"What about last night?" he said. "What about that? You needed me then. Remember? The way you were crying. The way you held me."

"Because Grandfather was dead, Alec. And because my feelings for you are very strong, and you had not talked to me for ten days. Because of all those things."

Kiyoko stood up and turned to face him for the first time. She reached out her arms, and the white comforter fell onto the porch. She hugged him, putting her naked body against him. She told him that she loved him, that they would be good friends. She seemed somehow unreal to him then, and Alec held her and felt as if the funeral had never ended, as if he still knelt beside her in that hot, grief-filled room, waiting for her to speak and knowing that she was lost to him.

35

BICYCLE DAYS

Alec must have walked past the old bicycle half a dozen times before he finally began to pay attention to it. The black paint had dulled to a milky gray, with patches of rusted steel showing through. The tires were thick and worn smooth, and the woven handlebar basket had a hole in the bottom. He could tell just by looking at it that it had been used by an old man, although the frame was so small it might as easily have belonged to a young boy. Though battered and scarred by the land and weather, it was still strong and durable, unchanged in all the important aspects. He stared at it a long time, thinking that, in a crazy sort of way, the bicycle actually *looked* a little bit like Grandfather. It was easy to picture him riding it, calmly working the worn pedals as he made his way out of the valley.

The sounds of people eating and talking reached him now as he stood outside the house; the final meal before everyone left to return to their own busy lives in their own parts of Japan. Kiyoko had told him that Yamadera was no longer so important to many of the people in her family, to those who lived too far away or were too busy to travel to a remote village in the north. And yet they had all come back this time, relatives and friends and neighbors. It seemed to Alec as if they were bound to one another by feelings and codes and passwords that he had never learned, probably would never be able to learn. He remembered the sense of solitude he had felt during his first visit to Yamadera, and now he longed for it, as though it too had died, as though Grandfather had taken it with him.

He knew that they were expecting him inside, but he didn't move. The idea of another long, awkward meal seemed impossible right now. So he just stood where he was and stared at the bicycle, and half wondered whether it was possible to envy an object. Because he did, in a way—envied the old bicycle its quiet post at the side of the house and, mostly, the simple closeness of its connection to the old man.

He had already walked up to the bicycle and grabbed hold of the handlebars before he noticed what his hands were doing, how sure they looked on the rusted chrome. He pumped the brakes, listened to them squeak. The brake pads opened and closed around the thick tires like the gills of a landed fish. He straddled the frame, rubbed his hand over the broad seat, the leather worn and shiny from years of constant use. Beyond the small grove of cherry trees, a cluster of parked cars marked the start of the dirt road that led out of the valley, eventually winding up to the paved road running along the crest of the hills. He put his foot to the pedal, and then the bicycle was moving, heading for the road, taking him with it. Twigs cracked under the tires. As he cut across the front of the house, he thought he saw Kiyoko step out onto the porch and stare at him. He waved once, then disappeared into the trees.

When the tires touched the packed dirt and rock of the road, Alec began to pedal harder. The bicycle was too small for him, and his knees rose practically to his chest. It made him think of the first bicycle he had ever owned—a bright orange Huffy one-speed, with a low-rider seat and stingray handlebars. For three weeks he had been the toast of his block. Until Jimmy Nichols's parents had bought him a bike just like it. Alec's mother told him that he had just learned a lesson about the sudden rise and fall of status in a country like the United States. Alec had wisely nodded his head, decided that skateboarding might be an easier way to reach the top.

He was nearing the crest of the hill now, where the dirt road met the narrow paved one. His legs burned from the steep climb. Still pedaling, he stood up in the seat while the bike bounced over a cluster of rocks. The vibrations shook his body, making his teeth knock together. He skidded to a stop at the edge of the paved road, which twisted and turned around blind corners.

He turned to the right, away from the small town. The tar was smooth and solid under the tires, and he glided like a hawk across one hill and then another. He thought he could feel the bicycle wake up under him, shake off some of its years and bruises. They worked together, an agile, confident team. No corner was too difficult. Even on the straight sections of road they weaved from side to side in sharp, swerving turns, testing their skill. They danced and played and sped forward all at once, and Alec felt himself transported in time. He imagined himself in other situations, in other places: curb jumping in the city with Jimmy Nichols; a family ride through Central Park one Sunday; up at the country house, tearing down a steep hill with no hands on the handlebars, half-crazy with the fear and freedom of it.

The road dipped and leaned down the hill. He removed his hands from the handlebars, raised them high above his head. The speeding bicycle wobbled for a second, and he felt his heart thrash like a fish in his chest. But then it was under control, all his, riding straight and gaining speed. The entire valley lay spread out below him. The wind tore at his hair and whistled through his open mouth. He turned his head sideways to breathe and let out a yell that sat in his ears for a brief moment before being dragged away by the wind. He let out another, stronger this time. The sound grew straight from his heaving diaphragm, and he listened, enraptured, the pavement speeding under him, his arms still raised above his head like a man about to be crowned champion of the world. And he felt it then, the freedom and confidence coming back to him from somewhere far away, rushing over and through him. He wanted to yell again, loud enough this time to reach his parents and Mark and Kiyoko and Jimmy Nichols and a hundred other people, to tell them how unbelievably good it felt.

Alec turned his head forward and saw the road disappear around a sharp corner. He did not reach for the handlebars. There was time enough only to feel the sudden loss of balance as the bicycle began to fall, throwing him headlong off the road and into the thorn bushes. He could think of nothing but the pain then, of how it had come up on him from nowhere, surrounding his chest and stomach like a vise, crushing the breath right out of his body. But when he stopped flying, he didn't feel it anymore, or anything else for that matter.

The world came back to him in beams of refracted light. Moonlight entered through the single window, bouncing off the walls, angling about the room. He saw the ceiling first. It was bathed in the shadowy green of childhood ghost stories, and for a moment he thought he might already be dead. He tried to sit up quickly, wanting to run away. Pain stabbed at his ribs and chest, making him gasp and almost cry out. Slowly, he eased himself back onto the futon. He could feel the blood rushing and pounding through his head, making him dizzy. He tried to think about where he was and what had happened to him. He moved his left arm, realized that it hurt, too. And his right knee. And both hands. He felt his teeth with his tongue, grateful they had been spared.

The ceiling continued to glow in the patched darkness. A narrow rectangle of light shone on one of the walls, a marionette of intricate shadows prancing about in the center, its invisible strings pulled by the swaying of a tree just outside the window. Gently, he turned his head so that he could see partway round the room. It was a room he knew, one in which he had stayed before. He remembered the colors and sounds of night in this room and the fresh laundry smell of the cotton futon and comforter. All around him people were breathing, some easily, others with a muffled catch in their noses and throats. He supposed they were there to take care of him, though he could think of nothing they might be able to do, even if they were awake. He listened a little longer and knew that Kiyoko was the one closest to him. He tried to remember when he had last seen her. The porch of the house came to him as a picture, and his waving to her. Then the bicycle and the speed and the blind corner and the car. The pain was what connected it all to the present.

He remembered the exhilarating sense of escape he had felt as he swept down the hill, the way the wind had torn at his hair and face like hands, pawing at him, menacing him, uplifting him. Crowning him Champion of the World, unconnected to anything, too fast and free for anyone. For a few seconds. And then he had lost control again. The world had reared up and come down on him, hurt him, until he thought his head might fall off. He worried that he had done something terrible to his body, something that wouldn't ever heal. And he wondered what would have happened if he had died here in this remote part of Japan, if his funeral would have been in Yamadera, who would have come.

Unanswered questions filled the room, threatening to drown him. He tried to sit up, as if moving to avoid them, and realized that his ribs were wrapped in stiff bandages. The pain caught him midway, exploding inside him, tearing through him like knives. But he held his position. Gasping and fighting, he managed finally to sit upright.

People left, and Alec remained in Yamadera to recover. He called Mrs. Hasegawa to tell her what had happened. She told him she would take care of him in Tokyo. But Alec said he would be okay where he was for a while, that he just needed time to get well and figure some things out. He told Kiyoko the same thing. She kissed him on the cheek the morning she left for work. And then he really was alone, except for Grandmother and two teenage girls who had stayed on to help her around the house.

Grandmother had taken to sleeping in a room on the first floor. Alec supposed she didn't want to sleep in the room she and Grandfather had shared for so many years. The girls also slept downstairs, but Alec never heard them talk to the old woman. For several days he never heard her speak at all. Once, he heard her humming to herself, the notes so sad he thought she must be crying. Sometimes he would see her from his window, standing between the cherry trees and the vegetable garden, her back to the house. She would walk now and then, but never very far. Her steps were no longer sure, and the wooden sandals looked too heavy for her frail legs.

He didn't move much those first few days. The local doctor who had first treated him said that two of his ribs were broken and his sternum was bruised. There were cuts and scrapes all over his body. The doctor suggested at least a couple of weeks of complete rest. So Alec stayed in his room alone. He listened to the two girls downstairs while they cleaned the house over and over again. Occasionally they would come upstairs with their damp cloths and dusters, but he would gently shake his head and they would turn and hurry down the stairs, whispering to each other. He kept the window closed. The room grew musty and began to smell of his own body. He tried to read the copy of *A Handful of Dust* he had brought with him but found himself skipping whole paragraphs. Usually he just sat by the window, feeling the heat of the sun through the glass. When it grew dark and his reflection appeared in the dusty panes, he would quickly turn away.

He tried to reduce everything to the bare essentials. He wanted certain feelings, but not others. Pain was all right. The brutal shock of it seemed more real than anything else. He didn't run away from pain. Sometimes he even looked for it, hungered for it: he sat up too quickly or rolled over onto his stomach. There was never any waiting time. Pain washed over him in an instant, taking his breath with it. He watched his hands as they gripped the futon, the skin whitening around the scabs that had formed since the accident. His fingers were long and slender, graceful even in this condition, and he found himself unable to look at them without thinking of the years he had spent studying the piano, his mother on the bench beside him, eyes closed, listening to the music and tapping her foot in her own determined way.

His mother. Suddenly she was back, their life together unrolling like a scroll until it was right there in front of him, scene by scene, his own faulty Chopin filtering through the background. An ocean of memory, each wave a moment, rising up and then cresting, about to break. And him, a child again, her little boy. There was no turning away from it.

She called them "bicycle days"—those days when she was teaching him to ride his bicycle in Central Park. Those days when she raced along beside him, laughing, one hand at the small of his back, the other hovering above the handlebars. She flew him like a kite, not letting him go until the wind was just right, until she was sure there wouldn't be an accident. But even then she never stopped running. Even when he was off and riding, thrilled and wobbling, he heard her behind him, keeping up, her heels frantically skipping and knocking against the pavement until it sounded like hailstones coming down around them. The noise was beautiful—the blood sounding in his ears, his rushing breath, her sharp heels and sudden, girlish laughter. A kind of music playing as they rode round and round, past park benches filled with other mothers and their children, all of them smiling, pointing, watching the blond woman run behind her child to catch him if he fell. But he never fell, never even thought he would. Every afternoon for a week she was there for him. She said she loved those bicycle days, the way they made her feel like a girl again. She said she had never had such a good time. And it seemed to Alec as he listened to her that nothing that good could ever stop, that all days would be bicycle days, and that he need only turn his head to find her there behind him, her arms outstretched, reaching for him as he rushed round the park with the wind in his face.

36

AIR

It was morning, five days or a week later. Alec woke just after sunrise, shivering. The room was cold and no longer smelled. He sat up slowly, his ribs stiff and painful from sleeping, and saw that someone had opened the window during the night. A mottled brown leaf rested briefly on the ledge before a light breeze floated it into the room. He reached over, picked it up, tracing with his eyes the veins and tiny holes in its surface. Fall had come without his even noticing. He thought of Rip Van Winkle then, wondered what the old man had really felt in the moment of waking under the tree, whether there was any chance he had felt somehow cheated and angry, not that he had slept for so long, but that he ever had to wake up at all.

Crumpling the dry leaf until it was dust, Alec got slowly to his feet. He walked the short distance to the window, looked out at the familiar patch of land. The cherry trees stood naked of their blossoms like soldiers in civilian clothes. Beneath their protection, the valley eased and stretched itself down toward the river, the rice paddies splayed like fingers. Already the air was filled with noise. Birds had picked up where the crickets had left off, their quick whistles making a carnival of the morning stillness. A raven picked and jumped its way through the neat rows of the vegetable garden. A breeze rose from the valley and lapped against the house. Alec felt it strong and then faint on his face.

He slammed the window shut. Time seemed to stop with the sound, and he felt it happening all over again—the frustration growing inside him, rising like heat. He tried to think about other things, about what he would say to the girls downstairs to make sure they didn't open the window again, or even come upstairs. He turned around and heard his own breath of surprise when he saw Grandmother kneeling in the far corner of the room where she and Grandfather had slept. She was ironing, light bursts of steam rising now and then about her small gray head. She didn't look up. Alec glanced at the spot on the tatami where he had thrown his dirty clothes, but it was bare. And so was the rest of the floor. Everywhere, the room had been made neat and clean. He looked behind him at the windowpanes, saw that they were no longer coated with dust. When he turned back to face her across the room, he heard her humming softly to herself, the same sad notes as before.

He took a few steps toward her kneeling form, then stopped, not sure what he wanted to say or do. She kept her face hidden from him, and he wondered if she was even aware of his presence. For a moment, he thought he might ask her to leave, tell her that it was important for him to be alone. Her humming grew stronger then, the notes reaching out and caressing him. And he felt suddenly and fiercely ashamed in a way he had not felt since he was a boy. Shame, warming and then burning his cheeks, pushing him forward.

He was almost close enough to touch her when she finally looked up at him. Her eyes found his without traveling any-where else, as if she had focused on them long ago in her thoughts. Led by their own sense of sight, her hands moved with sureness, coaxing heat from the iron, creating breaths of steam.

As he looked at her eyes Alec knew that he had expected them to appear lost in some way, filled with grief and regret and a deep longing for something irrevocably changed. Eyes touched with the sadness of the notes she hummed, eyes as unsteady and hopeless as the old-woman's legs that had given up supporting her. Eyes of a life that was all past now, all memory, its moments crowding the house until there was no room left for the living.

Grandmother set the iron down on its heel, removed the smooth shirt from the board on which she had been working. It was his shirt, and Alec understood in the instant it took her to fold it that her eyes weren't questioning anything just then, they were filled with doing. And he felt suddenly as if he could look right through them and deep inside her and know that she wasn't taking any of the emotional and physical realities of her life apart, wasn't analyzing them, but accepting them as each moment required. The way Grandfather had done. And for a moment it was as if the old man were back with them, as if he and Alec were fishing again, their thin rods swaying like reeds in the wind as they stood waist-deep in the rushing river, balanced and waiting for whatever came next.

The room seemed very clear as Grandmother reached behind her and brought out a plastic washbasin with a freshly ironed towel and yukata inside. Alec took it with a slight bow of his head and knew without seeing that her eyes were still on him as he got slowly to his feet and went downstairs to bathe.

37

TUNNEL
OF HEARTS

A lec stood outside the wall of glass doors that led into
Tokyo Station. He held his back rigid to ease the pressure
on his sore ribs. People hurried past him, some glancing twice at
the few scabs still visible on his hands and arms. An arc of late
afternoon sunlight reached him through a sliver of space
between the surrounding skyscrapers. He basked in it, feeling
with his hands the warmth in his hair, wondering what he
should do next. He had taken an earlier train than the one he
had told Mrs. Hasegawa he would be on. No one knew where
he was. Lifting his small duffel bag with care, he walked into the
street to hail a taxi.

The broad gravel path that led to the Meiji shrine was long and
curving, a sickle-shaped brushstroke of white. On the right side
of the path leading in, the peaked rooftop of Harajuku subway
station could be seen above the stone wall surrounding the

shrine grounds, standing resolutely amid the hiss and clatter of arriving and departing trains. Occasional shouts and blasts of rock music came from the student-filled streets beyond. Like a breeze, the raucous energy scaled the stone wall and crossed the gravel path, only to be blocked out by a band of trees that, like the path itself, curved round and out of sight. Signs were posted here and there, marking routes through the woods. Alec recognized the sign he was looking for and turned onto a rocky dirt path that ambled between the trees like a dried-out streambed.

Beneath the canopy of leaves, the world became a darker, more restful place. The air was cool with moisture. Alec breathed deeply as he walked, only vaguely aware of the other people he saw through the trees. There were not many, and most of them appeared to be on routes different from his. Only two people, a couple, were on his path, to one side of it, huddled together beside a tree. They looked up, startled, when he passed, and Alec saw the gleaming blade of a knife in the man's hand. But he noticed it then, a heart freshly carved in the trunk of the tree, blank and ready for the two lovers to claim it with their names.

He walked on. Eventually the woods fell away to reveal a small pond, its surface scattered with hand-size lily pads. Brightly colored carp surfaced continually, leaving the lily pads trembling in their wake. Separated from the pond by another path, a grassy embankment led up to a tea house. The sun seemed to have stopped its descent for the moment and now sat just above the eaves of the house, tingeing the bare wood a delicate, pale orange. A young man with a neatly trimmed mustache had balanced his easel on the grassy slope just below and was trying to paint the scene before the light changed. Alec considered going up to take a look at the man's work, but then thought better of it. If he took too much time, he would lose what was left of the day's light.

Another sign directed him onward. He crossed a wooden footbridge and continued along the path. The embankment on his right turned to woods again. He saw several people ahead of him, but they were all leaving, heading in the direction of the shrine itself or back up toward the entrance to the grounds.

The sign announcing the iris garden was painted with colorful flowers, only some of which looked like irises. Behind it the land dipped to form five evenly spaced planting rows, now almost indistinguishable beneath a tangle of weeds and dead vegetation. Along the rows and on into the distance, unrecognizable flowers raised their withered bodies, looking like meager tombstones in a horticultural cemetery. About twenty feet ahead, a bald man knelt amid the mess, digging into the earth with a trowel. His white T-shirt was ragged and stained, and his black cotton workpants were rolled up to his calves. Alec had not moved from in front of the painted sign. Several times he looked from it to the rows of withered flowers to the bald man with the trowel, who he supposed was the gardener. Finally he walked along the path to where the man was kneeling.

"Please excuse me," he said in Japanese, "but I am looking for the iris garden."

The gardener continued digging, occasionally using his free hand to pull weeds from the ground. Alec set down his duffel bag and waited, looking at the shiny back of his bald head. He tried again.

"Please excuse me, but I am looking for the iris garden."

The gardener paused, cocking his head as if he had heard an animal in the woods. Then he raised his face to Alec, but looked past him and into the sun. His face was as smooth and ageless as his bald head.

"It is growing late."

Alec could hardly hear him, his voice was so soft. He turned and followed the gardener's gaze. The sun had dropped and was now only partly visible above the tea house. He wondered whether the young man with the mustache had been able to complete his painting in time.

"Yes, it is," Alec agreed.

"This is an iris garden."

"Yes, but perhaps this is the wrong one. I am looking for the famous iris garden. I think it is supposed to have forty thousand flowers."

The gardener squatted on his haunches, his bare toes curling into the soil. "There are many flowers here."

"These flowers are all dead."

"They are not dead," the gardener said. "They are resting. You are almost two months late. This is the time of year when the iris rests."

"I did not know."

"Now you will know. For next season."

"The iris is my mother's favorite flower," Alec said, but the gardener had resumed his digging, the trowel tearing at the dead leaves.

"Have you been the gardener here for many years?" Alec asked after a while.

The man pointed to the soil beneath his trowel. "Yes, and now I am working on this row of flowers."

"It must be hard work."

"It does not matter," the gardener said. "When I finish this row, I will begin another. Perhaps you should return next season. The irises will be back then."

Alec studied him for a moment. "Yes, thank you. Perhaps I will do that. Well, good-bye."

Nodding, the man went back to his work. Alec carefully picked up his duffel bag and set off again. After a minute he looked over his shoulder. The sun had fallen below the line of the tea house roof, and its light, while still visible, could no longer be traced. The man's T-shirt and shining head stood out against the shadowy garden. A crescent moon was ascending the sky above him.

The woods were empty of people. A chill seemed to fall straight from the green-dark leaves above. Alec hardly felt it. He was thinking of the letter he had tried to write to his mother just after his accident, of how he had torn it up without ever putting down a word. And it was as if the blank page were still waiting in front of him, large and white as a sheet, a flattened-out ghost hovering in the gathering darkness. Now, as he made his way stiffly through the trees, their trunks carved with hearts and the names of lovers, he thought he might be able to try again. This letter would start simply. It would tell his mother what the land looked like just then, with the sun fading to purple and the green chill settling on him like frost. It would sit her down at the kitchen table and describe for her the decaying flowers of the iris garden and the soft voice of the bald man. It would be nothing special, this letter. But it would be real. It would fill his mother with his own words until she could paint the picture herself, the light dissolving but not gone, the moon rising over a wood full of hand-carved hearts, a tunnel of hearts, leading him up to the white gravel path and home.

38

CATCH AT THE IMPERIAL PALACE

A wind had come suddenly to Tokyo, surprising everyone with its force. Thunder clouds were pushed ahead of it, unfurled over the city. There was talk of an electrical storm. Television weathermen warned their viewers to take the necessary precautions. People began to change their plans.

It was Sunday afternoon, and Alec had the streets almost to himself as he walked the last few blocks to the Imperial Palace. He walked slowly and imagined that the city had been given over to him for the day, his own private museum. A veil of mist ranged over the wide avenues like a flying carpet. The near empty streets had the air of a playground. Wind ripped around corners and down into subway tunnels. It hummed against the large window fronts of stores and banks and restaurants. The few pieces of trash to be found held their own kind of rush hour, dancing wildly with the wind, swirling up into the mist, mocking all the street cleaners who had ever picked up a broom in Tokyo.

A light rain began to fall. Alec squinted and fastened the top button of his raincoat. The moat and stone wall that marked the outer boundaries of the palace grounds loomed in front of him. The boulders in the wall's surface had turned dark and medieval. Boon stood alone on the broad lawn in front of the massive gate and drawbridge. He was dressed in a yellow Windbreaker and faded blue jeans and hugged a canvas bag to his chest. He waved once when he saw Alec.

"The palace is closed."

Alec shrugged. "That's okay."

"I knew it would be. Thought we might play some catch instead."

"Hmm?"

"Catch. Baseball."

Boon reached into the bag, brought out two worn gloves and a nicked-up baseball. He offered one of the gloves to Alec.

Alec didn't take it. "You know my ribs still hurt. From the accident."

"I know. Maybe you could try throwing underhanded." He paused. "I thought it would be fun to toss the ball around a bit."

"It would. But I can't. I'm still pretty beat-up."

Boon put the gloves and baseball back into the bag, which he let drop to the wet ground. "Some other time, then."

"So. How have you been?"

"Keeping busy. The semiconductor deal in Taiwan looks as if it's going to come through for us."

"That's good. But how about you?"

"Fine. Everything's fine. And you? You look all right, considering everything."

"I feel all right, more or less. I've been doing a lot of thinking the last couple of weeks."

"Did I tell you about your high-tech report? It was terrific. One of the best I've read in a long time."

"Look, I've decided to go home. Back to New York."

The wind gusted. Boon wiped rain from his face with the back of his hand. "And do what?"

"I don't know. Just be there for a while. At home, with my family."

Boon shook his head. "That's too uncertain. I can give a call to the head office. Maybe they can offer you a position in New York. There's this guy you should see."

"No."

"Alec, listen to me. What you're saying doesn't make sense."

Alec put up his hands, as if to push him away. "Can't *you* listen to *me*—just for once? I'm going home to be with my family. That's it. I don't know any more than that. I have no plans to be in business, go to law school, anything. And you know something? I don't care if it sounds uncertain, because it doesn't feel that way to me. For once it's not 'I guess' this, or 'maybe' that. I'm going home, to be at home. No big plans, but done. Decided. And if you care about me, you'll accept that—the same way I'll accept who you are."

Boon's short hair was wet and dark, rain trickled down his face. The wind rose up again, and Alec almost didn't hear the soft "You're right." He waited a long time before Boon continued.

"I'm a lot older than you are. And sometimes it's harder to accept things when you're older. You get used to having your own way. If I talk business most of the time, it's because I'm not very good at talking about other things, personal things. The rules don't apply. Work is easier for me that way. And safer. I usually get my own way at work. I make the decisions, and people are supposed to accept those decisions. I saw you and I guess I thought we could really connect through work, that you would understand why I spend so much of life involved with it, and that maybe through work you would gain some confidence in yourself, learn to make your own decisions the way I did. I misjudged you, and I'm sorry for it. I called you selfish, but I have been too, trying to make you into who I thought you should be. Don't think that I agree with everything you've done and are doing. Because I don't. I still think you're throwing away a great opportunity. But the fact is you came to an important decision by yourself, without my help or anyone else's. And had a hell of a tough time, by the looks of it. That's something I have to respect."

Alec ran his fingers through his hair, feeling the water run down his neck and face, tasting it on his tongue. "I'm sorry about a lot of things."

Boon waved the idea away. "None of that's important."

The rain grew heavy. In an instant the drops seemed to double and then triple in size until they no longer danced but roared, pulsing against the soft ground and hard fortifying wall of the palace. With an effort, Alec lowered himself to the ground. He removed the baseball and one glove from the bag at Boon's feet, then stood up again.

"Are you still up for some catch? I'm good for at least one pop fly." He tossed the glove.

Surprised, Boon almost dropped it before pacing off and turning around. He pounded the glove with his fist.

"Okay, give me a good one now," he shouted. "Nice and high."

Alec took a hard look at him through the rain. Taking three steps for momentum, he put his entire body behind the throw. His chest heaved and his ribs felt for a moment as if they might cut a hole right through him.

But it didn't matter. He watched the ball take off from his fingertips up into the dark sky, its scarred form cutting a swath of its own kind of light. It had height, but distance too, and Boon took off under it, glove extended, his face turned up into the edge of the storm. Alec saw the beauty of it then, and, breathless, he watched Boon dive for the ball and catch it, his long body full out and flying, laughing as he came back to earth, leaving a body-length gash of mud directly in front of the Imperial Palace.

39

MORNING

Alec woke into the rich, purple darkness of the end of the night. The air in his room was cool and damp. He lay in bed for a moment longer, eyes open, wrapping himself more tightly in the warm comforter. And then he got out of bed, turned on the light, and started to pack.

He worked methodically, folding each piece of clothing and placing it around him on the floor and futon. He emptied the closet and the cupboard drawers. He untacked photographs and Japanese magazine clippings from the wall. He gathered his books in tall, leaning stacks. Soon he had become an island in his own room, surrounded by his possessions. He paused to look at them, wanting to place each one. He picked up the tea bowl Kiyoko had given him. He closed his eyes and ran his fingers over its simple, elegant surface and felt for a moment as if it were her he was touching with his blindman's hands. Across a river, she came back to him. Full-bodied, she filled him with her warmth until he was holding the tea bowl like a sweetheart, slow dancing to unheard music in the crowded little room.

Grandfather's black sleeping yukata lay folded on the futon behind him. Grandmother had given it to him before he had left to return to Tokyo. Like the waders he had worn fishing, the yukata was too short for him. He buried his face in the worn cotton and breathed in the smells and tastes of another world. He wondered whether he would ever again feel as close to it all—whether one day in New York he might fold himself into the dark cotton only to find that it no longer smelled of the sharp, green land and the people who had lived and died there.

He stopped moving and the room was quiet, as though it were listening. He looked through the glass doors and out over the city. Suspended in nothingness, solitary lights shone like stars from distant apartment towers. Others were awake at this hour, caught as he was in the unresolved time between night and morning. Alec pulled out his suitcases and began to fill them with his possessions.

When he had finished, he wrote his name and address in script on a sheet of paper, looked at it, then tore it up. He did this four times, changing from script to block print, gradually creating letters that resembled those written by grade-school teachers on classroom blackboards. He took the paper and went downstairs.

Mrs. Hasegawa already looked fresh and awake when he saw her. A portable heater blew warm air into the room. The room's only light came from a goose-necked lamp standing in the corner. Alec thought her skin looked smooth and cool in a way that it never had in the fluorescent light of the eating room.

"Are you packed?" she said.

"Yes."

She grunted.

Alec sat on a stool at the small kitchen table, drinking tea. He listened to the pulse of the washing machine from the nearby bathroom and watched her while she cooked, cleaned, and scrubbed. He lifted his feet so she could mop the vinyl floor beneath his stool. Finally, she began to repeat herself. She cleaned the outside of the refrigerator door twice, looking not at the door, but into the bucket of soapwater.

Shrimp were frying. The red light on the electric rice cooker was lit. Mrs. Hasegawa bent straight from the waist, then squatted from the knees to pick up an invisible piece of food from the kitchen floor. Her housedress was new, white cotton with yellow and red roses printed on it.

Alec said, "Your dress is very pretty, Mother."

She set down a plate of shrimp in front of him. "Eat," she said, then quickly turned away.

He realized that she hadn't looked at him. "The shrimp is delicious."

She set down a wooden bowl of rice. "Eat the rice, too."

Alec held up the paper with his address written on it. "Would you look at this paper, Mother? It's important."

"And drink your tea," she said, her back to him.

He ate in silence for a while, watching her while she cleaned the top of the stove. When his rice bowl was empty, he groaned loudly and put his hand over his stomach.

"Mother . . ."

"Eat more." She hadn't stopped cleaning.

"I'm already full."

"Eh! Full? Already?"

"Mother, why have you never let me help you with the dishes?"

She clucked loudly. "That is silly. You are a man."

"I do the dishes at home."

"Don't you like my cooking?" she said. "Eat."

But she had stopped cooking and cleaning for the moment. She stood by the closed window, looking out through it into the darkness, her hands dangling awkwardly by her side as if she no longer knew what to do with them. Her reflection formed in the glass, in spite of the room's faint light, and Alec wondered if she was even trying to see anything behind it. And then the heat of her breath fogged the picture and he couldn't see her face anymore.

He stood up and walked over to her, holding the sheet of paper in front of him so she could look at it if she wanted to.

"It's my address in New York," he said finally. "It's where I will be."

He put the paper in her hand, and her thick fingers closed around it, lightly crumpling the edges. She turned away from the window, away from him, so that she faced the sink. With her free hand, she turned the water on and then off.

"I can't," she said.

She still held the paper in her hand, off to the side of her body as though she was afraid to get too close to it. The edges were moving, vibrating, and Alec realized that she was trembling. Her body was so low and solid. But she was trembling, arm to hand to paper, in the still light of the kitchen. He took a step closer, put a hand on her shoulder. He spoke as softly as he could.

"We can say it together. Slowly."

She took a deep breath.

"It's not so hard," he said. "It won't be as hard as you think."

She looked at the paper in her hands but didn't say anything.

"It's my address," he said again. "It's where I will be."

"But who will I cook for?" she said, and her voice was so soft he could hardly hear it.

"You will cook for your family. They love your food."

"They do not eat as much as you."

"I'm bigger," Alec said.

Mrs. Hasegawa nodded her head at the truth of it. Alec watched her looking at the paper, the lines above her eyes deepening as she struggled to understand what he had written. He waited. She walked over to the stove and switched off the burner under the shrimp, then walked back to where he was standing.

"Shikushteen," she said hesitantly in English. Then again: "Shikushteen."

Alec smiled. "Yes, Mother. That's perfect. Sixteen."

She let out a quick breath of relief.

"Now try the next word: Grove Street. Sixteen Grove Street."

"Gorobu Shtreeto."

"Right. Sixteen Grove Street. Again."

She was looking at the floor now, concentrating. "Shikushteen Gorobu Shtreeto."

"New York."

"New Yorku."

"That's perfect, Mother," Alec said. "I love you."

She looked at him then, for the first time all morning. He held his breath while he watched her walk to the table and pick up his breakfast dishes. She scraped the food into the trash can and organized everything in the sink before reaching over and handing him the dish towel.

"Shikushteen Gorobu Shtreeto. New Yorku," she said.

Alec nodded. "I'll dry," he said.

40

MASKS

The bus kneeled down to him with a sigh. Still waving, Alec climbed on backward. The whole family had lined up in a row to see him off, their arms moving side to side in unison like a chorus line. They had brought out their best clothes for him—starched and pressed outfits in somber tones of black, brown, and gray. Mrs. Hasegawa's hair was even more voluminous than usual, and Mr. Hasegawa had clearly used an extra dose of his special tonic. The children had lined up according to age, though Hiroshi kept trying to squeeze in between the older two.

Alec reluctantly turned around, handed his ticket to the driver, and took a seat by the window. They had not stopped waving, and he thought their arms must be aching by now. Mrs. Hasegawa was wiping tears from her eyes with the back of her hand. He studied her face while he had the chance, wanting to know it exactly.

The bus exhaled, the doors closed the passengers in. The

driver shifted into gear, and the bus lumbered into motion. Alec waved with his palm flat against the glass, like the wiper on a car. The bus made a slow arc around the hotel parking lot, turning out the exit and down the street. He craned his neck to keep them in view. Mrs. Hasegawa was waving with both arms now, a colored handkerchief clasped tightly in one hand, its edges swirling wildly above her head. Her arms danced for him as the bus moved farther and farther away. And then she was gone.

They were all gone. In their place Tokyo transformed itself as the bus slowly made its way through the central part of the city to the highway entrance. Above, the sun was stretching, its rays barely reaching down into the streets. Like noh masks, neighborhoods changed continuously in the confusion of light and shadow, trying on old, familiar expressions and making them new again. Along the narrower, less commercial streets, local shops were in the midst of the hectic morning business, having arranged their goods on sidewalk stands hours before. Housewives walked among the fresh fruits and vegetables, squeezing a tomato here, a melon there, talking to one another about local news or why the things they wanted couldn't cost just a few yen less. An old man sold blocks of tofu from a window. Around him, the doors to pachinko parlors stood open, the electric lights and bells and clatter spilling out onto the quiet streets like a raucous invitation. A young man in a white paper hat and apron emerged from a soba shop balancing a tray of stacked dishes above his right shoulder. He hopped on an old bicycle and shot out into the morning traffic.

Alec watched him flow like water through the net of cars and pedestrians. He put his face against the window and thought how comfortable the man looked on his mad dash, how balanced and ready, his arm flexing like a sapling beneath the shifting weight of the tray. There was practice in his grace, but daring too, the bicycle weaving and dipping, the apron billowing and flapping, and him with his head held high, racing forward.

And then, suddenly, Alec was rising, rising up out of the city as the bus freed itself from traffic and sped up the entrance ramp and onto the highway. Neighborhoods fell away beneath him, as if they themselves were masks, shed for the moment by a larger world of brilliant color and promise. And he knew that he was in it this time. Not passed by, not stranded, but out of himself and in it, this world, its pulse beating everywhere around him, calling him back, leading him onward.

The bus roared on. Japan snapped by his window.

ABOUT THE AUTHOR

JOHN BURNHAM SCHWARTZ was born in 1965 and graduated from Harvard University with a degree in East Asian Studies. He lives in New York City, where he is currently working on another novel.